The Blue Hotel

The Blue Hotel

CHERRI PICKFORD

BLACK
lace

First published in 1993 by
Black Lace
332 Ladbroke Grove
London W10 5AH

Copyright © Cherri Pickford 1993

Typeset by CentraCet, Cambridge
Printed and bound by
Cox & Wyman Ltd, Reading, Berks

ISBN 0 352 32858 41

Chapter One

*I*n the night, Floy Pennington was a libertine. By day she was a bitch.

Ramon DuPrey took a deep breath and let it out in a slow exclamation, his eyes totally unable to rip themselves off her half-naked body. He could tell she was enjoying every second of keeping him on the edge of his bed.

As she slowly began to remove her bra, the tip of her tongue appeared. Through the full, glossy lips it showed briefly. It slid salaciously across her top lip, just once, before withdrawing.

There was no doubting she was accomplished at this performance; a cock-teaser of quite some skill. He wondered how many other men she had done it to before.

He slipped the zip of his trousers, the pressure of his erection bursting to get free.

She put her hands behind her. The clasp undone, the straps of the bra dangled. But she didn't let it drop. She held it with one hand at the cleavage of her breasts, the bra cups loose. It was as if she didn't want him to see the fulsome mounds, secreted only a flimsy black-silk thickness from his gaze.

She turned her back. Naked to the hips, her black

1

and shining hair flounced around the slender shoulders as she moved her head. He wanted to put his arms around that wine-glass waist, to nuzzle his mouth into her neck. He needed to smell her; to feel her silky skin upon his lips. His hands wanted to glide under her arms, to slip upwards within the protecting bra. They yearned to feel the weight of those glorious, mobile breasts. His fingers tingled. To take her nipples between each thumb and forefinger would be bliss. He longed to feel them pout in their dark brown rings, then harden in his mouth.

She dropped the bra slowly to the carpet. It swung away on a slim forefinger before she let it go. Now her breasts were naked but hidden from his eyes. He had the urge to grab her, to spin her around, to make her face him, but he was helpless.

Now her hands sank to her hips, smoothing at the curves and moving downwards. Slender fingers glided inside the waist-band of the under slip. She slid it down, in one seductive move.

This gone, she stood, legs splayed, the briefest of black panties hugging a perfect bottom, each cheek symmetrically round, a well padded pouch between. As she bent to pick up the slip, he viewed this pouch, its full-lipped vee running between her legs, little curls peeping out beside. He gasped, his solar plexus vibrant, his erection pulsing to greater hardness than before. It almost spurted.

Turning to the dressing table she found a hair band. Half towards him she raised her arms. For a moment while she tied her hair back, she showed one breast, highlighted by the dressing table lamp, full and curvaceous. He focused on its rampant nipple reflected from the mirror as a pair. As she glanced in his direction, she left him in no doubt she was fully aroused and ready for sex. Smiling sweetly, she snapped off the light in her room. He sat alone and sighed.

Yes. Floy Pennington was a libertine. She was also a

2

bitch. Worse than that, he was illogically in love with her.

The breakfast room was busy. Only one table stood empty, set for one. Occupying the whole of the great bay window, it stood alone.

As a stunning black-haired woman entered, heads turned to watch. The breakfast murmur turned to a hush.

Her step was light, but gliding; elegant and assured. She swept in, like a diva of the opera, lit up with the kind of accumulated exhilaration which comes with a third or fourth encore. Now centre stage, her audience waited for her to sit.

Floy smiled. She adored being famous.

'Good morning, Miss Pennington.'

Floy gave the young, white-coated waiter a cursory answering smile as he pulled back the chair at the solitary table. He waited for her to sit, and slid the chair under her trim, jersey-suited bottom. She scanned him overtly. He squirmed under her appraisal but stood his ground. He was too well trained, perhaps too afraid, to turn and run.

Yes, he was young – about nineteen – she thought. But he might suit her well. Young men were said to be sexually precocious once their shyness had been worn away by an encouraging female hand.

She liked his blondness. His blue eyes too. She would test him and see if he would suit.

'Do you live in, young man?'

His fair complexion coloured pink. His eyes darted with fright. They did not alight on hers for a second, looking anywhere except her face.

'Yes, madam. I live here while I'm on duty.'

Floy rested her elbow on the table, her chin supported by her out-turned wrist.

'And what are those duties, John?'

He looked nervously at his name tag, and then pulled himself up straight.

'I wait on table for breakfast, madam. Then I porter and do the paging. Some nights I do the night portering and any room service guests require.'

She smiled with satisfaction.

'And tonight? Are you doing room-service tonight?'

He blushed brightly now, looking around him nervously, aware that he had been talking for far too long.

'Y – yes, madam. Tonight I'm on.'

Floy leaned forward and whispered.

'Then bring me a cup of hot cocoa at exactly midnight.'

He bowed his head.

'Yes, madam.'

'Now. Has my post bag arrived yet?'

'I'll ask Mr DuPrey, madam. Will you be taking your usual breakfast?'

Floy kept him waiting longer while she considered. Across the parkland, early morning risers were returning from their walks. Pale sunshine back-lit the treescape in the middle-ground, throwing misty silhouettes of oak and beech into grey relief. A handsome young couple, arm in arm, honeymooning in all probability, strolled up the terrace steps. By the way they looked into each other's eyes they were obviously in love.

Floy wondered what that would feel like. It had never crossed her mind before. She had never been in love.

She turned to the young waiter.

'No. This morning I'll have some grapefruit, some natural yoghurt and a glass of lemon tea.' She looked down at her waist, for her own benefit, not his. She must lose weight. Staying at the DuPrey Country House Hotel had had its effect upon her waistline. Just now she needed to keep her figure trim and seductive.

Ramon DuPrey stood in the doorway of the breakfast room. He had been watching Floy Pennington keeping his trainee waiting at her table. They had been talking. But what about? John knew that he was not allowed to talk socially to guests.

Ramon tensed. She was up to some trick: playing the newly-rich lady; keeping the servants on their toes; waiting on her every whim. The bitch.

Ramon walked across the room carrying a silver salver with a bundle of letters. It had been the same thing every morning for the past week. A special delivery of letters for his very special guest.

As he approached, she glanced up. He knew what was going through her mind. He smiled knowingly.

She did not return his smile. Instead, she returned her gaze to the scenery. This too had been a ritual since her third night in the hotel. Since she had started her nightly sex performance for him, she had become more and more aloof by day.

'Good morning, Miss Pennington. I trust everything is exactly as you like it.'

He stood beside her table as always, waiting for her to acknowledge his presence. She was alluring, even with her hair taken up. It looked severe, pulled back from peach-blossom skin. Silky and unblemished, this skin was made all the more pale by the blackness of her hair. The style made her look older. It would have been too severe for many women of her age; perhaps just a touch past thirty. Businesslike and efficient, he thought. But she carried the look with aplomb.

The tip of her tongue came out. Erotically, it wiped white moistness of yoghurt from her lip. A thrill shot to his cock. Just once the salacious tongue traversed the top lip, lapping off all the thick white fluid before retracting. Ramon took a deep breath. The memory of the last time she had done that still excited him.

He waited.

She looked up.

He smiled.

She kept a dead-pan face.

'Yes, thank you, Mr DuPrey. Everything is satisfactory.' She looked at the letters. 'Are those for me?'

She said it with surprise, just as she had done every morning for the past seven days. It was as if she did not expect so much fan mail. She gave the impression that she marvelled that anyone should write to her at all. But it was false, just as so much about Floy Pennington was false. She needed adoration desperately, he could tell.

Ramon did a visual count of the letters.

'About the same number as usual I think.'

He caught her eye and held it. He needed to see behind the haughty stare, to make contact with the woman within. He needed to talk to her about their nightly erotic charade.

She shut him out.

Floy looked up at the youthful hotelier. As she had talked to the waiter, she had seen Ramon DuPrey standing in the doorway close by. One glance had been enough. His eyes had been intent, locked onto her face, looking for a sign from her. She would not give it. She had him on her string and she was certainly not going to let him off now. He would dance whenever she pulled him. He would dance to her tune and in her time.

Now, as he stood beside her, he kept a publicly respectable distance between them.

She took a lingering look, her writer's mind making cryptic notes.

He was perfect for her need. What a stroke of luck. She could have searched for months and not found a man to fit her better.

Well composed. Self-assured. Masculine, but not too much so. Italianate in his looks, he was swarthy yet refined. The Roman nose was regal, the face both strong and sensitive at once. His lips were full and firm. They were moist as they pouted outwards slightly as he watched her. Clearly he was fantasising about kissing her.

Above all his ideal physical attributes, he was sexy. He had an aura of sensuality about him which made her solar plexus heave. Every time she recalled how he

6

had stood before her, naked and unashamed, a slow throb started between her legs.

Now his dark eyes scanned her every move. Deep and intelligent, they searched, she knew, for something she was unwilling to give.

For a second, she recalled him naked, his sun-bronzed torso smooth and taut. Sinewy of limb. Spare and athletic. Well hung, but not overly so. Virile. Erect. Ready for action.

These were the terms which came to mind. She would note them again later in her room.

She shook herself and pulled her eyes away from his crotch.

'Put the letters on the table. I'll read them later.'

He obeyed immediately. She knew he would.

Sensing him hovering, she glanced up again.

'Yes?'

He faltered, schoolboyish. The air of confidence he usually held was gone.

'I . . .'

'Yes?'

'I want to talk.'

Floy smiled lightly, with surprise.

'Want?'

'I would like to talk with you. When you have the time.'

She broadened her smile, raising an eyebrow with surprise.

'What would you like to talk about – my bill?'

He looked embarrassed.

'No. Not that. I would like to talk about what we did last night. And about what has been happening for the last three nights.'

Floy raised a halting hand. She gulped her lemon tea. The whole breakfast-room was attending them with its eyes. Its ears strained for the slightest word of the muted conversation.

'I'm sorry, Mr DuPrey,' she picked up the letters, 'but I really must go. I have the book launch at ten thirty

7

and I must prepare. Have you made arrangements as I asked?'

'Of course. Exactly as you instructed. The Jade Room is all prepared. We will serve coffee at ten.'

'Thank you. You are so efficient, Mr DuPrey.'

Ramon did not want to be efficient. He would serve her, pander to her every whim. He would watch her; strip her naked; tease her nipples with his lips. He would lick her sex, pin her down and shaft her, passionately and strongly. He would kiss her skin all over, bite her until she squealed. He would bring her on ecstatically, with his fingers and his cock. He would make her want to fuck with him so addictively, so strongly, that she would yearn for him when he was gone.

No. Where Miss Floy Pennington was concerned, Ramon did not want to be thought of as efficient. He wanted to be her lover or her stud.

Floy stood. She smoothed her skirt. Then she wiped her lips slowly with the monogrammed napkin. Finished with that, she flirted it to Ramon, holding it poised above the carpet, just as she had done with her bra on each of the past nights. She dropped the napkin into his open hand.

'I shall need my pearls from the safe.'

Ramon pulled her chair back.

'Of course. Shall I bring them to your suite?'

Floy turned on him. Her eyes scanned his face closely, his breath on hers, the smell of his aftershave in her nostrils. In a fraction of a second she caught the expression in his eyes. Was it the look of a man besotted? Was he looking at her as she had seen the lovers on the terrace look at one another?

Setting her mouth straight, she produced a stony stare. The hope in Ramon DuPrey's eyes died, to be replaced by the water of impending tears.

'No. I'll come to your office.'

8

He bowed slightly and gestured to her to lead. She stood back.

'I'll come when I'm ready.' It was dismissive. She knew it and he knew it.

He bowed again and left, forging a path for her through the tense atmosphere in the room.

'Send John in to see me!' Scowling, Ramon put down the phone that connected to the kitchen. He began to pace the floor of his office. An hour had passed since his morning encounter with Floy Pennington. As usual she was keeping him on a string.

John appeared, white and apprehensive. Ramon narrowed his eyes.

'Why did you spend so long at Miss Pennington's table this morning? There were other guests waiting to be served!'

The youth lowered his eyes.

'She kept me waiting, Mr DuPrey. I wanted to get away, honest I did, but she kept giving me this funny stare.'

'What kind of stare?'

'She kept staring at my face and looking at my crotch. She asked some weird questions.'

'Weird?'

'She asked me what my duties were, and . . .'

'And what!'

He shook his head.

'Nothing.'

'All right. You'd better go. But I don't want to see any dallying in the breakfast room again! Understand?'

The waiter scuttled out.

Ramon was even more on edge. What was Floy Pennington up to now?

A shadow at the door made him look up.

'I've brought your morning coffee, Ramon.'

He focussed on the pretty maid hovering uncertainly in the doorway.

'Mr DuPrey, to you!' he snapped.

9

She stuck her nose up and plonked the coffee tray on his desk.

'My! A bit tetchy aren't we? What's up, lover?'

Normally Ramon would not have taken such talk from a member of his staff. But Jannine was different. They had an understanding. She would treat him formally in public. Only when they were alone was she allowed to sink to shared-bed informality.

He gave her a remorseful look.

'Sorry, Jan. I've got a lot on my mind.'

The girl looked over her shoulder, checking for eavesdroppers. She put a slender hand to his cheek. Her fingertips ran down the smooth skin to his chin.

'It's that Pennington woman, isn't it?'

He looked into the blue eyes of the petite blonde. For a simple girl she was very perceptive. But then, he supposed, any woman would become sensitised to everything her lover did when her place in his bed was challenged.

He didn't answer. Instead he took her chin with his finger and raised her face to his. She closed her eyes as his lips met hers lightly, in a lingering, sensual kiss.

'How charming!'

Their eyes swung towards the door.

'Oh. Miss Pennington. I'm sorry. I didn't see you there.' He cast his eyes down momentarily before lifting them to hers.

'It was quite obvious you didn't see me! Now, if you've quite finished, I want my pearls!'

Floy Pennington sparked briefly with anger. Ramon could see it in her eyes. Then it was gone. It was as if she had shut it off like a tap. But an aura of contained rage still emanated from her. This was amplified by the signal-red of her tailored suit, the open jacket overlaying a pristine white blouse. The blackness of her hair, set off against the red and white could not have been more dramatic, more indicative of her mood.

Jannine dipped courteously before the honoured guest and scurried away. But she did not escape a

10

whipping from the hard, dark eyes as she passed by her suspected rival.

Ramon's breath caught as Floy Pennington swung back to face him. Under the open jacket, her breasts were mobile, her nipples pointing at him through the sheer blouse. Clearly she was wearing no bra.

Floy stood motionless in the doorway. She would not move. Neither would she comment further. As Ramon unlocked the safe, her mind was rattling off phrases like a machine gun. *In Flagrante Delecto*? No, *Caught in the Act* was better. But it was too strong. They had only been kissing, and not passionately at that. Had his hand been on her bared breast, or up her skirt, then . . .

She pushed the thoughts aside. This was not the time. Later, when she had got herself under better control, she would sit at the word processor and add the phrases to her notes.

'Which box are the pearls in, Miss Pennington?'

She saw his eyes go to her breasts. He saw her looking and put his eyes down sheepishly. She smiled cruelly and thrust her breasts forward to increase the definition of the nipples through the silk. They stood proud, sending little tingling messages to her clitoris. The sensation of having him watch her stripping for the past nights had educated her body into responding rapidly to his eyes. The sensations which her abandoned acts created in her were becoming more unbearable with every night that passed. Her nipples, erect now, yearned to be sucked, the centre of her desire was moistening.

She made a rapid assessment of the front of his pin-stripe trousers. The bulge was a good indication of her effect on him. It was fascinating how she could pull his strings and make him rise.

Now she was wet with juices. She would have to go and change.

'Really, Mr DuPrey! Don't you know by now which box the pearls are in? They are in the white case. The

11

diamond necklace and ear clips are in the blue. The emerald brooch is in the green case with Tiffany written in gold.'

'I'm sorry. Most of our guests don't have as much jewellery as you have, Miss Pennington.'

That was the second time he had said he was sorry. It didn't fit his image. He was being subservient. It fitted neither his natural persona nor the one she was creating for him. She needed a strong man. She needed a man to take her forcibly, not one who would lick her feet. Despite the work she had put in on him, he was not measuring up. Perhaps the boy would serve her better after all.

'Here it is, Miss Pennington.'

'Help me put them on!'

Ramon lifted the pearls from the white leather case. His hands shook violently. He took a very deep breath in an effort to control himself, half angry at the way she treated him and half crazy with suppressing his desire for her. He wanted to show her who was the boss. If she had not been so important a guest, he might have locked the door, pinned her to the desk and taken her there and then. She wanted to be fucked, it was written all over her even though she did a good job in disguising it. That was part of her game. It was a game which was making him more and more angry with each day she stayed under his roof.

And he needed to screw her. What the hell were they both playing at with this insane cat and mouse affair?

The pearls were exquisite; a single string, graded down in size towards the clasp. A large half pearl set with a brilliant-cut diamond weighted the centre. Ramon thought they must be worth a fortune.

She turned her back on him, just as she had done the night before as she had shed her bra. A thrill coursed through him. Today her hair was up, baring her slender neck for his ministrations. He let out his breath and enclosed her throat in the pearls.

Close up, she smelled divine. There was a hint of perfume; heavy, laden with musk. But it did not mask her own scent, subtle but unmistakable to a man. He knew she was hot between the legs. Her sex would be revelling in the playing of her game. It sent a signal to his prick, already wide awake to her presence. She was driving him wild again, and she knew it.

It was a slender neck. Long and elegant, blending in a sweeping curve into the sloping shoulders which he so much wanted to kiss. But that was impossible. She was a guest in his office; he the owner and manager of a very select hotel. What would other guests think should any of them stray in?

'What are you waiting for, man!'

He shook himself.

'I'm sorry. I – I was looking for the clasp.'

'Hurry up! My guests will be arriving soon!'

'Yes, Miss Pennington.'

Nervously, Ramon fumbled with the necklace. His hands could not avoid the touch of her skin. Cool, it seemed to burn him.

He settled the pearls on her neck, ensuring that they were comfortable. His finger-tips tingled with electricity.

She turned, looked once in the mirror and walked out. Not one word of thanks passed her lips.

Ramon put away the box. He checked that the diamonds and the emeralds were there then locked the safe, spinning the combination lock several times.

Seated in a room of green marble and gilded furniture, Floy felt like a queen. Crystal chandeliers sparkled their light into the room which was reflected in great mirrors, their frames of ormolu with jade inlay. It was indeed a gracious hotel, built more in the French style than in the English.

Hotel staff, the blonde Jannine among them, stood at the ready. They waited to serve coffee to a select list of

13

buyers who were coming for the launch of her latest book.

Floy took Jannine in coldly. She was pretty. A fine bust and narrow waist, Monroesque in the way she pouted her lips. Her dress was too short for such an elegant hotel. She showed too much of her shapely legs. Floy could see the raw attraction for any male. But the girl was not well suited to Ramon DuPrey. He needed someone elegant, well educated and with a degree of culture which that girl would never have.

As Floy sat waiting, her publisher's assistants busied themselves with final details, seeing to displays and specimen copies of *An Impossible Plot*. It was her finest book yet. A mystery of such complexity that it would entrance her avid readership for years. And the TV rights had already been sold. That would bring her an audience of millions and an income of millions more. She smiled to herself at the thought.

A pile of books, each clothed in a dramatic dust cover, lay ready to be signed.

'Is everything in order, Miss Pennington?'

Floy looked up.

The brown eyes of Ramon DuPrey stared down at her. For a moment she was fazed. She had not sensed him arrive. She had not been prepared for what his presence did to her. Her heart pumped but settled after a few more beats. She flattened her excitement and set her face.

He was indeed handsome. His black hair, cut short, was parted sharply on the left. It neatly fringed his high, square forehead not a hair out of place. His Mediterranean complexion gave the impression that he spent much time in the sun.

'Yes, thank you, Mr DuPrey. Everything is in order.'

She purposely kept it short. The last thing she wanted was to strike up a conversation with him. There was work to do. Launching a brand-new thriller by Floy Pennington was a major event in the year, both for herself and for the book-store buyers who would shortly arrive.

There was an awkward silence. He picked up a copy of *An Impossible Plot*.

'May I look?'

She shrugged.

'That's what they're here for.'

While he was scanning the book, standing close to the desk, Floy took the opportunity to view him at close hand. She was aware that she had become a crotch watcher of late. The experiences she had had since she had arrived at the DuPrey had fixed her interest more and more on the bulges in the trousers of the younger men about the hotel. She knew what Ramon DuPrey had in his. She had viewed it in its erect majesty. But where it went to when it was not angry and ready for action, intrigued her.

Now Ramon DuPrey's bulge was hardly visible in the sharply pressed pin-stripe of his trousers. Perhaps he kept his male equipment trussed up tightly in the day and only let it loose by night. But when she had stimulated him by her behaviour in the office, the bulge had become clearly visible, upright and long.

She shivered with the mental pictures of it hot and naked before her.

'I've read them all, you know.'

He had caught her examining the vee in his trousers. Feigning to study the book in front of her for a moment, she looked up after a couple of respectable seconds, and after she had restrained the embarrassment flooding her face.

She was surprised that he had read her books. They were not the kind she had expected a man of twenty-five or six to read. She thought that, if he read at all, he would be into raunchy, womanising books. She would have expected such a virile man to have magazines of wide-spread, naked women. She had not expected him to read mysteries like hers.

15

But she was pleased. A smile appeared on her lips. He took it as encouragement.

'I think your detective, Sister Luke, beats Miss Marple any day. It was very clever of you to use a nun. She has a quite different perspective on life and crime. She seems to view the world from quite a different angle than the woman in the street. Of course, Miss Marple had some old-maid characteristics; but she was worldly wise in a strange kind of way. How did Sister Luke gain her worldly experience?'

Floy looked at him before answering, considering her reply carefully.

'Not all nuns hide themselves away in cloisters, you know! Some Orders work out in the world.'

'Of course, I . . . Anyway, I was only curious. I meant to say that she makes an excellent detective.'

He was being subservient again. Damn. She wished that he would assert himself more. If he put forward an opinion, even diametrically opposed to her own, he would fit her need better. But just because he behaved like this to her as a guest, he would not necessarily be the same if he had her naked in bed. Men, she understood, could change radically once they had their pants off. So far, he had resisted her too hard. He had watched her patiently as she had stripped; too patiently for her liking. Was he confusing his role of her host with that of a potential stud?

'Thank you for your compliments, Mr DuPrey. I'm flattered.'

'Would you sign this copy of the book for me? I'll pay for it, of course.'

She waved a hand dismissively.

'There's no need.'

She sighed and looked up again. He was in the category of admirer now, a quite different category than the one she had placed him in before. As a reader of hers rather than just a cocky male, he somehow seemed to be much more suitable for her need.

* * *

16

Floy lay on her bed. It had been a hectic day but a very successful one. The last buyer had gone at four. Now she was shattered.

She rang room service. John answered.

'Bring me a tray of tea and some buttered scones.'

His reply was hesitant. She smiled and put down the phone.

But, tired as she was, she could not rest. The sounds coming from the next room were too intriguing. the communication door near the foot of her bed was locked but it did not prevent all the sounds of seemingly continuous sexual athletics coming through to her from the honeymooners' suite.

She got up and went to the door. It was solid; she had tapped it earlier to see. There were no cracks, only a small keyhole showing a view of the far wall.

The groans; the squeals of delight; the cries of ecstasy and the rhythmic thud, thud, thud, of something against something else was driving her out of her mind. It was not annoying. It was stimulating. Her imagination ran riot, her body trembling with the pictures her mind produced. But still it was all conjecture. She had never seen anyone having sex. Until she had come here, she had never imagined that anyone could do sex like that couple were, seemingly all day and all night. She needed to see it for herself. She needed to know, in close-up detail, what it was that people did to one another which could take up so much of their time and interest.

Floy felt intensely lonely. She craved someone to share her fast developing desires. But the problem was there was a whole raft of needs coming to the surface of which she had previously had no inkling. The pressure which was building was becoming almost unbearable.

Yes, she had had feelings between her legs for many years, even if they had been ruthlessly suppressed. But it was the emotions which came with them that frightened her.

She understood that a woman's sexual parts could

17

crave for touching and stimulation. But there were other feelings now. They made her want to be held, tightly and with a degree of – yes, dominance.

Her whole life, it seemed, had been spent fighting against being dominated. Despite the mask of hardness she donned every day, she was becoming softer in her thoughts and speech. That would never do. What if she lost control?

A tap at her door brought her back to reality. She called out haughtily.

'Come!'

John entered and stood in her sitting room looking bewildered. She could see him through the bedroom door.

'Bring it in here.'

He came to the door and looked around nervously. She beckoned with one finger, hooking him further into her boudoir.

'Put it on the dressing table and pour me a cup of tea: weak with a dash of milk.'

He complied without a sound. As he stood with the cup in his hand, she gave him an encouraging smile.

'Don't be afraid, boy. I shan't eat you alive.'

She smiled to herself. That might not be true. In her present state, she might eat him alive. She might suckle that part of him which fascinated her most. She had heard that that was something people often did.

He came, handed her the tea and stood two feet from her. Putting the tea on the bedside table, she spoke to him softly.

'How much do you earn, John?'

'A hundred pounds, all found, madam.'

She scowled.

'That's not much.'

He brightened in self-defence.

'But I'm getting trained, too. Mr Ramon – that is Mr DuPrey is learning me the hotel trade.'

Floy smiled patiently.

'Do you want to earn as much tonight as you would in a week?'

His eyes widened. Then he looked suspicious.

'I don't do nothin' dishonest, madam.'

She nodded knowingly.

'I don't want you to do anything dishonest.' She reached into her top drawer and took out some fifty pound notes, put there just for this occasion. Peeling one off, she stood up, so close to the youth that she could hear his heart.

She whispered.

'Take this and come back for another one tonight, with my cocoa. And bring the key to this connecting door.'

His eyes widened.

'But . . .'

She lay a long finger on his mouth to silence the protest. Then she traced the line of the fine young lips. He quivered.

Her fingertips ran over the baby-smooth face and curled round his neck, drawing him to her. His eyes opened wider.

Her cheeks against his, she draw a deep breath through his blond hair. He smelled good: fresh and clean and wholesome.

He was trembling. She pulled back and studied him.

'Why are you so afraid of me, John?'

He set his eyes down.

'It's not allowed, madam.'

She put her finger under his chin and raised it so that he was forced to look at her.

'What is not allowed?'

'Mr DuPrey says we're not allowed to – to . . .'

She whispered.

'To what, young man?'

He tried to look away but she gripped his chin and shook it.

'We're not allowed to fratinate, madam.'

'Fraternise with the guests, do you mean?'

He nodded.

'But who will tell? Will you run to Mr DuPrey and tell him?'

He crumpled the fifty pound note in his hand and shook his head.

'They why are you so afraid?'

He shook his head again.

'Don't I excite you?'

Now he looked at her with watering eyes. But he did not answer.

Floy would have an answer. There was no way she was going to let him go before she knew.

Her hand slipped downwards. While one hand held onto the youth's chin, her other hand explored. The bulge her fingers found between his legs was small; not as large as she had expected.

'Please, madam. I – I gotta go now.'

She shushed him and stroked back a lock of hair from his forehead. Her other hand still cupped his warm knot. Her heart raced. She wanted to slip his zip and hold it naked in her hand. Her mouth needed to reach out for his young lips, to take a taste of his mouth.

She trembled.

Suddenly, he broke away from her and started walking backwards, his eyes fearful, the note crumpled in his fist.

Floy waved another note. His eyes lit and darted first to the fifty pounds, then to her face and back to the note.

'Remember my cocoa tonight, at exactly midnight. And bring me the key. I'll give you another one of these.'

Ramon sat uneasily in his office chair. It was eleven thirty. The staff had gone home or to their rooms. Most of his guests were gracious elderly rich people who took to their beds early. The honeymooners went early too, often not to be seen again much before noon.

The night porter was off tonight. Young John was to

stand in for him. It was time for Floy Pennington to make her usual entrance.

By her own admission a creature of habit, she had developed a pattern. First the jewels in the morning from the safe. Then at night she would come down and ask him to lock them up again. She would tarry a while then go, throwing out the subtlest of innuendos as she returned to her suite.

Then the night-time ritual would start. A totally changed personality, she would perform, just for him.

He looked at the page she had signed in his book. *To Ramon DuPrey: a dutiful servant. Florence Pennington.*

Ramon studied the dedication. It could have more than one interpretation.

When Floy Pennington arrived, exactly at her usual time, Ramon's heart was thumping. Dressed as always in a white, hotel bath-robe, loosely tied at the front, he could glimpse her black bra underneath. Her hair was down, taking several years off her age.

'Good evening, DuPrey. I would like you to put my necklace in the safe. Would you mind undoing the clasp?'

'Of course.'

He got up and went behind her. Again he trembled as he took the clasp. Her skin was warm, moist from the bath, the scent of bath oil on her still. It was a heady scent, strong and powerful. It made him reel while at the same time it was extraordinarily stimulating. Each night it had acted on him like an aphrodisiac. By the time he had taken off her necklace, he was as horny as he'd been when she'd undressed in front of him on the previous nights.

Before he faced her, Ramon adjusted his erection, hard and long and throbbing inside his pouch. To disguise it was part of the ritual; part of the game which seemed to entail each not showing how the other felt.

Right now he was hovering on the edge of control. Previously he had always kept the upper hand when making love to women. With this woman he had lost that advantage. She had him just where she wanted him: under her spell. And, so far, she had controlled him in every move of their strange relationship. Perhaps that was what excited him about her. She was a challenge. Somehow he must find a way of getting control over her. One way or another, he would tame this woman. He had the remaining three weeks of her stay to do it.

'Have you read any of the book yet?'

She nodded to the volume she had signed for him earlier. It lay closed on his desk.

This was unusual. Normally she didn't talk. A few curt words. Just cold politeness. Then the innuendo. Then she would go.

Tonight there was something different about her.

'I have read the first chapter.'

He saw a query in her eyes. It was plain she wanted more from him.

'I thought it was intriguing.'

She raised an eyebrow.

'Is that all?'

For a moment he saw again that she was vulnerable. She needed to be admired. He played on it.

'I thought it was brilliantly written.'

This time she flushed. He could see pleasure in her eyes as they lit just that little bit more.

'I'm pleased you like my writing.' She pursed her lips in the slightest embryonic kiss.

He played the cards he had been dealt.

'I admire it immensely. But I'm just one man. You must have thousands of devoted readers around the world.'

She smiled. It knocked Ramon sideways. It was the first open smile she had given him since her arrival. It made her appear vibrant; alive and naturally sexy. That creature which used her sensuality in a subtle and calculating way was banished for an instant. For the moment, the aloofness was gone.

'Yes. Thousands of devoted readers.' She smiled again. This time she was girlish and truly beautiful. The years dropped away from her. She could be more his age than a woman over thirty. Her age suited her though. Her figure, as he had viewed it minutely for the past three nights, was that of a model, tall and slim but not too much so. She had taken his breath away when he had first seen her semi-naked, the deep oval navel, the sweep of her waist flowing out over gently curving hips into elegant legs.

She set her eyes down coyly; uncharacteristically.

There was an awkward silence now. It was the kind of silence which hangs in the air when a man and woman want each other, each uncertain of how the other really feels. Each wants to reach out and touch, to kiss, to caress, to explore. But neither of them dares to make a move for fear of how the other might react, for fear of having read the signs and got them wrong.

'Was the buffet for your book launch satisfactory?'

'Excellent. You really are most efficient.'

This time it sounded much more like a true compliment than it had before.

'How is the writing of the new book going?'

She shrugged.

'I'm finding it quite difficult.'

Ramon rucked his brow in query.

'Surely it's not difficult for such a prolific author as you?'

She laughed.

'You really are a tonic, DuPrey. But since you ask, I'll allow you a secret, if you promise not to tell a soul.'

She leaned towards him as they stood, face to face, a couple of feet apart at most. Her eyes sparkled with fun. Had he not known that she was teetotal he would have suspected her to have had a glass too many. She was not drunk; but it was clear she was intoxicated. Perhaps it was his admiration of her writing. Perhaps it was the anticipation of her next move, if she followed the pattern of the past few nights.

23

Ramon leaned forward to her, an opportunity too good to miss. At last she was softening towards him. He whispered conspiratorially.

'I promise I won't tell a soul.'

'This book has a new twist. My publisher wants me to put in a new ingredient.'

'What kind of ingredient?'

Ramon was excited. He was getting worked up. This *tête à tête* was having an electrifying effect on his stiffening prick.

'A new and radical departure for me.'

His attention was riveted on her eyes. They shone, deeply as she confided, 'Sex!'

It was the emphatic whisper of the word which seemed to make it even more stimulating on her lips. Ramon was hard as iron now.

'Sex?'

'Yes, sex. My publisher thinks that we'll widen the readership if there's sex running through the book. It will be sensual but with a mystery too. What do you think?'

Ramon was taken aback for a second. He recovered quickly. Sex was a subject he could talk about all night, and practise too, when required.

'I think your publisher is right.'

She gave him another free and natural smile.

'Good. I'm glad you like the idea of sex. In my book, that is. But it's late. I think it's time to go to bed, don't you?' She gave him another coy look with the word bed.

Chapter Two

*F*or a moment Floy hovered in Ramon DuPrey's office. The earlier experience with the boy had made her body thrill. Blood was pumping through her, throbbing at her temple. The erogenous zones between her legs were alight, her secret lips swollen and sensitised, with a delicious wetness.

Her clitoris felt prominent, as if pushing against the flimsy material of the see-through panties she had worn. With her legs braced inside the bath robe, she could feel a gentle touching as her breasts heaved the material up and down.

She knew that her excitement showed. It was making her light-headed, her eyes wide and shining as she stood in front of Ramon Durey. If only he would reach out and pull her robe apart, slip his hand inside.

But he didn't. The proprietor was a model of propriety.

She could see his ridge clearly. It would be so simple to put out a hand and touch it, just as she had young John's. But she was scared. DuPrey was a man, not a callow youth. And it was bright and light and public here. It would be better to wait for the safety of her room; the darkness and the comfort of her bed.

* * *

Ramon smiled nervously, uncertain of what was expected of him.

'Would you like a nightcap? On the house.'

She smiled and shook her head.

'Thank you, but I've already provided for that. Now I must go. I'm a creature of habit, you know.'

He did know. He had noted the exact same pattern each night for a week.

With one hand on the door handle, she turned.

'I go to bed at the same time every night. And I rise at the same time too. I'm up by five-thirty. I usually work in the mornings. Then I walk. In the evening I work again until ten. Then I bathe and come down to you. To put my jewels away,' she added, as if an afterthought.

He knew that too. He had studied every move that Floy Pennington had made since she had entered his hotel. He had been unable to get her out of his thoughts in all that time.

He had watched her every moment that he could. He had seen her go across the park each day after lunch. He had wanted to run after her, to follow her into the woods. He had wanted to catch her there in some clearing, where the energies of nature always made him horny. He had wanted to play the satyr, a male spirit of Greek myth, his phallus of twelve inches curved and straining to discharge itself within her depths. He had wanted to move up behind her unawares, to fuck her hard and long in the grass before she could protest. And then he would melt, like a shadow, back among the trees.

'Good night, DuPrey. And thank you once again.'

With that, she swept out of the office, across the marbled hall and up the Grand Staircase.

Ramon quickly locked the office. He looked into the kitchen. John was there.

'What are you doing, John?'

The youth looked embarrassed.

'I'm making cocoa for a guest, Mr DuPrey.'

He gave John a wave and called good night, bounding up the stairs two at a time.

Ramon sat on the edge of his bed. He fiddled absent-mindedly with the gold St Christopher medallion around his neck, his eyes glued to the semi-naked enchantress.

Up to now, Floy Pennington's routine had been the same as usual. But tonight it was slower and more even seductive.

In the bath robe, she had flounced in front of the dressing table for a while. She had looked at him directly a couple of times. Clearly she was making sure that she had his full attention.

She had let her hair flow around her shoulders like a glossy black liquid. She had shaken it out, thrusting her head back haughtily as she did so.

Then she had stood facing him, had opened the robe to reveal the delicately-laced black bra, her full breasts weighting it heavily. As usual she wore the sheer slip. This time she spirited it away without turning from him, stepping out of it demurely.

Now she stood at the open-curtained window, in lace panties and bra, brushing her hair out in long sweeping strokes. She looked directly at him, but did not move away. Otherwise she didn't signal any acknowledgement of his presence.

He focussed on the vee between her legs and whistled. Tonight she had put on crotchless panties, her bush of black maiden hair filling in the missing piece of the delicate lace.

Ramon did not feel guilty. He did not feel like a peeping Tom. It was not secret or sordid. He was watching her and she was performing for him. They both knew it.

Apart from all that, he was in love with her. It seemed almost incredible to him that he could fall for any woman in a flash. But that was what had happened. It

27

seemed incredible too that it should have been Floy Pennington. But it was unmistakable.

In her room, separated from his by a narrow court-yard, she stripped openly. The separation seemed not to matter to her.

It did matter to him. It mattered almost more than he could bear. He could watch but not touch. This clearly was what she wanted. But it was driving him wild. Particularly when she froze him out by day only thawing as midnight approached. She was a witch.

She had cast her spell the moment she had set her haunting eyes on his. There had been no warning. As she had arrived at Reception he had looked into those eyes. There had been an energy exchange, like a bolt of lightning between them. He was sure she had felt it too. His heart had pounded, his hands shaken. He had fallen in love.

Then, with a haughty stare, her shutters had come down. She had blocked him out. He had had nothing more from her until the first night she had stripped in full view of his window. First, she had made sure he knew when she was going to bed. Then she had given him time to get to his room before undressing. It was in one way clandestine. In another, it was so deliberately open; not some sleazy key-hole affair.

Tonight she seemed bolder. Perhaps her intimate little confession in the office had worked her up too. But why was she doing this? What possible purpose did it serve?

She weighed her breasts in her hands, firming and lifting them provocatively in the bra, pulling at the nipples between her thumb and long forefinger.

Ramon slipped his zip. He slid out of his trousers, his erection straining to be free.

Then she turned away from him. Something had caught her attention. She was speaking.

Speaking? Who to?

Rage burst in Ramon as John appeared at her bed-room door holding a tray. The bitch! So that's what her *tête à tête* at breakfast had been about. And he recalled how she had refused his offer of a nightcap. She had already made arrangements with the youth. Damn her! What the bloody hell was the woman up to now!

Floy sat on the stool brushing out her hair. She did not close the curtains. Why should she? Part of the plan was to see how Ramon DuPrey responded. Would he be jealous? Would he seethe in his room and wait until morning to throw her or the boy out of his hotel? Would he rush round to her suite? If he did, would he rant at them both and leave. Or would he throw the boy out of her room and take her by force, in his anger at her daring to prefer the boy to himself?

She would not know until it happened. The riskiness of the whole affair was sending her to a height of arousal she had never felt before. The stool was wet with her juices as she faced the nineteen-year-old standing in awe with his tray.

'Did you bring the key?'

He looked nervously around him. Floy smiled. He obviously could not see his master at the darkened window opposite. He would have scuttled for his life if he had known.

'Yes, madam. I – I brought it.'

'Good.' She put out her hand. 'Give it to me!' She hooked him to her with her finger.

He came obediently but very cautiously, his eyes darting to her bra and to her crotch and back to her face.

'Put the tray down, John.' Floy softened her voice. He was shaking. If she was going to experience him, she would have to allay his fear first.

He set the tray on the dressing table and handed her the brass key at arm's length.

As she took it she caught his fingers and pulled him towards her. He resisted. She tugged harder.

'Don't you want the money?'

His eyes flicked to a fifty pound note lying on the dressing table. He nodded.

'Then,' she whispered, 'come here.'

He came to her, standing by the stool, her bare legs each side of his. She took his hands from where they hung by his sides. He held them stiffly.

'Am I so repulsive to you, John?'

He shook his head.

'N – no, madam. I think you're beautiful. Honest I do.'

She smiled.

'Thank you. I think you're beautiful too.'

She slipped open his white shirt and slid her fingers inside. He tensed. She thrilled. He felt so smooth; so warm, so lithe under her hand.

Floy slid her hand downwards, popping his buttons with her free hand as she went.

'Is that unpleasant, John?'

'No, madam. It's nice.'

'Good. I like it too. Have you ever made love to a woman?'

He shook his head shyly.

She dropped her bra. Taking his hand, she placed it on her breast.

'Would you like to make love to me?'

'I don't know, madam.'

Her hand was on his belt now. In a trice she had it undone.

'Would you like to fuck me then?' It seemed a better word, though it was the first time she had ever uttered it aloud. To ask a lad like this if he wanted intercourse or to make love to her, seemed pedantic. No – that, she decided, had been the correct word for the action she proposed.

'I – I don't know, madam.'

Suddenly, Floy made a decision. She stood up and went to the curtains. Then she closed them and walked back to her seat. The youth had not moved an inch. She opened up his shirt.

* * *

30

Ramon thumped the wall.

'The bloody cradle-snatching bitch! Wait until I see that John in the morning!'

His first instinct was to go round there and raise hell with them both. But he checked himself. Was that what she was playing for? Beside that, he could not risk a fuss. Heads would pop out of doorways at the first sound of scandal. The Proprietor in his dressing gown; the famous guest in crotchless panties and see-through bra; the servant boy half undressed in her rooms. It would be fodder for the local rag to chew on and would probably make the nationals too.

Ramon closed his own curtains and snapped on the light. He paced the room, his cock still up but with anger not with lust. He wanted to thrust it in her right up to the hilt, deep and hard. He wanted to use it to punish her, to pin her down – even tie her down – and screw the living daylight out of the prick-teasing slut. But was that what she wanted? Did she want to be forced and then threaten him with some law suit so that he would cancel her bill?

What the hell was he to do? Knowing that he was watching, she clearly was doing it to work him up for something. She had arranged it. She had also arranged beforehand with the boy to bring her cocoa. And what else had been on that tray? His binoculars had picked up something shiny that John had handed her.

Damn and blast the bitch. He was even more determined to get to the bottom of her game now.

He would bide his time and watch, and wait until he was sure. One way or another he would teach her a lesson she would not quickly forget.

Floy put her face to the warmness of John's chest. She rested there as he stood for her, obediently. The deep breathing of his diaphragm was relaxing. But the thump, thump, thump of his heart roused the passion in her. It was too much like the thump, thumping of the lovers next door.

She thought of the door. Now she had the key she could add some reality to her fantasies about them. She could see what it really looked and felt like to watch others making love.

Now as her hand slipped the obedient young man's trouser zip, the wetness of her excitement melted onto the seat. The crotchless panties let her sexual lips suck at the leather, working gently as she leaned into her reluctant lover's body.

Floy trembled as she slipped his trousers down. He stepped out of them, participating more now in the act.

She knelt.

As lightly as a feather, her fingers slid over the outline of his male form, tracing the elongated shape, the two large mobile eggs hanging in a silky purse. He sighed. As he began to swell to her caresses, he moved himself against her hand.

Floy thrilled. She had a male, albeit a young one, responding to her hand. She felt a sense of power and elation.

Quickly she shed his shirt. Next she pulled down his briefs, inch by trembling inch.

As the red head of his swelling organ emerged above the elasticated top, she leaned forward and kissed it, closing her eyes.

Now stark naked, the young man swayed against her. She ringed his rapidly burgeoning erection, working it gently as he moved. Milking it upwards she watched with wonder as the glans retracted between her coital thumb and fingers, only to emerge again as she skinned it down. Each time the head appeared, as if fucking her fingers, she kissed the eye.

Now he was hard and he moaned with every slow masturbation. She marvelled at the solidness of the organ in her hands. It was the first erect penis she had touched.

Now he thrust forward, thrusting harder with every stroke. As the head came through, she put her tongue to the under-side, to the little web of skin beneath the deeply grooved head.

Without warning there was a spasm. She had not known the signs. With one last thrust between her fingers, a fountain of hot thick liquid shot out over her face.

Floy watched with fascination as it pumped, spurt after spurt, over her neck, to trickle down the cleavage of her breasts.

The head now large, the single eye was wide open, pulsing strongly in her hand, even though the impetuous gush had ceased.

Once again, she kissed the eye, tasting for the first time the saltiness of fluid on her lips. Cupping his tight-drawn weighty eggs in the palm of her hand, she kissed the virgin stem repeatedly, from cherry tip to base.

Gradually she rose, her lips still moving over the tight young body, until she reached his lips.

They were quivering.

She touched them lightly with hers, still white with salty milt.

Suddenly, he pulled away. He bent, picked up his clothes, grabbed the fifty-pound note and ran.

Floy sat dazed before the mirror. The tip of her tongue appeared. Through the full, glossy lips it showed briefly. It slid salaciously through the pearl-white fluid, once across her top lip before being withdrawn.

Sliding in the slickness on the seat, she slipped out of her panties. Then she spread her fingers, working them through the adolescent male's fluid on her breasts. This seethed – she knew from biological studies – with energy and life. It was like an elixir of youth to her body, sensual and erotic. It seemed to sensitise her skin, to make it tingle with even more desire. Her nipples stood erect, almost painfully so, at the erotic massage of her semen-lubricated fingers.

She pushed a hand between her legs and brought it up glistening with her love-juice. She blended it with

33

that which had gushed so profusely from the nineteen-year-old John.

On her chest and breasts and nipples, she mixed the fluids, hers with his; an external union at least.

On the bed, she lay with legs open, on her back. Collecting the last slippery emission from her neck, she massaged it over the swollen clitoris, the centre of her need. It seemed to have a magic constituent which made the pip rise up with a sensitivity she had never known before.

A half hour later Floy still lay in the dim light of her bedside lamp, one long finger deep inside herself. The slow throb between her legs was almost unbearable. What must she do to alleviate it?

The hard nubbin beneath her finger's touch had come to life only since she had first encountered Ramon DuPrey. Each time she had been stimulated by him, it had grown, longer and more engorged.

As she rubbed it gently, it pulsed, but that was all. She assumed that it needed something more exciting to take away the ache.

Sadness was the predominant emotion in Floy as she lay. Loneliness came a close second. She would have paid much to have the youth beside her, to cosset her while she stroked him. Had it not been for her total lack of experience with the intimate parts of males, she would have stopped milking it before it spurted. Had she realised that he was about to climax, she would have taken him gently to her bed and pulled him deeply into herself.

Now she felt cheated. All she had left was the memory of a beautiful experience with the innocence of youth. And still the pain of unfulfillment resided deep inside her.

But that was not the young man's fault. He had been frightened and withdrawn. Only her fingers had made him rise and forget his fear until the end. Then, as she had kissed him with his own white fluid on her lips, he had flown. She assumed that he had been afraid of what she might do to him next.

It was already two o'clock when Floy remembered the key.

Next door, all was quiet. She had been too enthralled with her own liaison to take notice of the honey-mooners.

It might be a good opportunity to try the key.

The door opened easily. She let it show an inch-wide grey strip of the scene beyond.

The bed became visible as her eyes accustomed themselves to the darkness. Heat from the room escaped through the crack, fanning gently on her face like a lover's breath. It brought back the feeling of the breath of Ramon DuPrey, first at the breakfast table, and again as he had fastened and unfastened her pearls.

The lovers lay in beautiful nudity, his hand on her breast, hers between his legs. Even in sleep they had not relinquished their erotic hold on one another.

The rhythm of their breathing gave Floy confidence. Naked herself, she tiptoed into the room. Carefully she set the door ajar, off the latch for a quick retreat.

Moonlight struck through a gap in the curtains as she stood at the bottom of their bed.

The beautiful girl was fair; angelic in her sleep. Small but full breasts lay symmetrically, perfect in their round-ness, as yet innocent of any child's suckling mouth.

Her sleek, brown-haired lover's finger and thumb pinched a pouting nipple. Even in her sleep this was aroused. Floy's eyes wandered over the elegant curves of slender waist, to full hips, to the dimple of her navel. At the mound between the widely opened legs, Floy halted her appraisal.

Her heart pounded, both at the illicitness of her entry and with an excitement which thrilled her secret lips again. In all her life she had never viewed another woman's nakedness with sexual eyes. At the age of thirteen she had stopped even looking at her own nudity in any mirror. Only when she had reached the

35

ripe old age of twenty-four had she dared to look at herself, and then only in a functional way. She cursed the fate that had made this so, and studied the gently heaving stomach, the undulating breasts.

The girl was twenty-two at most, blonde and beautiful.

Her parted legs showed off the plump lips nestling between them, the beard of fine, golden hair running down on either side. Floy had a strong desire to kiss, to put her mouth to those young and plump leaves of erogenous flesh. She could smell the scent of the other woman, pungent in the air. It made her stomach tighten with strange desire. Her yearning tongue came out and licked her salty lips.

The man sighed and rolled over, relinquishing his mammary caress. With one leg straight down the bed, the other bent out at an angle to his body, he displayed to Floy innocently in his sleep.

Floy knelt at the foot of the bed, her eyes only three feet from the man's long but flaccid organ. Two large ovoids hung loosely, one lower than the other in their wrinkled sac.

The unsheathed purple mushroom lay languidly in the heat of the room. She desired to lick that too. She desired to see it come to life, like Ramon DuPrey's had done, a metamorphosis from slumbering slug to ravening beast. A *Manimal*.

Floy smiled at the new word she had created.

Then, as if tempted by some devil, her hand slid upwards, between the young husband's legs. This was madness, she knew, but the urge to experience other bodies, to feel and to explore them was too great to resist now.

Lightly her finger traced the ridge around the velvet-smooth helmet of the sleeping creature, lolling with its one eye closed. The finger moved upwards to the fine-laid mat of dark brown pubic hair. She stroked him sensuously, creating in herself that throbbing, hot sensation which made her juices seep.

He sighed and thrust his pelvis forward. The sleeping creature began to stir.

She thrilled. Again, she felt a sense of power. The realisation that the merest touch on a man in this way could make him stiffen, was even more exciting than what she'd experienced before.

Before her eyes the *manimal* began to grow. As it curved and opened its eye, rising sedately to lie against his stomach, she transferred her touching to the underside. Stroking at the web, she slowly ran the finger-tip down the centre seam. It stiffened to the touch, veins standing proud and throbbing.

Floy became frantic. She wanted it inside her. She needed to feel the hardness thrusting deep. Her sexual mouth needed to take it, to suck on it until it gushed as hotly inside her as John's had gushed in her hand.

She dared not move.

All she dared to do was palm his twin-lobed sac with one hand and caress the hardened shaft with her thumb.

Turning again, still half asleep, he groaned and covered the girl, forcing her legs wide. She let out a throaty moan.

'Oh, Jay. Not now.'

'Don't give me that, you tease. If you will play with my tool while I'm trying to sleep, you know what to expect.'

He growled and bit her neck. She moaned again and pulled her legs back further.

'Open up, I need to warm my cock.'

She murmured.

'You never stop warming your cock, you horny beast.'

He growled again.

Floy shook with excitement. She watched with fascination while, as if on automatic pilot, the stiffened shaft found its succulent mark. From her position crouched at the bottom of the bed, she watched the succulent lips of the young bride swallow the thrusting organ of her mate. The lips seemed to contract and relax and contract again as if sucking at his shaft, milking it for its fluid.

Now the thump, thump, thump which Floy had heard so many times took on a fleshy reality as the young buck served his doe, steadily, lustily, without a pause.

The suction of the mating went softly, *fuck, fuck, fuck*.

Again Floy smiled at the aptness of the word. Within its simple sound was captured all the lust embodied in this simple but erotic action. *Fuck, fuck, fuck*. No wonder it held such power when expressed, when whispered in a love-mate's ear. Now whenever she thought or used this word, she could re-create something of the exhilaration she now felt. *Fuck, fuck, fuck*.

Floy found herself panting. It was all she could do to stop herself from crying out. As one finger found her clitoris, the other crept up the bed. With a will of its own again, it snaked its way between the muscular young man's legs, until it reached the thrusting focus of the couple's sexuality.

Floy shook uncontrollably now. One finger drummed to the man's rhythm against her burning nub, while the other reached for his hardness. As it slid across the top surface of her stiffened finger, he moaned. Now, as his hairy sac rubbed the upper surface of her hand, his rhythm hastened, becoming frantic in its pace.

The girl emitted a cry with every thrust now, the same cries which Floy had heard so many times each day and night.

'Fuck me, you gorgeous man! I want to feel you inside me. I want to feel you come.' She began to squirm.

He thrust deeper; harder; making it difficult for Floy to hold her finger still enough for him to bear down on.

Slim red-nailed fingers clawed at the muscular buttocks of the man. One fore-finger searched out the rosette in the valley of his buttocks and began to probe. This made him writhe on her finger and work harder. He gasped and growled again.

It was this finger working in his secret hole that made Floy start to shudder. Her whole body began to convulse. It was as much as she could do to stop herself from jumping up and throwing the girl out of her bridal bed. Floy's body was wracked with the desire for that thrashing manimal inside her own molten sex.

Her pelvis jerked to each of the couple's thrusts.

As the girl screamed, 'Fuck me, Jay,' Floy bit the bed sheets hard to stop herself from shouting, *Fuck me too*!

Just as unexpectedly as it had been with John, the man came. Floy could feel the pulsing of his fluid through the channel in his shaft. The contractions became gradually less violent, until they steadied to a tick as he subsided onto her hand.

Floy was in a fix now. Sprawled at the bottom of their bed, her hand was trapped between the sheets and his pulsing member. She dared not move it.

But in one way she didn't care. The exertion of her own muscular contractions had made her weak. All she could do was rest and hope that they would not discover her.

What if they did? That would be too bad. She would claim she had been sleep walking or some such unbelievable thing. After what she had done to young John tonight, she would probably be slung out on her ear in the morning anyway.

'That was incredible, Prissy.' The voice was dusky, muted as he spoke into the flaxen hair. 'I don't quite know how you managed what you did with your fingers, but it was the best performance yet.'

She giggled.

'I only fingered your arse. I've done that a dozen times before.'

The sound of kissing reached Floy.

'Well you can do it again, any time. My God, it made me come like a volcano.'

Floy could feel the softness of his penis now as it slid out of the woman's love hole. She could feel the warmth of the female juices, slippery on her hand. That brought her little nubbin to life again.

Even though her body had had convulsions, she was still as taut as before. Nothing had happened to release that awful tension which had strung her out for days. She shifted her position.

A slim, red-nailed hand stroked the buttock above.

'You, Jay Polland, are a ram, do you know that?'

'But you like being tupped, Priscilla Polland, so don't pretend you don't.'

'Of course I do. I wouldn't take kindly to being woken twice a night by your scrumptious squirter if I didn't. But I need you again, Jay darling.'

'Didn't you come, sweetheart?'

'Nearly. But, as always when you screw me, I just seemed to hover on the brink. I need your tongue.'

'We've tried fucking every way I know, angel.'

'I know. I think I just need to try some more. Perhaps tomorrow you can have me in the woods. I've always fancied that.'

He laughed.

'You cock-starved hussy. I'll have you in the breakfast room if it'll make you come.'

She giggled.

'I don't think Miss Pennington would approve of that.'

'Fuck Miss Pennington.'

'Don't you dare.'

'It was only a figure of speech, sweetheart.'

'Lick me, Jay. I can always come when you lick me. I won't sleep now if I don't come.'

Floy made a silent groan to herself. Mentally she exhorted Jay Polland to lick his wife so that she would orgasm and go to sleep again.

But would that satisfy the girl? At this rate it would be daylight and the enraptured lovers would discover Miss Floy Pennington at the foot of their bed.

Thankful that the divan was quite high off the floor, Floy slid her legs under it. In an emergency, and at a squeeze, she could hide the whole of herself. But it surely would not come to that. Surely they would finish soon and go back to sleep.

With her legs under the bed and supporting herself on her elbows, Floy watched the man rise to his knees. She quivered as he worked towards the bottom of the bed, his feet over the edge, within inches of her face. With his head deep between the young woman's open legs, his tense buttocks were almost above her. His testicles hung loosely in their sac. His manimal, though still large, hung sleepily between strong legs. If Floy had been allowed to – if she had been brave enough – she would have sat upright and taken it in her mouth.

She dared not. All she could do was lie and watch the pendulous sexual organs of the lovely male as he licked at his young wife.

Floy cursed her unquenchable curiosity. Tonight had been the wildest of her life. Even a month ago, when the publisher had dropped the sex bombshell on her, she could not have imagined in her wildest of fantasies that she would be doing what she was doing here.

What if Ramon DuPrey, unable to restrain himself any longer, was to rise to her challenge and come in what remained of the secret darkness of the night? What if he was to enter her room and find the key in the communicating door? What if he was to open it and find her, the respectable Floy Pennington, lying on her back half under the bed of two irrepressible lovers, looking up at the husband's crotch.

She blew her cheeks out silently. Crotch-watching for her would never be the same again.

The action above was becoming more heated. Floy groaned. Surely they would tire soon. This was bizarre; crazy in the extreme. The most bizarre thing was that it thrilled her more than anything in her life before.

To her alarm the man slid off the end of the bed, his knees each side of Floy's head where she had quickly slipped under the divan.

'Oh you beautiful, beautiful man,' came a passionate

accolade above her. While the masculine equipment above Floy hardened quickly, the plum-like weights dangled only inches from her lips. She could have bent her neck and licked them.

Still she dared not.

Never again would she need to wonder how a man was constructed for sex. As the shaft stiffened, the covering hood rolled back from the mushroom head. Then the plums retracted upwards, she assumed for protection in preparation for the impending mating with his bride. The veins stood out on the eight-inch shaft, shorter than Ramon DuPrey's but apparently none the less effective for that.

Later when she was to re-run this scene in fantasy, adding to it her own imagined licking of Jay Polland's plums and the sucking of his manimal, Floy was to be amazed at her lustful thoughts.

She wondered why men had one testicle larger than the other. Why did one always seem to hang lower? According to all the statues she had seen, it was always the left one. Though, she recalled, one learned professor had claimed that men of genius had a larger right testicle. Witness Rodin and Da Vinci. All their men in sculpture, in paint and in charcoal, had shown the right one dangling prominently below the left. The professor had presumed his theory about genii to be correct because those two notable men had used themselves as their own models for their work.

Now, as the testicles of this man worked above her, his erection rubbing on the counterpane, she could see that he was no genius. Perhaps an expert – a sexpert – a veritable olympian as this sport. But according to the largeness of the left oval nestled up tightly in its hairy purse, he was only *Homo Vulgaris*, a common, ordinary man.

But what would she not do for one like him inside her now.

The undulations of the lovers brought Floy back to the insanity of her situation. With each violent flexing of the woman's pelvis, the bed pressed down on Floy's abdomen and breasts. She gasped and held her mouth wide open, petrified that any sound from her would bring the disaster of discovery. Ignominy and estrangement of the other guests in the elegance of the hotel would be even worse than the wrath of Ramon DuPrey when he faced her in the morning. She could control him. She had set herself that task. But she could not bear to see the admiring eyes which praised her every morning and evening in the dining rooms and cocktail lounge turn to sneering disgust.

Floy shook herself and looked up.

Jay Polland had widened his stance. The manimal stroked wildly on the bed, twelve inches from her face. Each downward thrust of the bed springs squeezed the breath out of her. She was being pressed under her female counterpart by proxy of the bed, unable to respond.

Gasps and shrieks coupled with the exertion of pelvic thrusting reached a crescendo. Jay let out a moan as he subsided, the blonde Priscilla gasping out each contraction of her orgasmic bliss.

Floy shuddered and panted silently, trapped by the lovers' weight above.

A wet warmness on her face made her look up. Like a leaking tap, the fascinating male organ of Jay Polland was dripping its nectar as it sagged above her. Beads formed in the eye and dripped into her mouth. Floy was mesmerised as they swelled and dropped with each spasmodic tick. She closed her mouth. Still he dripped.

Her tongue came out spontaneously to taste the sweet saltiness of a young man's seed; the second time that night. And still she had the ache of unrequited arousal between her legs. She sighed.

He climbed back on the bed. For Floy, the relief of going undiscovered was immense.

'You're the most wonderful licker, Jay Polland.'

Floy's hopes sagged. They were talking again. She

stared up at the ceiling. It was getting lighter, the impending dawn showing through the curtain.

'I'm glad you liked it, sweetheart.'

There was a long and poignant silence before Priscilla spoke again.

'Have you licked many others, Jay?'

He chortled.

'A few. But I thought we agreed not to talk about past lovers. It's only us now, remember.'

'I just wondered how you learned, that's all.'

'Would you want me to be a virgin?'

'No, of course not. I'm glad you're such a ram.'

Another long silence followed. Floy eased her position. She would be stiff in the morning.

'Jay?'

He sighed.

'Yes, my sweetness.'

'Do you think the Pennington woman can hear us through that door?'

He chuckled.

'Who cares if she does.'

'She looks very sad. I know she tries to be so superior, but the sadness still shows in her eyes.'

'Does it. I hadn't noticed, pet.'

'Liar. I caught you ogling her tits in the cocktail lounge last night. And that black cat suit she wore was positively pornographic. I could see, you know, her shape between her legs, as clear as day.'

'I know. I couldn't take my eyes off it. That was a come-on if ever I saw one.'

There was the sound of a slap on bare flesh.

'Don't you dare get any thoughts about her, Jay Polland!'

'Why not? I can fantasise, can't I? She's just about the most fanciable woman I've come across in ages. Apart from you, my sweetness.'

There was another slap.

'Don't you let me catch you even thinking of touching her.'

44

He laughed.

'The woman's a tease. She's one of those bitches who flash their bodies, flicker their eyelids at you and then slam your cock in the door when you try to get in the room. Didn't you see how she flaunted herself at DuPrey in the bar last night and how she treated him at breakfast this morning? You can see he fancies her like crazy. He had a hard-on as he stood at her table. And she knew it, the cow. I saw how her eyes kept flicking to his crotch.'

'Perhaps they're secret lovers. Perhaps he creeps in next door and rogers her all night.'

'We would have heard them if he did.'

'Perhaps he sucks her silently, like you suck me.'

'You, Prissy Polland, have got a lurid mind. Anyway if he sucked her properly, like I suck you, she would cry out like you do. You're not the quietest of women in bed, you know.' There was another slap. 'Ouch, you little vixen!'

'She was probably jilted in her youth. Women become bitter like that when someone they love lets them down badly. I pity her.'

Floy's eyes were running with tears. She nearly sniffed. It is said that eavesdroppers never heard good of themselves. She shook her head with the sense of unfairness of it all.

She did not blame Jay or Prissy. They were simply saying how they felt. It had not occurred to her before that people would talk ill of her; only that they would admire her for her success. Only she knew that the frigidity was partly feigned. But the sadness: that was another thing.

Floy sighed silently. But it didn't matter what others thought. Only she knew the truth. And she had set herself on this crazy venture for a reason good enough to outweigh any condemnation from this young pair or from Ramon DuPrey.

She had misjudged DuPrey. Her scant knowledge of men had played her false. But neither had he matched

45

up to the image she had set for him. He had not met her requirement either. Why else would she be lying, playing peeping Tomasine beneath this nuptial bed?

As far as Floy was concerned, she still had her plan and would follow it to the letter. To the casual observer she might seem haughty and aloof. Regardless of that, Floy Pennington would not be put off her goal.

'Promise me you won't go near that Pennington woman, Jay.' The words were said through a yawn.

He replied sleepily.

'Why would I do a thing like that when I've got you to exhaust me.'

'You might go through that door while I'm asleep.'

'And tie her to her bed-rails and screw her mercilessly?'

Floy's heart nearly stopped. Her mind raced. Had she given herself the wrong target from the start? Should she have set out to snare this randy bridegroom instead of working on DuPrey? No, that was crazy. How could she have done that? DuPrey was a far sounder bet in the long run. If only he would react as she had planned, there would be no problem.

But she had gained valuable experience in one short night. Perhaps tomorrow night would bring her what she wanted from DuPrey.

It was nearly light when Floy eased herself from under the bed. She looked down on the lovers and smiled. They lay entwined, his thigh between her legs, her arm around his waist.

Tiptoeing to the door, Floy went to her room. She smiled as she took a rose from the vase on her sitting room table.

Quietly she slipped back into the lovers' boudoir, placing the rose on the pillow between their faces.

Once again she thought how beautiful they were; what a picture of sensual youth and unquenchable desire. She hoped that it would last for them. They had a valuable gift; a gift of freedom to act and to express their natural needs and passions. If only she could have done the same at their age, she would not be here now.

But through them she had had her first close encounter with the sexual act. They had provided a true experience of sensual love, albeit by proxy. Even though they had no awareness of what they had done for her, she should reward them somehow. Even though they thought her a sad and frigid cow, she would not hold that against them.

Floy lay on her bed in the growing light of dawn. The sadness that welled up in her had quenched the ache between her legs. The warm excitement which had coursed through the whole of her body from her toes to her clitoris to her lips had gone.

Now the memory of the thrusting manimal of Jay Polland was a shadow. The gushing organ of young John was even less memorable. Why was it such things faded so soon from the mind?

Perhaps they were not truly her experience. They were not acts which actually impinged upon her own body. Perhaps to have recoverable thoughts of intensity and feeling one had first to have the pressure of another body on one's own. Perhaps to quench that excruciating need, to explode that tension which had built through her body, she would need to feel the thrusting of the male inside her own deep cavity.

Time would tell.

Maybe the lightening new day would provide some answers. Maybe Ramon DuPrey would throw her out. Perhaps he would freeze her out. Perhaps he would ignore her lascivious and underhand enticements and shut his curtains on her tonight. Perhaps . . .

Floy slept.

Chapter Three

*B*reakfast-time was tense. Floy was late down. The usual red-nosed businessmen, the colonels and their blue-rinsed wives, had gone. Only Jay and Prissy Polland remained.

Floy watched Ramon DuPrey hovering just outside the door.

She put on her iciness for the reduced audience, although this morning apprehension underlay her apparent calm.

The honeymooners were furtive. They kept glancing over to her table and looked away again immediately she cast her eyes in their direction.

She smiled. On reflection, leaving the rose on their pillow had been a cruel trick, though sweetly meant. They had looked so innocent lying there, even though their innocence of the flesh had long since gone. At some time she would make up for her covert intrusion into their lovemaking.

Tension also came from the waitress, Jannine. She bristled with hostility when she came to take Floy's breakfast order.

'What would Madam like for breakfast?' Floy knew that the girl's manner was deliberately sneering.

Floy did not retaliate. She looked Jannine over coldly

48

and made her wait while she read unnecessarily down the menu. Before ordering, she decided to gain control. The competitor in her disliked it when anyone tried to best her. She fixed her stare on the blue eyes of the waitress and did not move it one millimetre.

'Where is John this morning?'

The blue eyes flashed angrily.

'He's run away.'

Floy did not flinch. She would not give the girl the satisfaction of knowing she was surprised.

'Run away? Was he not happy here?'

The serving girl flared angrily.

'He was until – '

'Until?'

Floy watched Jannine flick a glance at Ramon. He stood in the doorway, looking anxious. The girl was obviously undecided whether or not to spit out her anger at the guest. Floy saw that she knew about herself and John. It was clear from her hostility. At least the below-stairs staff were efficient in the passing on of gossip, if they were efficient in nothing else.

'I don't know anything about it, Madam! Now – what can I get Madam for breakfast?'

Floy ordered cursorily: yoghurt and toast and lemon tea. She looked away from the waitress immediately, and studied the brilliant spring morning in the park.

Heat was already rising in the far-ground, the distant woodland hazy blue. Floy decided that if she was not asked to leave, she would break her routine and walk this morning. It would give her time to consider several things.

Whether she stayed or left would depend on how Ramon DuPrey reacted to her. As he approached across the room, she saw him out of the corner of her eye.

'Good morning, Miss Pennington. Is everything to your liking?'

Floy turned and gave him a measured smile. So, he was playing a denying game too.

'Thank you, Mr DuPrey. Everything is exactly as I like it.'

With Jay's eyes riveted to her, Floy did not even glance at Ramon DuPrey's crotch. She hardly looked at him at all. But she did give Jay a subtle knowing smile. He looked down immediately, clearly embarrassed at being caught watching.

Ramon was aware that something was going on in the breakfast room. He had seen the honeymoon couple studying his other guest. Even at a distance, he had sensed the tension between Jannine and Floy Pennington.

This morning he was tired. He was tired of the charade between Floy Pennington and himself. He was tired of the game she was playing with his staff. In the absence of the petulant Jannine from his bed, he was tired of having his prick teased to the brink of explosion, unable to do anything with it except rub himself off. He was tired from pacing his room and the corridors, and of not having slept more than a couple of hours all night.

When Floy Pennington had closed the curtains on him, to hide her molesting of his trainee, he had raged. He'd nearly stormed round there. But had the impulse been for the protection of young John? He doubted it. A nineteen-year-old youth was quite capable of looking after himself sexually. If nothing else, he would have learned something about a woman and her sexual needs.

Ramon reasoned that his anger must have been from jealousy. The realisation had stopped him in mid-stride and he had slumped back on his bed.

This morning there had been a note on the porter's desk. John had been called away unexpectedly. A relative was ill.

Ramon had cursed Florence Pennington loudly. Staff were difficult enough to find without her driving them away. Jannine would be the next; he could tell.

But he could not ask Floy Pennington to leave. Her presence here was causing a buzz in Stokey Magna. Self appointed news-seekers from the village had been arriving, ostensibly for cocktails, or the occasional lunch. They had gone away, excited at having seen the famous author. In general, the takings were up. Floy Pennington's patronage could be the break for which he had been looking for a long time.

And then there was Floy Pennington herself. He had sworn to get even with her for her treatment of him. The least he would do would be to have her, if only once, before she finally escaped him. If he ordered her to leave, that would be the end of that. But he would have to bide his time and read her signs. The last thing he wanted was to be flung noisily out of her bedroom.

But, after all other considerations, the bottom line was that he was still in love with the wretched woman. Though God only knew why.

Floy looked up as Ramon put a tray of letters before her. He hovered.

'Thank you, DuPrey. Was there something else?'

She watched Ramon hesitate.

'No, nothing else, Miss Pennington; except – '

'Yes?'

'Will you need your pearls or diamonds? You see, I have to go out this morning. It's my morning off and I thought I might . . .'

Floy waved his explanation aside.

'No, I shall not need anything this morning. Perhaps this afternoon.'

The morning sun beat hotly on her back as Floy walked across the park. In the distance, two figures ambled hand in hand. Behind, a black-suited man hovered on the terrace steps. She ignored both him and the lovers and continued towards the wood. Slinging her camera over one shoulder, she walked jauntily.

A couple of hundred yards away across the open

grass a knot of cows mooed. They sounded as if they were in pain. A huddle of men stood around.

She took her camera and spied them through the telephoto lens. A bull, huge and bulky, stood with its nose to the rear of one cow. From between its legs hung a heavy set of pendulous testicles. A penile rod shot out. It was so long and thin that Floy was amazed. Focussing sharply, she watched, enthralled.

The bull mounted and drove its phallus in. She marvelled as half an arm's length of it sank up to the hilt.

With two or three long thrusts he was finished. She heard a distant cheer. The bull dismounted, its phallus dripping, already looking for another cow.

Floy strode on, trembling. The sheer cold-bloodedness of the act stimulated the animal in herself. She wished that she could somehow do that with a man. To experience what she needed without the burden of emotion, selfconsciousness or shame.

Shame? Ah, yes. How could she justify her recent actions? Sorrow about John tainted the purity of the morning. She had not realised that he would flee, either from her room or from his job. She had not realised that any man, particularly one approaching his reproductive prime, would decline to take a sexual opportunity offered by any reasonably attractive female. Now she doubted her attractiveness to men. Was she flawed?

In her mind she had always regarded men as being wagged by the mindless fleshy tails between their legs, rather like a tail would wag a dog. But she had been wrong. She had been wrong about the lad, and wrong about DuPrey. She had assumed that, at the slightest inference that she wanted sex, he would be round hammering at her door.

His reticence in responding to her performances in her boudoir had forced her to revise her strategy. To her annoyance she had had to become more lascivious and more devious by the day. The annoyance had grown as she had found herself increasingly stimulated by her own wantonness. Thrilling more intensely as she increased the degree of exposure of her sexual parts to the lenses of his binoculars, she had become addicted to the feelings she had generated in herself.

Now she was craving carnal knowledge and experience. But something deep down inside her would not allow her to ask for it openly and honestly. She was a coward and a sneak. Why else had she crept in on the lovers? Why else was she following them to the woods? There was no doubt why they were heading there.

But had Ramon DuPrey played the part which she had written for him, she would not be here now. The ploy to use John to make him jealous had been forced upon her by DuPrey's reluctance. It had been a valuable experience but had not yet produced the result she wanted.

Surely if she kept on the pressure, the virile Ramon must soon succumb. If she continued to play her part of cow – which Jay and Prissy had so correctly observed – and stimulated DuPrey enough, he would drop his gracious manners. He would revert to his animal nature and become like the bull: dispassionate and irresistibly strong.

Ramon let Floy Pennington get away. He did not want to be seen following her across the park. He would take his stallion around the perimeter. Then he would walk him casually back through the woods and with luck come upon her by surprise.

He slung his field glasses over his shoulder and went to the stables.

Saddling up, he viewed Floy's big red Bentley, its creamy-coloured soft-top snugly up, shining opulently beside the battered Mini of Jay and Priscilla Polland.

He waved to the mechanic from the village as the man emerged from underneath the Mini, smeared with oil. The mechanic made a discouraging face and a hopeless gesture with his hands.

Ramon mounted, gave the great black beast a subtle

53

signal, and cantered towards the back-ride of the park.

The wood was dark to Floy's eyes. Patches of bright green lit by dappled sunshine painted the grassy floor. Ahead, she could see the brightness of a clearing through smooth grey beech trunks. She trod quietly, not certain where Jay and Prissy had gone.

The memory of the young bride's exhortation to her husband to take her in the woods was prominent in Floy's mind.

Fired with expectation, she crept carefully on. She was unrepentant. Already a blatant voyeuse, an extension of her sin would require only a few more Hail Marys – should she ever bring herself to confess.

At the edge of the clearing she came upon the couple. Already they were naked, their clothes strewn with abandon across the dewy grass. Floy took cover behind a wide trunk of oak, only ten feet away at the most.

She held her camera to the scene.

They were fooling about, Jay's erection strong and hard and pointing at his quarry as she ran from him. Her hair streamed in the sunlight, golden as a nymph's. Her arms out, her breasts bouncing, her laughter tinkled round the glade as he chased her.

Floy's camera clicked and whirred in her expert hands.

She felt exhilarated at the couple's freedom to express themselves. Such carefree sensations must be a joy.

Jay had Prissy cornered now, hedged around by a bramble thicket. Dancing and laughing, she tried to dodge him and escape. He lunged at her, his legs splayed wide, his arms set outwards to grab her.

Floy zoomed in.

With a goatee beard and pointed ears he would have made a veritable Pan.

She snapped the shot.

Now Jay had his prize, and Floy had him; the scene recorded for her reference in less demanding times.

With one quick move Jay grabbed Prissy's wrists.

54

Bending into her waist, he hoisted her over his shoulder and weighed her like a sack.

He turned toward Floy's hiding place. Camouflaged by young branches shooting from low on the tree, Floy did not dodge back. She was confident of not being seen.

The zoon lens focused. The shutter whirred.

As the couple approached, Floy marvelled at the young man's physique. As he strained under his kicking, back-thumping, squealing load, every muscle in his athletic torso tautened.

His wiry brush of pubic hair was almost hidden by his erection, bigger and more vigorous than in the night before. His face grinned wickedly as he approached a fallen oak trunk, four feet in diameter at least and only three good strides from Floy's refuge tree.

Floy found the sight of the round, upturned bottom of the captured Prissy almost as arousing as the young man's body. Those plump, blonde-fringed leaves of flesh that Floy had wanted to take in her mouth glowed pinkly in the morning light.

She zoomed in on the syrupy lips and snapped, quivering with expectation. Her clitoris was swelling, sensitised by the eroticism of the scene. She nearly whistled with surprise as the masterful Jay lowered his naked woman stomach down across the fallen trunk. He must have already prepared for this situation. As quick as lightning he produced a loop of rope, slipped it round his lover's neck and pulled. This took her head down the far side of the log, her arms hanging to the ground. With other ropes, he quickly snared her wrists and ankles and trussed her tightly.

The delectable Prissy was now spreadeagled, head down, bottom up, legs wide apart, hands tied tightly behind her back. She cried and struggled but her lover had done his preparation well.

He knelt in front of her, facing Floy's position. She could see the sparkle of lechery in his eyes.

Throwing his head back, he laughed loudly.

'Now my little vixen, you're mine to do what I like with, you naughty, wicked girl!' He took a switch of young supple branches – also, it appeared, previously prepared – and, bending over her, began to thwack her bottom. The leaves at the ends of the switch wrapped between Prissy's open thighs and flicked against her moist and tender flesh.

Floy trembled as she zoomed in and snapped again.

She trembled more as the girl cried out with the pleasure as much as with the pain.

'You bastard, Jay Polland! Just you let me go this minute, or I'll never speak to you again!'

'Oh no, my sweetness. You wanted to be done in the woods, and you will be well done!' He thwacked again. She yelled, feigning anger, Floy could tell.

Floy sank to her knees, her thighs shaking with the referred pleasure coursing through her. She could almost feel the switch on her own buttocks, the leafy tips stinging her own pouting lips.

Floy felt the erotic ache deep inside her body building to explosive pitch now, as she watched Prissy's sex spasm open and then close with the stimulation of the switch.

'Now, since you've been so wicked, I'm going to leave you to the animals. The wolves will come and lick your naughty bits while I go and find another nymph to stick my horn in!'

He strolled nonchalantly away across the clearing.

'Jay Polland, you bloody bastard! Come back here at once and fuck me like a man!'

He took no notice, skipped between the trees on the far side of the clearing, and was gone.

Floy gulped. He had actually left his Prissy trussed up and helpless.

She zoomed in on the pink love-lips of the bound bride. Prissy's succulent bottom filled the viewfinder, bright in the sunlight. The girl strained her buttocks to get free. The golden hairs quivered as the lips they surrounded opened and closed. Each pubic whisker was clearly in focus; the engorged pink labia gleamed wetly.

Floy snapped, uncaring of the wind-on motor's whirr.

Her heart was doing a hundred and eighty. Her legs shook uncontrollably. She could feel wetness between her own legs.

Something in Floy took her over. All common sense and caution left her. She put down the camera. Her pulse raced as she slithered on hands and knees, inching towards the open legs of the tied-up blonde.

Even if she craned her neck Prissy would not glimpse Floy approaching from behind. Neither would Jay see her if he returned from the woods at the same place he had left the clearing. She was well hidden by the massive fallen trunk. And she could crawl back to cover before he could reach his young wife.

The leaves rustled under Floy as she approached.

'Jay, you bastard! I can hear you. Just you come round here and face me. I'll give you a piece of my mind!' Prissy strained at the ropes tying her wrists behind her back.

Floy undressed. She peeled off her jeans and soaked panties, and shed the white blouse, now wet too with perspiration.

Lying on her stomach, she raised her torso on her elbows, her face nuzzling between the legs stretched out before her. With her forehead cushioned by Prissy's sun-hot, red-striped, elastic buttocks, she rested momentarily and breathed the other woman's scent.

Then she pursed her mouth. At first contact with the plump youthful lips a wave of shock ran through her, thrilling in her tautened abdomen, and deep between her legs.

'Jay, you pig! Just stop that! I thought you agreed to bonking, not licking!'

Too preoccupied with the erotic sensation of kissing another woman's secret parts, Floy took no notice of the protest. Her tongue found the hardened nub of Prissy's clitoris. She licked it, savouring the taste.

The helpless girl shuddered, Her vulva spasmed rhythmically. This spurred Floy on. Again she felt a sense of enormous power. Just as she had with the men, she could conjure pleasure from another body, and give pleasure in return.

As Floy tickled the proud nubbin, Prissy's scent was pungent. She could smell her own scent too. Until quite recently that had been a smell to abhor; to wash away at every occasion.

Now this aroma acted on her senses like no other perfume had. Even the bath oil she had purchased especially from France and used to lure the halpless Ramon each night had not half the power of this aroma.

Trembling helplessly with total abandonment to the illicit act, Floy felt her mouth working continuously. Her tongue stroked sensuously at the erectile tissue, her nose slid between the glistening lips.

Those lips writhed now to every tongue-rasp. Floy knelt, not taking her mouth away from the struggling woman for an instant. Her hands grazed the downy buttocks, stretching and spreading them wider to increase Prissy's sensations and to gain better access for herself. She dug her thumb-nails into the hollows on each side of Prissy's pulsing lips and sucked hard on the swollen nub.

Prissy cried and panted ecstatically.

Floy paused to consider the situation. The girl's cries could bring her husband racing back.

'Oh, Jay. You're the biggest tease I've ever known. But fuck me. I need to feel your ram!'

Floy was just in time to see a flash of pink among the trees. She grabbed her clothes and retreated to cover, her naked breasts tickling through the leaves, her breath panting uncontrollably.

The ecstatic Prissy was now screaming for more.

'Don't stop now, lover, ram me!'

Floy assumed that Prissy had her eyes closed, because she kept on pleading even as Jay walked jauntily towards her across the glade, his face alight with pleasure, his ram, like a jousting lance, at full tilt.

Calmly and without a word he rounded the log. Leaning his spread hands on the hollow of her back, he splayed his legs and aimed.

Floy's camera snapped just as the purple tip homed in on the expectant, eager sex-mouth.

As he thrust and thrust and thrust, Prissy screamed once and shuddered, her body convulsing against the tree trunk.

The beautiful Jay withdrew and stood, the tool of his manhood dripping; beating in the sunshine.

Floy managed one last close-up of the dewy tip before she sank, shuddering, to the ground. Among the leaves she shook in silent agony. But still the tension in the whole of her body would not be released.

She had reasoned that the more and more abandoned the sexual acts she took part in, the more likely it was that she would reach orgasm. She had been wrong.

It was almost unbearable to watch her erstwhile love-mate, Prissy, quivering in ecstatic convulsions over the trunk. And she – despite a frantic finger on her super-sensitised sexual nub, despite the taste of Prissy on her lips, and the memory of that soft and beautiful spasming flesh in her mouth – she still could not obtain relief.

Floy looked up. The lovers sat on the trunk now, Prissy sobbing in Jay's arms. She stroked his cheek and kissed him.

'You beautiful, darling men. How did you know that was what I needed? All the lovemaking we've done this week, wonderful as it was, was nothing compared to that.'

He stroked her tenderly.

'Shhh, my sweetheart, shhh.'

'Promise me you'll tie me up like that and whip me and lick me and fuck me just like that again.'

He laughed.

'If that's what it takes, my darling. But I only tied you and beat you and fucked you. I didn't lick you.'

59

She gave him a playful push.

'Fibber. I felt you. It was the best licking you've ever done.'

Jay looked at her with puzzlement.

'It must have been the foxes, sweetness.'

Floy was crying. She sat against the oak tree, her eyes streaming silently. Her solar plexus heaved. She worked her hand in her own damp warmth for comfort more than stimulation. She was soaked; she had been so ready, but she had not had release. She raised her head to the canopy above and, closing her eyes, whispered, 'Oh sweet Mother of God. What am I doing to myself?'

The neigh of a horse caught Floy's attention and brought her back from her self-pitying reverie. She picked up her camera and peered round her tree. She focused.

Across the glade a bronze-skinned man sat upon a magnificent Arab horse. Dressed in white jodhpurs, black helmet and black coat, the rider surveyed the clearing. His disposition, the huge and glossy Arab, the red tack, together with glinting polished brass, signalled to her: power and certainty. She recognised him at once.

The magnificent beast stood champing. The two young lovers strolled, arm in arm, to meet him. The rider looked down and smiled upon them. The young woman reached up and stroked the horse's head, her lips pressed to its muzzle. As she stretched up to take its ears in a caress, her perfect breasts pressed against thin material and hung highlighted in the mid-morning sun.

The young woman put up her arms to the rider. With seeming ease, he swung her up before him, her legs straddling the horse's broad neck.

Floy thrilled at the imagined feeling of being on horseback; of being naked; of that long black mane sweeping at her own open sex-lips.

The trio turned and moved towards Floy's tree, Jay leading the stallion while Ramon held Prissy around her waist.

Tears streamed down Floy's face. Such total acceptance and such simplicity were surely more valuable than anything money could ever buy.

Setting down the camera, she hastily pulled on her jeans. Then, blouse in hand, she turned and made her way back towards the open park. Still afraid of being discovered, she felt like a thief. She had stolen sexual pleasures from Jay and Prissy and from young John. In her desperate need for experience she had used them.

But could she stop now?

She answered no. The stakes were too high. There was too much money at risk. She dared not stop or change her plan, and must see it through even if there were other Jays and Prissys and Johns. She must see it through, even at the risk of hurting Ramon DuPrey.

Guilt about the others she could cope with. They had suffered little or no harm. But Ramon was different. She hoped he was more able to handle things she might do to him. No matter what happened to make her soften, it was imperative that she remain cold and hard where he was concerned.

Striding across the open parkland, Floy was so preoccupied with her resolutions and her plans that she did not hear the thundering hooves. It was the shouting voice which captured her attention.

'Floy. For God's sake, run!'

She smiled. If Ramon DuPrey was going to play the knight on galloping horseback in an attempt to gain her attention, he would be disappointed.

The thundering got louder. So did his shouting.

'Floy! For God's sake look behind you!'

There was an angry bellow.

She spun.

Surprise turned to terror as she saw the bull charging

at her. It was within a hundred paces and a streak of black horse-flesh closely at its tail.

She quelled the terror and stood. It seemed like madness but she would not show her fear.

The bull neared, panting. It let out another bellow.

Floy stood her ground. She had lived so long on the horns of her personal dilemma that she could not believe she could die now on the horns of a bull.

As it approached, she prayed. She asked God for forgiveness of her sins of the past week, of the wickedness she had wrought.

When the bull was within a yard, she flung herself aside. The ground came up to meet her. She took a bite of grass.

A set of bovine hooves thudded past.

She looked up.

The bull had stopped, was turning.

A black shadow flew over her as Ramon DuPrey's horse cleared her and pulled up to a stiff-legged halt in front of the bull.

It snorted.

He shouted.

It bellowed.

He heeled the horse's sides.

The horse reared.

The bull charged.

With amazing skill Ramon turned the horse. Almost simultaneously it lashed out and struck the charging bull with flying hooves. The creature swerved and careered on.

Then it stopped and turned again, prepared for a charge at Floy.

'Floy, get up! Quickly, woman!'

She obeyed. This was no place to debate who was the boss.

Ramon came up behind her. With one sweep he grabbed her under the arms and hoisted her up.

Clutching the edge of his saddle she managed to heave her legs over the horse's mane.

Now she was on, straddling the muscular neck.

Ramon executed a sharp toreador's turn and the horse powered towards the house. Shouting and the roar of an engine behind them made Floy glance round. A Land Rover and half a dozen men were racing across the grass.

Saying nothing, Ramon clasped her tightly around the waist. In turn she clasped the horse's mane.

He cantered.

Now she felt what Prissy had felt, the rubbing of the steely muscles beneath her lower lips. This, and the excitement of the narrow escape, and of the warmth of Ramon DuPrey against her back, made Floy pant. Her heart was racing, her pulse drumming at her temple.

The horse slowed to a trot with no discernible command from its rider.

They entered the stable yard. Her Bentley was standing in the open garage, a beaten-up Mini beside it. Ramon halted the horse. Still he said nothing. Still he clung to her, both arms tight around her rib cage; his face buried in her shoulder now, breathing deeply.

She stretched her neck back. She sighed as she felt the warmth of his face on her cheek, the heat of his body against her back, the heat of his breath coursing through her blouse to warm her breast.

'Thank you, Ramon. You were very brave.'

'It was nothing. I thank God I was near enough.'

He breathed deeply into her hair.

She patted the horse's neck. 'He's beautiful. What's his name?'

'Charlemagne.'

'Have you had him long?' It was small talk. With his arms around her, her breasts nestling onto his wrists, she needed an excuse to stay; an excuse to allow him to continue to hold her.

'Charlemagne was my father's horse. I keep him for stud. There's a mare coming tomorrow morning. Would you like to watch him cover her?'

Floy thrilled. She knew that he would feel it. She

knew also that he was coaxing her. He was deliberately stimulating her with talk of mating the horse; to have her watch, perhaps in the hope that she would allow him to mount her afterwards. In the hay-loft? In the stall with the stallion nosing at her sexual parts?

Why could she not simply say: yes, Ramon, I know what you want. Come to my room and mate me like the bull and the stallion.

But it would not work. She knew it would not. Still she must goad him into action, make him angry like the bull. Only then would she get what she needed and avoid getting what she must deny herself at all costs.

'How did that bull get loose?'

'I don't know. Something must have spooked it.'

'Why did it charge me!'

The conversation was still strange. It was contrived. But so many of their conversations had been the same: polite and uncommitted or evasive.

Floy still sat astride the horse's neck, Ramon's hands were still tight around her, still he did not move to dismount.

'You clearly excited Jasper.'

'Jasper?'

He laughed.

'The bull.'

'You're joking! Me excite him? How could I do that?'

Ramon moved one hand. It slid down her stomach and slipped between her legs. Floy felt it warm against her wetness. Part of her thrilled to have it there, another part of her wanted to flee, just like John had flown from her.

The realisation that she was afraid of Ramon DuPrey hit her hard. She had not let herself be overawed by the bull, but she was frightened by the man and the emotions he was arousing in her.

'The bull must have scented you. It has been known for a woman in heat to draw a bull from half a mile away.'

He still held her tight between the legs. Floy leaned

64

back against him. She wanted him to move the hand, to slip it inside her jeans. She wanted it to massage her engorged lips and work her swelling bud. She sighed and closed her eyes.

Suddenly, panic welled inside her.

She cocked her leg over the mane, vaulted to the ground and ran.

Ramon was dismayed. He sat on his mount wondering what he must do to capture the enigmatic Floy Pennington.

Raising his hand to his nose he smelled the scent of her strong on his fingers where he had held her intimately; where his hand had covered the crevice of her soft and heated sex.

It had seemed right at the time. She had leaned into him, indicating that she liked the way he held her. She had been frightened and so it had been a natural thing to do.

And she had made conversation, as if wanting to prolong their closeness. She had trembled at his mention of mating Charlemagne to a mare. He had felt her solar plexus tighten, her legs grip the horse more tightly. Her heart had pumped against his wrist. Her breasts had heaved.

When answering her question about her attraction for the bull, the only way he had been able to prove it to himself, and to her, had been to see if she was wet. He had guessed that she had been watching the young newlyweds in the clearing. When he had first spotted her, she had been too near them in the woods not to have witnessed their wild sexual abandon.

Perhaps she had been peeping even as Jay Polland had thrust his Pan's horn into the luscious Priscilla, trussed to the tree trunk.

Through his binoculars Ramon had watched as he had approached the clearing. The horse had smelled them first, opening its nostrils, pawing at the ground. At first he had wondered what he had stumbled on. A wild orgy? Then he had recognised his guests and smiled.

They were young. Why should they not have fun on their honeymoon; to have memories which would last them all their lives. All too soon the mortgage and the gas bills, the babies and the broken down cars would cripple them emotionally as well as financially.

Under the strain, Jay would probably find another lover who was still free of cares and who would fuck and romp with the same abandon that Priscilla fucked and sucked and gambolled now. She would become embittered by the ties of family, imprisoned in the home. He would leave his pretty young wife of today and start again. Men of prodigious sexual appetites often did.

But what of himself and Florence Pennington? He had not even made a start with her. Despite her night-time activities he had been unable to get past her icy barrier in the day-time.

Again she had slipped out of his grasp, just when he thought he had her. Now all he had was her sexual scent on his hand. As he breathed it deeply, his own horn hardened, already almost erect with her heat against it and the jogging of the horse.

The horse smelled her too and pricked his ears, pawing at the cobbles with a hoof. Ramon patted the black neck. The stallion was frustrated too.

At least tomorrow the stallion could be certain that he would get his end away.

Not so with himself and Florence Pennington.

But there was no way he could continue in this vein. He had lost control and must get it back. As a rider of powerful horses, he knew the penalties of letting a mare have her head. She became just that: headstrong; diffi-cult to ride, and temperamental.

He would see what Miss Pennington would do tonight. Then he would make his mind up. Perhaps he would abandon the whole idea of making love to her, and just take her roughly. If not that, he must forget her and get back into Jannine's good books and into her bed.

At least Jannine was simple. All right, she was moody; but only when she thought he had his interest trained on another woman. In bed she was like a steam engine, hot and spitting; rhythmic in her motion. Her crevice was small and tight. It had the most amazing muscles. She seemed to be able to grip and suck him in at will. But somehow there was a missing ingredient. No matter how she sucked him and fucked him, he was never satisfied.

The moment he had set eyes on Floy Pennington, he had known instinctively that she had the missing ingredient he had been searching for. She made him instantly horny; something that no other woman had ever done. She made his solar plexus flutter, but that was not all. Somehow they were soul-mates. Perhaps she did not acknowledge it, but he had seen indications that somewhere deep inside her there were feelings which she would not let go.

He wanted more than just to make love to her. Sometimes he wanted to ram her with abandon; sometimes to explore every millimetre of her wonderful body with his tongue. He wanted her mind, her emotions and her wit. He wanted her soul.

The intellect which showed through her writing was a challenge to him. Few women he had known could match it.

And she wanted him. Or seemed to.

But the bitch was either playing hard to get, or she was a repressed lesbian, or she was taking delight in hating his masculinity. And so far, he had not decided which.

In contrast, Jannine was instantly available. The great thing was that she made all the running. He did not have to chase her. She would touch him up behind the cocktail bar when they were working. She would make him so hard that it was impossible for him to go out and serve for fear of revealing his arousal to the guests.

She would slide her hand inside his zip in the office despite the risk of getting caught. It was this very risk that seemed to excite her most. Once she had been on her knees in the kitchen giving him head, sucking on his hardness, when a guest had walked in. She had pretended to be looking for a dropped saucepan lid while he had hurriedly grabbed the chef's spare apron to hide his dripping shaft.

Yes, Jannine was easy. She was simple in her needs. Not like the unfathomable; the frustrating; the frustrated Miss Pennington.

Floy stood with her back to her sitting-room door, still shaking from her encounter with the bull and with the stallion – Ramon DuPrey. She touched herself between the legs. The memory of his hand there still lingered.

She sighed. Why in God's name had she set out on this course? If she had not taken on this damned book she would not be here now. She could have told the publisher to find another author. But then, there was the money. He had been particularly successful in selling the rights. TV and film rights could turn thousands into millions. There was no real choice. She would just have to work hard at the book and get it finished. Then she could review the situation and perhaps return to simple mystery and murder and suspense.

She smiled to herself emptily. Were there any such things as simple mystery, murder or suspense? Was there anything simple when it came to human relationships and actions?

Floy went to shower. She stopped herself. The shower would wash away the lingering sensation of Ramon DuPrey's hand. She would leave it for a while and smell of sexual arousal.

She did change into a clean pair of jeans, and found a pristine white blouse. There was something which she had to do. She had lost control. It was imperative to reassert herself. Running from him like a silly schoolgirl had been stupid. Now he would know that she was weaker than she wanted him to think her. He would know that she had liked him holding her and, by her wetness, he would have known that she was in heat, like an animal.

Also, she had thanked him only cursorily for saving her. Good manners demanded that she make amends for that.

Voices escaped noisily from Ramon DuPrey's office.

'Yes, Mr DuPrey. No, Mr DuPrey. But what can I do, Mr DuPrey?'

Floy pushed past the receptionist despite the girl's outstretched hand. As an important guest of the hotel she would not stand aside while he dressed down his staff. And, beside that, Floy Pennington must live up to her reputation as the bitch, must be seen to be active and in full spate.

As she flung open the door, she was surprised to find Mr and Mrs Polland standing like juniors in front of an angry headmaster.

Floy bristled. So, after all, DuPrey was admonishing them for their naked cavorting in his woods.

He looked up sharply as she entered.

'One moment please, Miss Pennington. I'm in conference.'

She did not budge.

'I need to see you. And I need my diamonds for tonight. I have a guest for dinner.' It was a lie but what of that? She was the bitch.

DuPrey ignored her. This made Floy indignant, but she waited all the same.

'I'm sorry, Mr and Mrs Polland, but you'll have to settle this car repair bill. The mechanic fixed your car and he needs to be paid.' Ramon waved an oily piece of paper at them.

'But we haven't got that much. We've only enough cash to pay the price we agreed for our accommodation. That bill's almost as much!'

Prissy was in tears. They rolled down her cheeks as she turned and glanced at Floy, then looked back at DuPrey.

Ramon DuPrey put out his hand in desperation.

'I'll take a cheque for the accommodation. You can give the garage man your cash.'

Prissy looked up at Jay and then back at DuPrey.

'Apart from a bit of money Jay has saved to start his new business, that's all the money we have in the world. We wanted to have the best honeymoon ever; something to remember all our lives.'

DuPrey took a deep breath.

'But I can't help it if your car needed fixing. You did ask me to get the man up to look at it.'

The Pollands spoke together.

'Yes, but we didn't think it would cost that much!'

'Well, I'm sorry, but you'll have to dip into your savings.'

DuPrey got up. To Floy he seemed to have shut the case.

'Yes, Miss Pennington, which jewels did you say?'

Floy put up her hand.

'Just a moment, Mr DuPrey. How much money is involved here?'

Three pairs of eyes looked at her with surprise.

'Three hundred and fifty pounds.'

She stiffened.

'Add it to my account. Now, can I have my diamonds?'

Three mouths dropped open. Prissy was the first to collect her wits.

'But – but you can't do that. It's very generous, but – '

'Nonsense. But if you feel badly about it, treat it as a loan. You can pay it back when Jay's business is up and running profitably. Mr DuPrey will give you my address.'

Floy smiled at the tearful Prissy and touched her face lovingly.

70

'You're so beautiful. I envy you your young love. I don't like to see you sad. And you deserve to have a good start. Keep your savings, child. Invest them wisely, with my blessing.'

Ramon held out the case of diamonds, his mouth still wide open. To his amazement Floy Pennington touched Priscilla's forehead with two fingers. She made the sign of the cross, took the case and left.

Chapter Four

*F*loy was in the shower when she heard a knock on the outer door. Her heart leapt. She calmed it. If it was Ramon DuPrey, she would still keep to her plan. She would keep him on the edge of uncertainty.

Wrapping a towel around herself she went to dispel the mystery.

Prissy Polland stood in the corridor. She looked nervous.

'I – I came to say . . .'

Floy motioned her inside. She did not relish passers-by seeing her in towels.

She smiled at Prissy. In the light and close up, she was very pretty. Her blonde hair bounced around her face with a natural curl. Her skin was clear, her complexion vital.

'I came to say thank you for paying our bill.'

Floy smiled genuinely.

'That's all right. I appreciate your thanks.'

Prissy looked round the room. Her eyes alighted on the word processor.

'Mr DuPrey said you were writing a new book. I've read some of yours you know. I read *Murder in the Cloisters* when I was only fifteen.'

Floy smiled again. She was surprised that the young woman read her type of book.

'I'm glad you like my writing.'

Prissy hovered uncertainly, going to the bowl of rosebuds and fingering them admiringly. She obviously wanted to talk. Floy beckoned her into the bedroom.

'Come through while I dry my hair. It'll go knotted if I leave it.'

Prissy smiled widely, clearly pleased to be permitted to stay.

Floy sat at the dressing-table. She switched on the hair dryer.

'Let me do that,' Prissy said. 'I work in a beauty salon.'

'Thanks.'

Prissy worked studiously at the hair. Floy enjoyed it. She rarely went to a hairdresser except to have it cut. Her style was self-managing as far as possible.

'You're very beautiful, you know.'

Floy looked in the mirror at her hairdresser. She was surprised at the compliment.

'It's nice of you to say so. But is it really true?'

'Of course it is. I wouldn't say it just to please you. I hope I'll be beautiful like you when I get to your age.'

Floy smiled.

'How old are you?'

'Twenty one.'

'You're really lovely now, I'm sure you'll be a stunner when you're my age.'

'And as sexy as you, too?'

Floy laughed freely. She was almost embarrassed at the comment.

'I'm not sexy, am I?'

'You're a tease in that cat-suit you wear.'

Floy held her breath.

'It doesn't cover you up, really. It shows everything off, even between your legs. And it makes Jay hard to watch your bottom in that tight black velvet.'

Now Floy flattened an expression of amazement.

'Does it?'

'Yes, My Jay says he'd like to feel your arse. He says you're very sexy. He says . . .'

Floy studied the reflection of Prissy's bright red face. Now she smiled with amusement at the girl. There was obviously nothing like calling a spade a spade where Prissy Polland was concerned.

'What does Jay say I am? A cow?'

Prissy blushed brighter.

'I was going to say that he thinks you're really fuckable. Why did you say cow?'

Floy pondered her answer. The girl was being forthright. She needn't have been honest about the 'fuckable'. And there was some other reason why she was here. The only way to find out was to wait until she spat it out. Floy decided to be forthright too.

'I overheard him say I was a cow.'

Prissy's eyes watered.

'Did you hear us through that door?'

Floy nodded. It was not strictly true but she could not confess to her clandestine visit to their room.

'Can you hear us bonking?'

Again, Floy smiled at another apt description. That was most of what she had heard most of the time – bonking.

'Yes, I can hear you.'

'Do you mind?'

'No, I don't mind. I find it strangely stimulating.'

Prissy showed surprise.

'Do you like sex?' She brushed Floy's hair vigorously, as if she was nervous of the answer.

'I think so.'

'Don't you know?'

'I've never done it.'

Prissy stopped brushing and stood back, astonished.

'You've never fucked?'

Floy shook her head and smiled, her eyes twinkling. This girl was a tonic. She was so open, so refreshingly uninhibited.

'No, Prissy. I've never fucked.'

Prissy scowled.

'But why not? Are you a dyke?'

Floy creased her brow.

'Are you a lesbian?'

Floy increased her frown. The way she had nuzzled between this young woman's legs that very morning made her wonder if she *was* a lesbian.

'I don't think I am a lesbian. I don't really know.'

'I don't mind if you are.'

'Thank you.'

'I lived with a woman before I met Jay. She was beautiful like you. She taught me a lot. I was only sixteen. My old lady threw me out when I wouldn't let her boyfriend screw me.'

Floy smiled her acknowledgement of Prissy's confession.

'Why haven't you had sex? It's really wild you know. It makes all your body tingle. You get all hot and kind of tingly, especially between your legs, sort of swollen and nearly painful with excitement. And if the man's good, it makes you writhe and moan. Jay's very good at it. The problem is, I don't come yet when we fuck.'

'Come?'

'Orgasm.'

'Of course.'

'He hasn't got it right yet. He is trying hard. But he licks me all right.'

'I know.'

Floy snapped her mouth shut. The words were out now and she could do nothing about it.

Prissy looked round at the communication door to her room. The brass key was still in the lock. Floy's heart pattered with apprehension. She had been found out.

Prissy's face became stern.

'You put that rose on our pillow, didn't you?'

Floy sat up straight and looked Prissy's reflection in the eyes.

'Yes, I'm afraid I did.'

Prissy cocked her head on one side. The look in her eyes was more of puzzlement than of condemnation.

'Why did you do that?'

'I thought you looked so beautiful, lying naked together.'

'Did you watch us fucking?'

Floy's face drained.

'Yes I did.'

'Why?'

'I've never seen anyone having intercourse before.'

Prissy threw her head back and laughed.

'People don't have intercourse any more. That's what the Victorians did, isn't it? Now, people fuck each other's rocks off. They lick and suck each other. They stick vibrating things up their arses, tie each other up and whip them until they shout with pleasure.'

Floy was coming alight. This was talking dirty. She had known other women who talked like this. But at that time she had been totally unaware of what it really meant. She had been shut and guarded, her legs always tight together, her mind closed to such bawdiness. The words had had no significance.

This girl was free and open. She held her legs open too. In bed she had splayed them as if ready for sex at any time.

Lately, Floy had noticed how tightly she had kept her own legs together, even when she lay in bed. But that was changing. With her clandestine sexual adventures she was opening up too. In fact, she felt that Prissy was someone she could talk to frankly.

'Ramon DuPrey wants to fuck you. Do you know that?'

Floy was taken aback somewhat.

'Did he tell you?'

'No, but you can see it in his eyes. And he gets a hard-on whenever he goes near you.'

'You're very perceptive.'

'I watch men's cocks all the time. Don't you?'

Floy nearly blushed. Since she had been at The DuPrey Hotel – since the time she had seen Ramon DuPrey naked in his room – she had developed a habit of watching the bulges in men's trousers.

'Why don't you let Ramon DuPrey do it with you? I'm sure he's very good at it. I wouldn't mind a ride with him myself. He's part French you know. Frenchmen are usually good at sex.'

'Really?'

'Mmmm. Really, really good!' Prissie's laughter tinkled just like it had around the clearing that morning.

Floy smiled as Prissy stood back to admire her handiwork on Floy's hair. She swivelled to face Prissy.

'That's very nice. Thank you very much.' She looked up at the young blonde, her legs set wide in ragged jeans, her hands on her shapely hips, her nipples hard under the cotton of a white T-shirt. The vee in her tight jeans bulged prominently, presumably with the mass of blonde hair Floy had seen. She was the picture of rude health. A raunchy, sparkling young woman, ready to handle any man she chose. Her libido seemed to light her and to flow freely from her in an exciting way. The only other person Floy had felt this from was Ramon DuPrey.

Looking at Prissy made Floy sad to think how she had been at that age.

Prissy stepped close; close enough for Floy to put her hand out and place it on one slender, fine-haired arm. Prissy looked down on her, smiling.

'Do you fancy me?' She thrust her breasts out proudly.

Floy looked her straight in the eyes.

'I'm not quite sure. I admire you tremendously. You're so open and honest. I find your body irresistibly attractive. I want to touch you and caress you. Is that what fancying means?'

Prissy knelt between Floy's feet. She looked up with a soft expression. Taking Floy's hands in hers, she whispered.

77

'Where have you been all your life? Haven't you lived at all? Don't you know anything about sex and loving and people and what they need?'

A tear rolled down Floy's cheek. Prissy reached up and kissed it lovingly away. Letting go of one hand, she eased away the towel from Floy's body and removed it. Then she ran her finger over the downward curve of Floy's breast. At the nipple she stroked until it stood up hard. Then she took the finger and kissed it.

'You really are beautiful, you know. You really should believe it. I'm not a lesbian, but I like women's bodies. I don't see any reason why one woman shouldn't make love to another. It doesn't make me gay. All people are beautiful in one way or another. You've just got to look for the good bits and ignore the bad.'

Tears streamed down Floy's cheeks now. She stroked Prissy's hair.

Prissy caught her hand and kissed the tips of Floy's long fingers.

'I think, behind that icy shell you put on, you're a soft and loving woman. Why don't you let go? Why don't you let someone love you?'

Floy's tears flowed freely.

Prissy stroked them away with her fingertips. She nodded knowingly.

'What can I do to take that sadness away? I want to do something to repay you for your kindess to us.'

Floy breathed deeply and shook her head.

'I don't know, Prissy, my love. I wish I did.'

Floy continued stroking Prissie's hair and running her fingers across the youthful face.

'To tell you the truth I'm frightened.'

'What are you frightened of? The way you flounce around downstairs gives me the impression you wouldn't be frightened of anything or anyone.'

'I'm frightened of myself.'

'Why?'

'I'm discovering things I didn't know about my body. I have feelings I never suspected until this week.'

'Why's that so bad?'

'I can't afford to lose control. There is too much at stake.'

'Money?'

'Yes.'

'Money isn't the most important thing in the world.'

'It is to me.'

'But why do you need to lose control just to let yourself be loved?'

'I don't know. I've been dominated all my life until recently. I dare not let it happen again.'

Prissy's eyes showed sadness. Floy could see them watering.

'But if someone loves you, that doesn't mean they would dominate you.'

'A man would.'

'Only if you let him. Anyway, whoever told you that?'

Floy shook her head. She didn't know. It was just one of the control factors she had been brought up with.

'Have you ever had your breasts sucked?'

Floy shook her head.

'Have you ever had anyone touch you or lick your clitoris?'

Floy shook her head again.

'No, I told you. I've never had sex like that or any other way. I've never had anyone do anything to me.'

Prissy reached up and stroked her face lovingly.

'Have you ever been cuddled?'

'I don't remember. My mother died when I was young. I was brought up in an orphanage. Until I saw you lying on your bed last night, I'd never seen a man and woman hold each other tenderly. I've seen many bodies, but never seen them as sexual. Only functional.'

Floy looked down and then back into Prissy's eyes.

'I'm sorry. It was very wrong of me to look at you like that when you were asleep. I feel like a thief, taking a view of you without your knowledge.'

Prissy stood. She slipped her blouse off. She sloughed off her jeans and skimpy panties. She braced her legs widely, standing wonderfully nude and totally unashamed.

'Look at me. Don't be ashamed. Don't feel bad. I would have done the same. If I had been you with a key to that door I would have been in there making out with us.' She grinned a face-wide grin. 'People take sex too seriously. It's for fun. Enjoy it.'

'I'll try.'

'Do you like my tits?' She lifted them proudly towards Floy.

'I think they're prefect.'

Prissy brushed her pubic hair.

'Do you like my bush?'

'It's incredibly bushy.'

Prissy bent her leg up and put it on Floy's knee. She looked down and teased her pubic hairs.

'Jay likes the way my hair goes right round to form a sort of beard round my lips. Do you like that?'

Floy was shaking with excitement. She could smell the same stimulating, pungent smell she had smelled that morning. It had stayed in her nostrils for a couple of hours. Again it made her clitoris thrill.

She had never imagined that looking at another woman intimately could turn her to jelly. That morning when she had watched Prissy tied to the tree trunk she had lost control, the compulsion to touch her had been so great. She had buried her lips in the very area which Prissy was showing off so proudly now. But she had done it so covertly that Prissy did not know. She felt the need to confess. But she could not.

'I think that everything about you is perfect.'

Prissy pulled Floy's hands and made her stand.

'And you are too. It makes me go all wobbly just to look at you.'

Floy smiled.

'I'm glad.'

Prissy ran her hands lightly over Floy's face. Her

finger-tips traced her lips and skimmed down over her breasts. The continued down to her waist and then back in to her mount of Venus, black and thick and flat, a contrast to Prissy's bush.

Prissy knelt. She put her hands around Floy's buttocks and placed her lips to Floy's smooth pubic mat. She kissed it lovingly.

Floy widened her stance. Prissy nuzzled in between her legs, kissing with small pouting motions. Floy thrilled. The excitement of being touched there by another person was making her shake.

As Prissy kissed, Floy kneaded her hair. Her fingers wandered down her slender neck. She stroked it sensuously.

Prissy stood, led Floy to the bed and gently pulled her down beside herself.

Floy felt like a child. She allowed Prissy to put her arm around her neck and shoulder and to pull her face into the crook of her own neck.

Naked beside the young woman, Floy felt small. Her pulse beat loudly in her ears. But the gentle rise and fall of Prissy's chest was soothing.

Prissy stroked her back with one hand. The other pulled at Floy's buttocks so her pubis pressed on Prissy's own.

Prissy kissed her forehead.

'It's hard to be loved sometimes. You really have to trust and let go.'

Floy closed her eyes and tried to relax. The heat of the young body on her felt good. She felt shamed. For all her apparent worldliness she knew virtually nothing about sex or love compared with this girl.

Prissy's small but perfect breasts came warmly up to hers. Their nipples kissed.

Prissy pressed one though between Floy's legs. Now her warm leg nestled against Floy's moist lips. Prissy's own lush sex sucked on Floy's thigh in warm companionship.

Floy felt humbled. This girl was giving herself freely,

only hours after Floy had secretly stolen lascivious pleasure from her. She had kissed the sex-lips and licked the clitoris and stroked the pubic hair now pressed so close to hers.

'Were you in the woods this morning before you got chased by that bull?'

Floy nodded.

'And were you near that clearing when Jay tied me to that fallen tree?'

Floy nodded again. She was confessing to the gentle interrogation but could not say the words.

'And you took some pictures?'

Again, Floy nodded. She was more and more ashamed.

'I heard the camera wind on. I'd like some copies.'

Floy was surprised. She pulled her head back.

'You didn't mind?'

'I've never been turned on so much in all my life. Was it you who licked me?'

Floy could say nothing. She nodded.

'There, I said you were soft and loving. That was marvellous. Jay never does it like that, even though he tries hard. But you had me so excited. When he began to fuck me, I just exploded. That was the most excruciatingly wonderful sex I've ever had. I've never come with Jay's cock before.'

Prissy put out her lips and kissed Floy tenderly. Floy wept tears of joy.

Where was all the obscenity and the vulgarity she had been told sex consisted of? What had happened to the rudeness, the filth and squalor of the body which lurked in every darkened corner of the baser instincts of men and women? This was beautiful. It was kind and loving. It was stimulating and yet relaxing. It was love, unashamed and undemanding. It was natural.

Floy kissed Prissy tenderly.

'I love you Prissy Polland. You are the most wonderful young woman I've met.'

'I'm glad. You see. You can love someone without

strings. Why don't you let Ramon into your room tonight? You wouldn't have to do anything but let him lead. He's bound to be experienced.'

'I dare not. I couldn't just say, Ramon I need you to – to fuck me, could I?'

'Why ever not? He'd come in his pin-striped trousers.' She laughed.

'I couldn't. I don't want Ramon to love me.'

'Why?'

'I can't tell you.'

'All right.'

As if to reinforce her acceptance, Prissy raised herself on the bed. She lifted her breast and gently pressed the nipple to Floy's mouth. Floy took the gift and enclosed the hardened nub within her lips.

She closed her eyes and suckled.

Then they slept.

Ramon paced his office. Floy Pennington had not been down to lunch. Neither had she been for high tea as she usually did. It was five o'clock and he was getting worried. Was she all right? Was she suffering from shock? Should he check her room and see?

Perhaps she was working. Yes, that was it. She was catching up on the lost morning. She would surely be down to dinner.

He ran his fingers through his hair. This was crazy. He could not get Floy Pennington out of his mind. Every minute of the day, she occupied some corner of his thoughts. It was driving him mad.

Tonight must be the make or break time. If things did not come to a head one way or another he must withdraw and let her go her own way.

Should he check her room now? No, she might take it as an intrusion. The last thing he wanted was for her to throw him out. If he did get in, he would have to seduce her slowly. To rush her might court disaster. If he was to lose his head and rush things, she might later accuse him of rape. His reputation and that of the hotel could be ruined.

No, he would have to watch for her signs and make a considered judgement. After all, his hand in the heat between her thighs might have left her with some yearning for him to do it again. But maybe not. Would she have fled from him if she'd liked it?

Why were women so damned complicated when it came to sex?

The evening was tense. Floy Pennington appeared on time for dinner. Ramon was relieved. She looked stunning. Her hair shone more than usual. There was a light in her eyes which Ramon had not seen before.

She seemed unusually bright and chatted with the Pollands at their table. A change seemed to have come over her. Perhaps her generous gesture to the young couple had relieved her conscience in some way. She had appeared to be very money-conscious until now.

Ramon had observed among former guests that those with conspicuous amounts of wealth were also conspicuous in the way they hung on to it. Perhaps the iceberg had melted a little.

She was wearing the black cat-suit again. It was a strange contradiction of attitudes. At one moment hard and cold; another, sensuous and alluring.

As he had led her to her table, she had not shown any sign of friendship. That too was strange considering that he had saved her life. But then, perhaps his hand on her body had done the damage after all. Perhaps that had made her go cold on him again.

If so, why was she wearing the revealing suit? The soft downward vee of her pubis drew the eye of every man in the room, including Jay Polland.

Floy refused her table.

'I'll sit with Mr and Mrs Polland tonight, Mr DuPrey. Kindly have a place set at their table.'

Ramon bowed slightly. She could tell that her haugh-

84

tiness had him confused again. Good. That put her back in control.

Prissy was bright. Her face shone. Her eyes were alight. To Floy she seemed to have blossomed since their intimate afternoon. Perhaps she needed a woman in her life as well as a husband. It was an intriguing thought.

'I told Jay about – about what we discussed, Miss Pennington.'

'Please call me Floy.' She looked at them both and whispered. 'I hardly think we can be formal now that the secret of my voyeurism is out.' She turned to Jay. He looked at her boldly, not a hint of censure in his eyes.

'Put me out of my misery, Jay. Are you angry at me?'

He smiled.

'Why should I be? Whatever makes Prissy happy makes me happy.' He squeezed Prissy's hand as she reached across the table to him.

'We don't see any reason why people shouldn't enjoy each other in any way they like, providing no-one gets hurt.'

Floy took a deep breath. No, that was important. She thought of her plan. The only aspect of it that bothered her was that Ramon DuPrey might get hurt. But again, the importance of the outcome weighed heavier than that.

'You've gone sad again, Floy.'

Prissy took her hand too, holding Jay's and hers in a ring around the table.

Jannine brought soup and broke the intimacy. She glowered at Floy and stuck her nose in the air at the Pollands. Prissy whispered when she'd gone.

'She's Ramon's regular, I believe. I think she's had her nose put out of joint by someone.' Prissy winked at Floy.

Floy did not respond. She didn't want to know anything about Ramon DuPrey's love life.

'What business are you starting, Jay?'

The dinner went on with time-filling conversation. In the openness of the dining room, with many pairs of ears fully cocked in their direction, they were careful not to broach the subject they all know to be foremost in their minds.

It was not until they retired to a corner of the cocktail lounge that Floy felt the closeness between Prissy and herself return.

Jay was at the bar ordering drinks.

'How long are you and Jay staying?' Floy could hear the urgency in her voice.

'We've got to go tomorrow, early.' Prissy looked at her sadly.

'Must you?'

'I'm afraid so.' She put out a comforting hand to Floy's arm. 'We can meet again.'

Floy nodded.

'Of course.'

Jay put down the drinks and sat beside Prissy on a Regency settee. Floy sipped her bitter lemon slowly.

'Jay and me have been talking,' Prissy said.

Floy looked up.

'Yes,' Prissy paused, looking at Jay nervously, 'we were wondering if you'd like to come in and sleep with us.'

Floy put down her glass; her face questioning.

'I don't understand.' She looked with puzzlement at them both.

Prissy traced some spilt martini with her finger.

'I told Jay you were afraid of men. I told him you had never done sex with anyone, properly that is.'

Floy's eyes watered. Prissy continued.

'Well, if you came and slept with us, we could pleasure you. We could show you what to do so that you wouldn't be frightened of Ramon or anyone.'

Floy was aware of her mouth hanging open. She was also aware that Ramon was staring at the trio intently from the bar.

'I don't know what to say.'

'Don't say anything. It's the least we can do for you.'

'But – '

'But nothing. Don't chew it over. Just finish your drink and we'll go up.' She grinned. 'There's nothing like getting an early night.'

'I can't, Prissy. I've got something very important I must do tonight.'

'What's more important than learning to make love?'

Floy took a deep breath. She had no idea that sex could be such an open subject. With these young people she might just as well be talking about the weather. It was all so natural and so normal to them. Where was the sleaze she had been warned of?

'I have to be in my rooms by eleven.'

Prissy smirked.

'A secret assignation?'

Floy was aware of blushing.

'Something like that.'

'Well,' Prissy looked at her watch, 'that gives us two hours.'

'But what if – ?'

'Don't worry. You don't have to do anything if you don't want to. But if you do want to have sex with Jay, it's all right with me. You don't have to be afraid of him. Anyway, I'll be there to see that he does it gently for your first time. He gets carried away sometimes.'

Floy was in a turmoil. Prissy was graciously offering to lend her husband, as she might offer to lend a dress for a special occasion. Jay sat grinning at the whole prospect. She must have looked worried. Prissy put a reassuring hand on her arm.

'It's all right. I won't let him come inside you. He won't make you pregnant.'

Floy smiled to herself. No, he wouldn't. There was no fear of that.

'If you like, you can just watch us doing it. And then you can play with Jay's ramrod if you'd like to.' She grinned, 'I'll show you how to make it as hard as iron.

87

You can rub it between your legs if you want to, just to get the feel of it first.'

Floy shook her head in disbelief. She was being offered a crash course for virgins. How to stimulate a man in easy lessons.

Prissy leaned over the table conspiratorially. She whispered.

'And we'll show you some wicked little toys we've got. They'll make you all wet just to see them.'

Floy was quivering now. She was being offered the path to sin and damnation, and her body was loving the very thought of it. But was she losing track of the reason she was here? If she allowed herself to get diverted into sexual pleasures, she might not accomplish her task.

But then, what had she been doing already if not having sexual pleasures, albeit not very orgasmic ones?

Both Jay and Prissy were already naked when Floy edged through the communicating door into their dimly lit bedroom. They sat her at the bottom of their bed. Prissy had lit a joss stick and Floy found the sharp aroma cleansing to the nostrils. It made her breath deeply. She relaxed.

As Jay held back Floy's hair, Prissy slipped down the zipper of her catsuit. Slowly she peeled it off, putting her lips to Floy's bare shoulder as she did so.

Floy had worn nothing but the cat-suit. She had deliberately exposed as much of her sexual detail to Ramon as she could.

They laid her naked on her back. Jay came up beside her, his body hot against her own, Prissy lying by her on the other side.

Jay stroked Floy's face gently with a slender finger. Prissy sucked softly on one breast.

'Do you want to watch us first? Or shall we do a massage rota. We all massage each other in turn. The only rule is that you must massage every single millimetre of each other. There are no places which you're allowed to miss. It's scrumptuous.' She grinned.

Floy lay and pondered. She decided.

'Before we do anything, I've got a confession.'

They leaned over her, all ears and smiles.

'Last night, when I came in here and you were asleep, I did more than look at you. I touched Jay's penis and his testes. Then when he got aroused and started making love to you, I crouched at the bottom of the bed and watched.'

Floy closed her eyes, unable to look at them, she was so ashamed.

'I wish we'd known.'

'I was petrified you'd discover me.'

'Oh, what a shame. We've been wanting to try a threesome.'

Floy decided to confess all. She felt lighter of her guilt already.

'When Jay was giving you cunnilingus – '

'Cunny what?' Prissy giggled. 'Do you mean licking inside me?'

'Yes, when he was doing that. I crept under the bed. But my head was out. I lay between his legs and watched his – '

'His cock?'

'I watched his cock throbbing.'

Prissy grinned at Jay then at Floy.

'Isn't it a marvellous cock.'

'I wanted to reach up and take it in my mouth.'

'Why didn't you?'

'I couldn't. I didn't even know you then.'

Prissy gave Floy a wise nod of the head.

'Ah.'

'Then when you finished and went to sleep, I crept back to my bed and cried with frustration.'

Deep in thought, Jay stroked Floy's nipple soothingly. Prissy kissed Floy tenderly on the lips. Suddenly, her eyes sparked with fun.

'I know what we'll do.'

Jay grinned.

'What shall we do, sweetheart.'

'We'll let Floy do it all over again. Properly this time. We'll let her touch and lick and do anything she wants to.'

Floy's heart raced. This was wild. But her body was vibrating with the excitement of it all. What harm would it do? But would it be the same with their permission as it had been when furtively done? She would not know unless she tried.

The door to the honeymoon suite opened easily.

The lovers lay in beautiful nudity, on their backs, Jay Polland's hand on Prissie's breast, hers between his legs.

The rhythm of their breathing gave the impression they were really asleep. Naked herself, Floy tiptoed into the room.

Prissy was beautiful, her breasts rising and falling gently.

Jay's finger and thumb pinched a pouting nipple. It was aroused. Floy's heart pounded. Excitement trilled in her labia once again.

Prissy bent her leg, showing off her own plump lips, displaying the beard of fine, gold hair on either side. The scent was still pungent. It tightened Floy's stomach to a knot. This time she knelt at the bottom of the bed and leant forward to put her mouth to the warm and fleshy lips.

'Mmmm.' This time Prissy sighed.

Jay rolled over, relinquishing his mammary caress. With one leg straight down the bed, the other bent at an angle to his body, he let Floy inspect him.

As she knelt at the foot of the bed her eyes were only three feet from the half-hard organ. His testes hung loosely in their wrinkled sac.

Floy's hand slid upwards, to feel and to explore him.

Lightly her finger traced the ridge around the helmet of his *manimal*. Then upwards to the fine-laid mat of dark brown pubic hair. She stroked the hair seductively, stimulating a hot moistness between her thighs.

He sighed and thrust his pelvis forward. She thrilled. Again, she felt a sense of power as the creature reared, curved and rose sedately to lie against his stomach. Then she transferred her touching to the under-side. Stroking at the web, she slowly ran the finger-tip down the centre seam. It stiffened to the touch. She leant forward, putting her lips to the web of skin. As her tongue-tip came out and tickled it, the creature pulsed and tightened. He moaned. From snake to ram, the transformation was complete.

Without warning Jay turned, growled and straddled Prissy, forcing her legs wide. She let out a throaty moan.

'Oh, Jay. Not now. Can't you see we've got company?'

'Don't give me that, you tease. If you will fantasise and play with my cock while I'm trying to sleep, you know what to expect.'

He growled and bit her neck. She moaned again and pulled her legs back further, opening herself wide to him.

Floy watched with fascination as the shaft found its mark again. Now she knelt beside them as it disappeared between Prissy's glistening leaves of flesh. Prissy contracted and relaxed them, as if milking his shaft for its fluid.

He began to drive it in and out; the thump, thump, thump making Floy's pulse throb in unison. Her hand snaked its way between the muscular young man's legs. She cupped his sac, shaking uncontrollably as he thrust and pulled and thrust.

Instinctively she pulled his hood of skin back tight with two fingers on either side of the shaft as it drove. He thrashed now, the bed undulating with every stroke.

Jay gasped.

'Oh my God, Floy, that's incredible. Don't let go.'

91

Prissy was emitting a cry with every thrust now.

'Fuck me you gorgeous man? Show Floy what it's like. Make me come with your cock like you did in the woods.' She began to squirm.

He thrust deeper; harder; making it difficult for Floy to keep her hold.

Prissy's fingers clawed at his muscular buttocks. One fore-finger searched out his rosette again and began to probe. He writhed on her finger.

'You wicked little tart,' he growled.

Floy started to shudder. Her whole body began to convulse. She was racked with the need for that thrashing stem inside herself, her pelvis jerking upwards to every thrust.

As Prissy screamed, 'Fuck me, fuck me!' Floy could stand it no more. She was about to pull Jay off and throw herself onto her back for him to transfer his ram to her, when they both let out a deep and guttural groan.

Prissy writhed in ecstasy. Jay rolled off her and onto his back gasping, his phallus pumping, his stomach heaving with every spasm.

Shuddering, Floy collapsed between his legs. She took his slippery shaft between her fingers and worked the foreskin gently, milking it so the thick white fluid oozed out. The pumping pulses eased as Jay's erection subsided, becoming soft and pliable in Floy's hand.

Floy was almost as shattered as Jay and Prissy. Her body quivered from head to toe. She was so wet that her thighs slipped and slid over one another where she lay.

Lying on her side between Jay's legs, Floy pressed her face to his slack scrotal sac. She buried her lips in its crinkled hairiness.

Now softening, the root of his penis still made little ticks against her mouth. She lapped the saltiness, her tongue moving slowly up and down.

It was intimate; loving; and so erotic it made Floy burn with energy coursing through her again.

Prissy moved round and down beside her. She slipped her hand between Floy's legs and slipped two fingers deep inside the fleshy cavity.

Floy's own hand mimicked Prissy's, her stiffened fingers sliding easily in the lubrication of Jay's semen mixed with Prissy's love-juice.

Together they lay, connected in an accepting circuit, Floy suckling delicately on Jay, as she and Prissy worked each other with slow and comforting movements of their fingers.

Floy woke and stretched. She was on her back, her legs splayed widely, a manly hand deep between her legs. A gently sucking mouth on each nipple brought her back to full alertness.

She stroked two heads of hair lovingly as their mouths suckled, pulling her nipples into rampant nubs.

'That feels so good. I feel so relaxed.'

Jay left her nipple and kissed her lips tenderly.

'Did you come when I was fucking with Prissy?'

'I don't know. I think so. My body went into convulsions.'

'Are you still randy?'

She smiled.

'I'm randy all the time these days. I don't seem to be able to do anything about it.'

'Perhaps you want a man inside you?'

'Perhaps I do. I'm so confused. I wanted it just then, but you ejaculated before I could claw you away from Prissie.'

'Sorry. We can try again when I've got my strength back.'

Floy reached up and stroked his face with her musk-scented fingertips.

'I think you're wonderful. But I'm not sure now if that's a good idea.'

'I won't make you pregnant.'

She smiled.

'That's not a problem.'

'Then what is?'

Floy sighed deeply.

'The problem is, I think I'm falling in love with you both. You're both so beautiful. So kind and loving.'

'Is that a problem?'

'I dare not fall in love with anyone.'

'Why not?'

'I don't truly know. All I know is that I have to keep my independence.'

'Are you in love with DuPrey?'

Floy looked up into Jay's dark, clear eyes as he gazed down on her intently. His face was only inches from her own. She turned her head away.

'I dare not be.'

Jay pulled her head back gently with his fingers, forcing her to look at him again.

'Why not?'

'I can't tell you.'

Jay kissed her gently and returned his lips to her nipple.

'What's the time?'

Prissy looked at the bedside clock.

'Quarter past eleven.'

Floy sprang up.

'Oh my God! I'll have to go. I'll be late.'

Prissy and Jay knelt beside her. They put their arms around her and hugged her tight.

'Go and do whatever it is you have to do. Come back and sleep with us if you want to.'

Prissy kissed her on the lips as tenderly as she had that afternoon. Jay kissed her too.

Floy slipped away. As she closed the door behind her, she felt sad. She felt as if she had abandoned friends at a time when she needed their comfort the most. She had felt relaxed with them. Much of the sexual tension had somehow gone. But still she needed a proper release.

She hesitated. Should she go back? She could abandon her plan? Why not leave it? Was she being obsessive? Ramon DuPrey would have to wait another night.

But her deadline was looming. She could not waste any more time. She needed to know what she needed to know. She needed to feel what she needed to feel.

But was it really necessary? Why didn't she stop torturing DuPrey and simply call him up and ask him to her room? No, she knew that would not work. And she knew what would happen if she did that.

The only way to solve the problem was to go on. Damn, why had she ever embarked on this insane course?

That was stupid. She knew why. And she knew that it was more important than making love with Jay and Prissy or hurting Ramon DuPrey.

Chapter Five

*F*loy raced down the Grand Staircase. It was already after half past eleven.

Her heart raced too. Her body still pulsed from the warmth which her sensual interlude with Jay and Prissy had fired deep inside her. Even though she had not received sexual gratification from either Prissy or Jay, the touched and holding and the giving of pleasure to them had generated a plethora of sensations which she had not known were possible.

Her skin tingled. She was sure she was flushed all over, not just her face. Those secret places which had lain dormant for so many years of her adulthood now seemed to have come to life.

The nimbus around each nipple responded to the rubbing of the bath-robe as she scrampered down the stairs. The air rushing through the loose folds of white towelling sensitised the inner surfaces of her thighs. That forbidden place, her anus, seemed to want a finger's touch now; just as Prissy had done to that rosy, winking hole of Jay's

Floy had not showered. There had been no time.

In all that time with Jay and Prissy, she had lain naked apart for her pearls. It was a strange thing that she felt naked in public without them. At one time, she had regarded such baubles as decadent. Now they had become a part of her, a necessary component of the person she had been forced to become.

The pearls were sticky on her skin. When she had fetched them from the office just before going in to dinner, Ramon had not been there. A young woman at reception had reached them out for her.

Now Floy prayed he would be there. She needed to advance the plan; to bring it to fulfilment so that she could move on to what she needed to do next.

Ramon looked up with relief as he saw the white form through the frosted glass of the office door. His hands shook. His knees trembled. He steadied himself for Floy Pennington's entry.

What mood would she be in tonight? She had been so cold and unappreciative to him at dinner. But she had appeared so warm and friendly with the Pollands.

How could anyone be so compartmentalised in her emotions as that; especially with someone who had saved her from certain harm.

He was certain that it had been his hand between her legs that had made her run. But at that time it had seemed such a natural thing to do. Now his face was drained with apprehension as the door opened without a knock. Would she have changed from Hyde into Jekyll; a white witch changed from black?

He was surprised.

She stood in the doorway, radiant and tangled. Her hair previously so glossy, so smoothly brushed out at dinner, looked a mess now. But her eyes shone. Her cheeks were flushed with that kind of exhilaration which Ramon had seen so many times before in sexually satisfied women.

Floy Pennington had been making love. He was certain. She looked girlish. Her face had that impishness which comes from knowing a great secret and keeping it close between herself and her lover.

Ramon was devastated. He felt dejected; rejected;

jilted; and angry. But why should he? She had not made him any promises. She had not given him any encouragement by day. The very opposite was true. It had been only her visits to the office in her bath robe, the ritual of the necklace and the lascivious striptease which had led him to hope she would be his.

But this was cruel. She had taunted him. And all the while, she had another lover. But who?

Young John? No, he had not returned.

One of the colonels?

The businessman in his fifties?

Jay Polland? Surely not. He was on his honeymoon, and if the staff were to be believed, he was sexually occupied for most of the day and night.

Then who? Who had brought Floy Pennington to the radiance she showed now?

'Good evening, Mr DuPrey. You look as if you've seen a ghost. It's only me in my bath robe.'

Ramon shook his head.

'I'm sorry, I was thinking of something else when you came in.'

She ignored the remark.

'Will you take my pearls off and put them away please.'

He moved round the desk and stood behind her.

'I was wondering how you were after your fright.'

It was a lie, but he could not tell her what he had really been conjuring in his thoughts. He could not tell her that he'd pictured her naked under some anonymous young buck, her legs spread wide, her breasts undulating with the rhythm of the man thrusting into her. He could not tell her that she smelled of love juice, that it drifted to his nostrils and was making him horny.

She pulled her hair up to give him access to the clasp.

'You needn't worry. I'm quite alright.'

Ramon breathed deeply, partly to control his shaking, but also to test the scent in the air. Her hands smelled unmistakably of semen. Ramon could not mistake that aroma.

Floy Pennington was acting out of character. She was normally so clean. She had not bothered to shower. Did she need to let the love-smells linger so she could savour their making for an hour longer?

He picked the string of pearls off her neck and opened the safe.

As he put them away, she went to the door.

'Good night, Mr DuPrey. I want to go to bed now.'

Ramon frowned as he closed the safe. There had been no thanks for his rescue. No thanks – as usual – for helping with the necklace. She had not stopped and dropped her little innuendos. No, the game was over. She had been served by some other stallion.

Ramon mounted the stairs dolefully. He called good night to the night porter and made for his room.

Inside, he snapped the light on and went to close the curtains.

His mouth dropped open. In the lighted bedroom opposite stood Floy Pennington in bra and panties. She glanced across and looked away quickly.

Ramon quickly put out the light and grabbed his binoculars.

Yes, she was at it again. And this time she was alone. His cock revived. It had hung despondently since she had acted so cursorily in the office. Now it was taking an interest in its prospects once more.

He focused on her breasts, full and weighty in their half-cup slings.

She put her hands behind her back for the clasp.

A query went through Ramon's mind. If she could unclasp that, why couldn't she fasten and unfasten her necklaces? He pushed the thought aside.

Tonight she did not turn away from him. She undid the clip and held the bra to herself for a few seconds as usual.

As usual, she swung the bra aside and dropped it on the floor, first letting it hang from one finger. But tonight she stood facing him. When she tied her hair back, her breasts rose tightly, two perfectly symmetrical lobes of sheer delight.

Ramon slid down his zip, his erection under pressure in the pouch of his black briefs. He sloughed these and his shirt off.

Picking up the glasses he re-focused. They were good binoculars – the best. He could have reached out and touched her she seemed so close; the detail so sharp, the colour clear.

She was massaging her breasts. She had oil on them. The taut surfaces shone in the light of the lamp. The pink-brown nipples stood up proudly each in a perfect circle of its darker moon.

Her thumb and forefinger plucked the nipples, her lips pouting as if she wanted to suck on them herself.

Ramon shook. His hands trembled. His cock curved up, full-veined, its head, stretched smooth, purple in its ardour.

Even if she had been enjoying herself earlier, she was getting ready to go again. His heart sank. Was she torturing him with her display, only to introduce a raunchy lover from the sidelines? At any moment would a stud appear from the shadows, spread her widely on the bed, and have her before his very eyes?

With her back to him now, she was sliding off her panties. Inch by tantalising inch she pushed them down. The silky rounds of perfect buttocks swelled and burst from the restraining lace.

She bent deeply to pick up her bra. Two prominent lips fringed with jet-black curls pouted at him beneath the rosebud of her secret hole. Now he was rigid; as taut as steel. She seemed to be displaying her most secret places as if to invite his cupid's arrow to wing across the space and penetrate her.

Then she snapped off the light.

Ramon was too angry to stay still. He flung down his binoculars on the bed. She was a cock-teasing bitch and needed to be taught a lesson. He snapped on his light and stood at the window, glaring at the darkened room ten feet away across the light-well of the building.

Ramon stood, undecided. Planting his hands firmly on his hips, his cock was angry, ready to bury its head between those plump and teasing lips. His legs stretched wide, his pelvis pushed forward, straining his erection to its fullest size.

A glimpse of white flesh in the darkness of the suite opposite did not escape him. She was watching him. She was not the innocent undresser he still feared he might be accused of spying on.

He turned sideways to her and stretched, his hands placed on his head. A few bending and stretching exercises of the sort he normally did in the mornings would give her something to watch. As he arched backwards, tensing his stomach, his cock stood proud and ready, his balls large in their pouch.

She closed her curtains.

Again, she was shutting him out. His anger began to boil. Without thinking things through he grabbed his robe and jammed his keys in the pocket. He charged out through the door, down some steps, along corridors, and soon stood outside her room.

Fool that he was, Ramon knocked softly. He should have banged.

There was no reply. He cursed.

He knocked louder.

Still there was no answer.

This time he did bang, his anger taking charge of his normally even temper.

There was no audible movement inside the room. Then from the staircase came the sound of voices. They got nearer. There were guests coming home late. A moment more and he would be discovered, the hotel owner standing in a bathrobe outside the room of a woman guest.

Ramon decided. The whole thing had got out of hand and it was time he put a stop to it one way or another.

Just as the late revellers reached the corner of the

corridor, he slid his pass-key into the lock and slipped like a white shadow into Floy Pennington's suite.

In the dim light coming through the uncurtained window of the sitting room he could see the bedroom door. It stood open. An invitation? He knew exactly, to the inch, where to go. The bedroom was dark. The thick curtains she had just drawn cut out all light from the window.

He inched his way by sense towards her bed. He could hear her breathing. She was not asleep; not even pretending.

Flinging off the bath robe he dropped it to the floor. For a moment he stood sideways, close to her. He knew that she would see his erection silhouetted against the lighter grey of the sitting-room doorway. Was this what she had been working towards each night? To be taken without making a move in public to encourage him? To have sex without the responsibility of having given herself up to a man? Had she done it so that she could justify the act to herself afterwards? Would she say he had had her but she had not had him?

'So you've come.'

'Yes, Miss Pennington, I've come.'

He knelt by the bed, close to her head. Her breathing sped. It was as if she was panting with anticipation. He could see only her outline, his eyes not fully adjusted to the darkness. She was lying on her pillow looking up, her black hair fanned out against the whiteness.

Ramon steered his mouth towards the breathing, towards the warmness of her breath.

When his lips touched hers there was a rush of energy. It caught his breath and shot through his solar plexus, driving his cock into a paroxysm of little stiff beats.

She breathed heavily under his lips, her own lips immobile; soft but unco-operative. He sensed that she was scared.

Softly he touched her cheek with the tips of his

fingers and caressed the smooth skin which he had yearned to touch for days.

This seemed to calm her.

Now he smoothed her hair back to trace the line of her slender neck. His fingers sought a mystery as they caressed her silken skin. Was she naked?

With gentle stroking movements Ramon moved his fingers downwards. Yes she was devoid of clothes, as naked as a wood-nymph.

For the first time, his fingertips found the object of their desire – those perfect breasts. Mobile beneath his fingers, they were heaven to touch. His fingers pulled a nipple just as she had pulled at it in her tantalising display for him.

He thought he heard a little gasp of pleasure, but he could not be sure. He whispered near her ear.

'You are the most exquisite woman I have ever seen. Do you know that?'

There was a small expiration of surprise in answer.

'Do you say that to all the women you conquer?'

Ramon stopped. That was a strange word to use. Was he conquering her or she him? He was apparently performing her desire to the letter. She had stirred his interest each day with the ritual of the necklace. Then she had seduced him from her window, night by frustrating night until he had answered her call.

She had let him into her room. She could have bolted it. Now she was allowing him to kiss her, to caress her wonderful breasts. So who was the victor, he or she?

'Love is not a conquest, Miss Pennington.' It sounded strange. He was in intimate contact with her marvellous body, yet it was as if they had only just been introduced. 'May I call you Floy?'

'If that pleases you.'

She didn't say: and may I call you Ramon?

'You were saying?'

Ramon took a couple of seconds to pick up the gist of what he had been saying. She wanted an explanation?

'Love is not a conquest, Floy. When two people love,

fully and exquisitely, there is only giving. There is no taking. He gives to her and she to him. In the giving, the other receives.'

'You've very eloquent. And very romantic, DuPrey. But are you going to ravish me?'

Ramon took a deep breath. It was a curious question. No woman would normally lie back and ask it so coldly. She would at least pretend to be fighting for her honour. Most of the women he had had before wanted only to be loved; there were a few who actually desired to be taken by force. These seemed to get their pleasure without loving in return. It had taken all his skills and experience as a lover to make them change. He had had to intoxicate them deeply with physical sensations, and teach them the delight of engulfing a rigid, spurting cock. Then he would withdraw. He would refuse them more. Only then would they come on to him, craving for him; ready to give before they could receive again.

Still he was in doubt. Did she want to be taken summarily or made love to? He'd better play it safe. The last thing he wanted was an accusation of rape.

Ramon's lips found a nipple. It was already firm. He moved the tip of his tongue in salacious circular movements around the nimbus, feeling the little pimples in a circle at the rim. The nipple stood rigid.

As his hand slipped downwards to her navel, he moved his mouth to her other breast. There the second teat soon rose up, as erect as its fellow.

Her abdomen was tense. Ramon could feel it taut under his hand. It seemed to flutter with excitement, yet she held it in, unrelaxed.

She didn't move. She just lay there, allowing him to explore her nubile nakedness.

Sucking on the nipple, his lips pulled at it, and let it go; pulling again to make it even harder. He wanted to drive a wave of sensation downwards, to between her legs, where she should be weeping if he was doing his part right.

His hand was there now, stroking gently at the soft

maiden-hair. Carefully, millimetre by millimetre, he moved his fingers until he found the soft firmness of her clitoris, warm and mobile to his finger.

She splayed her legs.

Moving his mouth up her breast, a small kiss at a time, his lips found the hollow under her chin. She put her head back slightly to grant him access. Her vulval lips were moist to his fingers. He smiled and bit her neck gently. He probed gently and then stopped as his experienced fingers found her maidenhead.

She was a virgin!

She shuddered almost imperceptibly at his touch.

He resolved to go on. His lips traced the line of her jaw until he found her mouth again. This time it was open, her breath panting.

The kiss was tender on his part, permissive on hers. She held herself available to his lips. She did not resist him, but neither did she participate. But there was no doubt in his mind that he was creating sensations she could not deny, although apart from the slippery moistness upon his fingers she gave little evidence of what she felt.

He stroked her cheek with the backs of his fingers. Those of his other hand worked sensuously at her clitoris, then moved downward, more deeply between those luscious lips. She was more slippery now, something which she could not hide no matter how aloof she remained.

'*Are* you going to ravish me?'

Again, it sounded so unreal; so formal;. so utterly cold.

'I'm going to make love to you as you have never been loved before.'

'And how will you know whether you have achieved that?'

'Believe me, I'll know.'

'And how do you propose to do it?'

'You'll see. But before I begin, I want you to know one thing.'

105

'And what is that?'

'I want you to know that I love you.'

She said nothing. Lying naked before him, her legs splayed wide, available to his every move, she remained silent. But as he knelt beside her she raised a hand and moved her fingers lightly over his face. Only once, they traced his cheek, and then his chin, before subsiding to their former place beside her thigh.

'I've loved you since the first moment our eyes met across the reception desk. You're the most exquisite woman I have ever had the privilege of touching.'

'Thank you.'

She said no more.

Ramon kissed her tenderly. He moved his mouth out across her cheek, traced the line of her jaw, reached her neck and traversed down it slowly.

Now he moved his hands; fingers smoothing, then teasing, then pressing hard. He scratched down and around her breast; to the centre-line of her still-taut abdomen, then downwards to her navel.

She shuddered slightly.

He was achieving what he wanted. Pressing into the wonderfully firm flesh, he gauged the success of each movement from the heightening of her tension.

Somehow his own urgency had gone. Although still fully rampant, his erection had outlasted the indescribable thrill transmitted from his fingers in their first touching of her. He had been near to explosion, but had held back. For this first time of loving Floy Pennington he would have to sacrifice himself on the altar of her pleasure. He would have to bring her to climax without his cock. He knew all too well that the minute it touched her, the moment it felt the moist heat between her legs, it would spout copiously and hot. All would then be lost, for the first time at least.

Now the journey of his lips continued, taking in her navel with the tip of his tongue. A brief excursion to the smooth black hair of her mound of Venus, and then a purposeful detour down the outer thigh.

At her toes he stopped, kissing and caressing each one in turn; sucking and then moving on. Placing her feet firmly on his shoulders he moved upwards, his moist-lipped target in reach. He could smell that familiar musky aroma which made his erection strain almost to bursting. He loved it. There was no better feeling than the anticipation of burying an iron-hard prick in an adored, moist sex.

First came the surface inside the knee, sensitive and tight. As he moved towards the centre of her womanhood, her legs frogged back. He drew a deep breath. The pungent feminine attractant made him as wild as the bull. His cock strained as it rubbed over the bed sheet, focusing its single eye on the lusciousness between tensed thighs.

He slowly licked the taut skin. She shuddered slightly, bending her legs back further with his advance; opening herself up wider.

The progress up her inner thigh was slow, a millimetre at a time. He strained her legs even wider, her feet still on his shoulders. Now he reached the hollow lying on one side of her secret lips. He licked it sensuously with his tongue-tip. A thrill went through her body.

Floy was losing control. Her body was reacting to the man's demand and seemed not to care any more for decorum, modesty or the ingrained injunctions which had always shut it down.

Now his tongue was lapping at the inner surfaces of her thighs, each movement sending shivers upwards and inwards until the whole of her body began to tingle with a delicious tension. This drove her nipples to a greater, more painful hardness. Her lips pouted, her solar plexus contracted so tight that it made her sexual lips – those untouched, unloved lips – tremor with her heaving stomach.

If he did not take her soon, she would surely set upon him like a wild animal and drag him into herself, pulling on him, making him charge her until the dam of tension burst.

Ramon's mouth contacted the outer lips, succulent and warm. He rested, letting his hot breath heat her more.

Now his tongue tracked up the lips and took the swollen nub of flesh which nosed out between them. As he slowly lapped, it hardened. She raised her pelvis from the bed, her stomach taut, her feet turned outwards. He brought his hands under her thighs and gripped her, his thumb nails digging into the taut hollows of her loins, spreading the cock-hungry mouth wide for him to suck. Thrusting the tip of his tongue downwards, inside her, he dug his nails in hard.

She began to writhe, riding his tongue so that it rasped her nub.

She panted. She moaned.

She threw her head back, her neck stretched tight, her eyes closed in ecstasy. Then as the riding of her purse of heated flesh on his mouth reached a height of fervour, she let out a small scream of relief.

A great shudder rippled through her body and was gone.

Ramon came with her, the excitement of her climax too much for him to hold his ejaculation. As her pelvis subsided, she let out a deep-seated moan and relaxed.

He took a breath too and let it out with slow satisfaction.

'I love you, Floy.'

His words were sighed, almost inaudible, as he lay between her legs, his erection beating, his mouth kissing occasionally at her sexual lips.

The click of the light-switch and the glare of the bedside lamp startled Ramon from his sensual bliss. He raised himself and looked up. As he did so, Floy Pennington pulled up her legs; withdrawing from him; shutting herself off.

He knelt at the bottom of the bed; dazed.

She drew a bed-sheet over herself, pulling it prudishly up to the cleft between her breasts just as she had held her bra in her striptease performances. Her dark eyes were shallow. He could see no pleasure there.

'Thank you, DuPrey. That was interesting. Now I think you should go.'

Ramon was devastated. He stared; his eyes wide with disbelief. His mouth dropped open.

'Don't kneel there staring. You've had your pleasure. Now, it's time you went!'

Ramon put his face in his cupped hands. Was this a nightmare? If it was, he wanted to wake up.

But the pungent smell on his hands told him that he was not dreaming.

He took a deep breath and looked up, his eyes watering so that her face seemed blurred.

'I – I don't understand.'

Her face was flat; ungiving.

'There is nothing for you to understand.'

'But I – I thought you wanted to make love.'

She let out a sharp exhalation through her open mouth.

'What gave you that idea?'

Ramon shook his head.

'You enticed me here.'

'True. It took you a long time to come.'

Ramon felt shattered. She was criticising him. She was actually complaining that he had not taken her titillation at the window more seriously. She had wanted him to come to her earlier.

'I don't believe this.'

She shrugged.

He shook his head again.

'But I thought you wanted to make love.'

'You're repeating yourself.'

'But it's true.'

'No, Mr DuPrey. It is not true! You assumed that because I invited you to my bedroom, I wanted to make love to you. It was you who wanted to make love with me. You have been advertising it for the past week.'

'But. But . . .'

'But nothing! I think you should go!'

Ramon was suddenly very angry. It did not boil up slowly. It did not swell and grow until it showed gradually in his face. It was as if someone had turned a switch.

'You bloody bitch!'

He sprang up and stood over her, his penis erect and hard again, this time with anger.

A glint of excitement passed her eyes and then died.

'Get out!'

'Not until you tell me what this whole charade is about, I won't!'

'I'll call the night porter. You'll look foolish to your staff.'

Without thinking, Ramon's arm swung. His anger had to go somewhere.

The back of his hand caught her face, jolting her head sideways. It stung him, so he was sure it had hurt her too. But he was glad.

He did not look back to see if she was hurt. Right now, he did not care!

As Floy entered the busy breakfast room, heads turned to watch. As usual, the breakfast murmur decreased. Then it turned to silence. She had a large and angry bruise on her cheek.

One table stood empty, set for one.

She stepped lightly, but her usual self assurance was contrived. The exhilaration which comes with a third or fourth encore did not fill her this morning.

Floy kept her eyes ahead. She did not welcome the attentions she was getting. She pulled her own chair under her blue denim jeans.

'Good morning, madam. What would you like to order?'

Jannine grinned down on her, clearly delighted that

110

someone had given her a lesson. Floy ignored the question. She had to get back in control.

'Has my post bag arrived yet?'

'I'll ask Mr DuPrey, madam. Now, what would you like to order?'

Floy did not keep her waiting while she considered. She wanted to be alone.

'I'll have some toast and coffee.'

Jannine bobbed mechanically.

Across the parkland, the usual early-morning risers were returning from their walks. There was no sunshine to light the treescape in the misty middle-ground. There was no sunshine in her heart.

The honeymooning Pollands did not come. Perhaps they were making love. Perhaps they had left early as Prissy said they would.

This morning she did not wonder what it would feel like to be in love.

Ramon stood in the doorway to the breakfast room. He carried a silver salver with a bundle of letters on it.

As he looked across the room at Floy Pennington, she glanced up. His face did not give its usual smile. He knew what was going through her mind. He saw her try to make a smile to give him, but it did not develop. She returned her gaze to the scenery.

Ramon called the waitress then went back to the office.

For Floy there was no 'Good morning, Miss Pennington. I trust everything is exactly as you like it?'

Instead, the petulant Jannine stood beside her table with the tray of letters. She plonked it down and went without a word.

Floy felt old, even with her hair let down. It looked girlish about her face, but stark against the paleness of her skin. This morning the skin was blemished, even though an hour with foundation and dark powder had

111

taken away much of the evidence of the bruise. It could not disguise the half-shut eye.

The tip of her tongue came out to wipe her lip. Just once it traversed the top lip before recalling the taste of his kiss. It retracted. She took a deep breath and released it as a sigh.

The letters were the same as usual; adoring and full of praise. There was a review from a trade paper; complimentary as always. She was bored.

Pictures of the naked man filtered into her mind, his erection curved in silhouette against the greyness showing through her doorway. She shut the pictures out.

This morning, as he had stood in the doorway of the breakfast room, one glance had been enough. His face had been fierce; his eyes locked onto hers, looking for a sign of remorse from her at what she'd done.

Now he was gone.

She took a lingering look at her memories of him, her writer's mind recalling the notes it had taken.

He had been perfect.

She recalled his dark eyes; full of love. She recalled the stricken way he had scanned her face, searching for some explanation of her behaviour.

For a second, she imagined the feel of him as he had lain between her legs, his tongue rasping at her clitoris, his mouth kissing lovingly at her sexual lips.

She remembered their last breakfast conversation.

I want to talk.

She'd stopped him with a cursory wave. She had made some cutting remark about her bill.

He had been embarrassed.

No, not your bill. I would like to talk about what happened last night.

She gulped her coffee, gone cold as she had lingered over the night's events. He had been a wonderful lover. Could she have wished for more? But it had not been what she needed.

Floy stood at her table. She smoothed her jeans. Then she wiped her lips slowly with the monogrammed napkin. Finished with that, she set it carefully on the table without first holding it poised as she usually did.

Today she would not need her pearls. But she would like her diamond clips. They would brighten her face. They would help to lift her mood.

Setting her mouth straight, she produced a stony look and set out across the breakfast room, forging a path through the intense interest she could sense.

Ramon paced the floor of his office. An hour had gone past since he had sent the letters to Floy Pennington. He had vowed to keep right out of her way. The less he saw of her the better it would be for him. She might yet bring an assault charge. She might accuse him of rape or gross indecency.

He had loved her. He had made love to her in every way open to him at the time. In return, she had used him for some perverted reason best known to herself. She had discarded him like some hired gigolo who had licked her to order. The way she had sat in her bed – looking so coldly at him, her eyes shallow and cruel – made him think that she was capable of anything.

A shadow at the door made him look up.

'Good morning, Mr DuPrey.'

Ramon focused on the woman hovering uncertainly in the doorway. He was shocked. She looked vulnerable, and hurt; her face swollen on one side, the eye partly closed.

Giving her a remorseful look, he didn't answer her. Instead, he searched for his safe key, embarrassed at her presence in his office.

'What jewellery do you require, Miss Pennington? I'll open the safe.'

She cast her eyes down momentarily before lifting them to his.

'I'd like the clips, if that's not too much trouble.'

'No trouble at all, I assure you.'

They were being too polite. They were playing a game again, just as they had played games all week. It was dishonest. Why could she not have said, discreetly when alone with him, I would like to experience sex with you. Will you come to my room? But understand that it is not for love. And when it's done, please don't be hurt. Just melt away as if it had never happened.

But she had teased him. She had lured him to her bed with her body, flashing it like a beacon across to his room. She had lured him blatantly.

Perhaps she had kidded herself. Maybe she had believed that he had not been there, watching her every move. Perhaps she undressed like that as normal. Had it been the illicitness of his watching that had convinced him that she had been doing it for him? He was confused.

'The blue box I believe, Miss Pennington?'

She smiled weakly.

'You remembered.'

Ramon could see tears in her eyes. She sniffed. An aura of sadness hung about her. This was reflected in her faded jeans; the prominence of her breasts hidden by the fullness of a black sweater. It dulled the blackness of her hair and paled her face. It made him sad too. Where was the beautiful woman he had fallen in love with? Where was the fire and verve of yesterday? Where was the hard creature who had demeaned him after he had made love to her?

Jannine entered unexpectedly, dipped cursorily before the guest and scurried away, shooting Ramon a scathing look.

'Here you are, Miss Pennington.'

He handed her the box with the diamonds. She hesitated before she took it.

'On second thoughts, I think I'll take the pearl necklace.'

Ramon turned to the open safe. When he brought out the white box he found she had moved close. He stiffened. She was too close for comfort. His heart beat wildly even though his mind was angry at her. Without opening the box of pearls, he handed it to her.

She took it and opened it herself.

'Would you put them on?'

He studied her sternly, her face so close to him that he could feel the warmth of her breath.

'No. Not this time. I think you can put them on yourself.'

As he looked into her eyes, they watered. She put out a hand to touch his arm.

Ramon let her. At the warmth of her touch, his heart pumped madly and he began to tremble. What was it about this woman that made his quiver whenever she was near?

'Ramon?'

'Yes, Miss Pennington.'

'Ramon. I'm – '

He kept his eyes on hers; unwavering.

'Ramon, I'm sorry.'

She turned and fled.

Ramon sat heavily in his chair. Elbows on the desk, he put his face in his hands. She had looked so doleful. Clearly she was experiencing the aftermath of her cruelty the night before. No doubt she had thought that she could play the rich and famous guest, and demand anything she wanted. Had she thought that he was there to serve her sexually as well as provide her with accommodation and food? Put it on the bill, he could almost hear her say.

He breathed deeply. He'd shut her out this time. Well, that would teach her a lesson. Perhaps she would not play with the feelings of a lover so lightly another time. With her gone from the office, his anger had returned.

Floy worked like a demon on the book. She had to. She had to get it done or she would be in trouble. And she had to try to get her mind onto something other than thinking about what she had done with Ramon DuPrey. But it was proving to be impossible to forget. He was so much a part of the whole thing; the reason for her staying on here.

When Floy wrote she worked fast. One thing that writing from experience did was to enable the words to flow from feelings. One did not have to make them up. One had to chase sensations around the body and the mind, grab them and put a name to them and get them down before they slipped away.

It was not easy, finding words for the things she had been experiencing lately. But her dialogue with Prissy had helped a lot. Those sexual words she'd learned were so expressive of their actions. They made her tremble even to think them. But it was not easy finding words for how she felt about her experience with Ramon DuPrey. And that experience had not solved her problem. She had a huge gap in the area she needed most right now.

It was noon before she switched off the word processor. A salad brought up from the kitchen lay half eaten, the lettuce curling, a glass of apple juice undrunk. Her mind was clouded. She could not think. She was satiated with sensation and emotion coming at her from all angles and she could not stop one of them and hold it down.

She was wet; her erotic centre stimulated into weeping at the sensuality of her writing. The tension in her body had reached an almost unbearable pitch. She had obtained a temporary release from Ramon's love-making. It had helped a little, but that deep ache had quickly built again.

Her visit to the office had opened up those things she was desperately trying to push down. The visit had been foolish. She should have forsaken her baubles today. But she had been drawn there. There had been a desperate need to see him, partly to say how sorry she was; partly out of need to be with him, even for a moment.

But he had shut her out this time. Now she knew

how he must have felt at her treatment of him. And she had run from him like a schoolgirl, just as she had fled from him in the stable yard where he had held her intimately on his horse.

What was it about Ramon DuPrey that was tying her in knots? This kind of thing had never happened to her before. But then, she had never ventured into the world as a sexual being before, to be lured by its sensations, its sights and smells; caught in its subtle and not so subtle snares.

Floy went out. A walk across the park would clear her head. The bull was gone. The cows grazed peacefully, their sexual needs served.

The afternoon sun shone brightly; too brightly for her tearful eyes. The bruise hurt; the half closed eye puffed up. She went to the stable yard to fetch her sunglasses from the car. They would do two jobs: shade her eyes and hide her bruise.

As the Bentley's door clunked behind her she heard neighing from a loose box. Passing it on the way to the park, she glanced in.

A young brown mare stood tethered at her head, her hobbled hind legs placed astride and waiting. A groom held her tail aside, immodestly revealing the moist, chestnut-coloured lips of her distended vulva to the champing stallion.

Charlemagne threw his head back, sniffing at the mare; another groom hanging on his halter. The horse had to be restrained; his ardour contained until she was ready.

Floy took off her glasses and leaned against the door post. Her inner thighs trembled as a knife-like phallus grew out from Charlemagne's sheath, long and black and hard.

Too strong for the groom, the stallion charged forward, mounted the mare and with one thrust sank his phallus into her. She threw her head back and whinnied. The stallion rode her briefly with a couple of hard, uncompromising thrusts. Letting out a shriek he tossed his head, pulled back, sniffed at her and turned away.

The groom led him out, brushing Floy with his black and shining coat. She shuddered and stared, transfixed. Animal sensation poured through her as pearl-white semen trickled down the vulva of the mare. The other groom wiped it carelessly, winked at Floy and removed the mare's hobbles.

Floy raced across the yard. Her body was in turmoil. Her mind whirled. Why had Ramon DuPrey not served her like that? Why had he not burst into her room unrestrained? Why had he not dragged her to the edge of the bed, turned her on her stomach, her knees on the floor her legs hobbled to the bed frame? Why hadn't he driven his great phallus into her like a stallion to a mare? Why had he not pulled at the mane of her black hair, dragging her head back while he rode her, and drove his pelvis hard against her? He could have thrashed her until she had whinnied. He could have withdrawn, sniffed at her, turned his head and left her dripping with his pearly fluid.

No. He had loved her. He had been soft. He had kissed her and caressed her. He had told her that she was exquisite. He had brought her to an orgasm, yet left her unsatisfied.

And instead of being grateful for his tenderness, she had responded with derision. And so he had hit her and then he'd left.

Jay had had Priscilla over the log, like a dog would serve a bitch. But when Prissy and he had stripped her on their bed, he had been kind and gentle and understanding too. For Floy he had not played the part of animal. He had undertaken to treat her gently. He had vowed not to hurt her for her first time.

Floy clenched her fists. She wouldn't have minded being hurt, for heavens sake! Like the mare she had wanted a good hard fucking, not love.

* * *

118

It was early afternoon when Ramon watched Floy Pennington run from the stable yard and set out across the park. Smiling knowingly, he viewed her from the window of the cocktail bar. She walked rapidly, her head up, her fists clenched. Clearly she had recovered from her ordeal. She was not cowed now by his treatment of her.

Quickly he went upstairs. At her suite he stopped briefly, looking around like a thief casing a joint.

Slipping his key into the lock he let himself in. He had lost his gold St Christopher, presumably in her bed. He had hoped that she would find it and return it to him. She had not.

The word processor stood dead on the desk of the sitting room. Papers were strewn about, a scatter of screwed-up sheets on the floor.

He searched the bedroom. Nothing. Not under the bed. If the maid had found anything, she would have put it on the bedside cabinet. His staff were totally honest.

On the way out he stopped at the desk.

A manuscript lay there. The title caught his eye. *A Mysterious Love Affair*.

He recalled that she had told him her publisher wanted her to build sex into her plots. Was this the first one?

Intrigued, he flipped back the title page.

Lara van den Berg drove fast. She drove just as she lived her life: aggressively and at high speed. There was no other speed for her.

The open-topped Bentley Mulsanne swerved off the lane and through massive gates. The gilded iron frames hung from stone pillars, each topped with a sphere of gold. A pigeon flew from the ivied stone and winged its way towards a splendid house.

The sun was already climbing into the morning sky, driving a mist away across the parkland. The former mansion, now the most desirable hotel for many miles around, looked blue and seemed to float in the distance, like a desert mirage in the steamy deer-grazed landscape.

Lara was impressed. This would do for a wild, abandoned, sexual adventure. It would suit her very nicely

Ramon stopped reading. He let out a long breath. Without a doubt, Floy Pennington had written about the DuPrey Country House Hotel. Now his interest was really fired.

The Bentley glided along the avenue lined with hundred-year-old oaks, the long black hair of the young millionairess flowing freely in the slipstream. With a whish of gravel it came to rest at the foot of the stone-ballustraded staircase.

She looked at the building, colourful with blue clematis woven among ivy strands. It was more French Baroque than English Classical; an anomaly in the Berkshire scene.

As a young, uniformed footman scurried to open the door of the ruby red Mulsanne, the new guest was already scanning him. No, he was too young for her. She needed older men.

She dismounted: tall, elegant and refined. She . . .

Ramon hurried forward through the script. Who was this mysterious black-haired beauty and why was she being written into his hotel?

Lara made her entrance boldly. She was never one to sneak around. Heads turned, murmuring as she swept across the squared marble floor. Before the reception desk she halted, and although the male clerk was seated there, she rang the bell. Lara van den Berg was not a woman to be kept waiting by any man.

A handsome man appeared from an office on the side. His lapel badge proclaimed: Manager – Pierre Cocteau. Lara analysed him rapidly. He looked far too young for such a position, twenty-six at most. But he was quite old enough for her.

He smiled at her broadly. It was more than friendly. It was a devastating, sensual smile.

120

'Good morning, may I help you?'

For a moment she was stunned. His face was beautiful, in a manly way. Mediterranean in complexion, with dark eyes that were fiercely intelligent, interested and alert. There was a sexuality about him that she had not experienced before in any man. He emanated a bold eroticism, as if he wanted to take her there and then. It was the look of an experienced man who loved to dominate women.

But there was honesty in the face, and an impressive air of confidence. All in all, here was a man who believed in himself and knew that he could have the women he wanted.

As his eyes met hers, there came a flash. It was as if a bolt of erotic fire had jumped the few feet between them, hitting her hard in the solar plexus, burning down to the erogenous inner surfaces of her thighs.

'I want a suite of rooms. Probably for a month.'

Lara fixed him with the eyes of a woman who knows what she wants too. From that moment, she wanted him.

Ramon shook his head. This was unbelievable. Floy Pennington was writing about her own arrival at the hotel. She was writing about their first encounter. He had sensed that she had felt that bolt of lightning too, even though she had shown no sign of it. Now here it was in black and white.

Quickly he left the room and hurried to the office. Switching on the photocopier, he furtively fed the manuscript pages through. When the door opened he was flustered.

It was Jannine. The maid looked angry.

Guiltily he hid the papers behind his back.

'I thought you said you weren't interested in that Pennington woman!' Her eyes flashed with challenging fire.

Ramon hardened towards her. He would not be questioned by staff in that manner.

'Miss Pennington is a guest. I give her what attention she deserves.'

Jannine sneered.

'Does that include screwing her whenever she rings for you?'

Ramon reddened. He faced up to her, the illicitly obtained papers in his hand. He must get them back quickly. Floy Pennington could return at any moment.

'I think you'd better go.'

'Not until I get an answer. Did you have her last night or not?'

'No. I did not.' It was true. He had not screwed Floy Pennington, although now he wished he had, hard and mercilessly until she had screamed for him to stop. 'What the hell's got into you, Jan?'

The maid smiling coldly.

'You haven't, that's for sure! You haven't got into me for a week. I thought you were my regular. I was wrong. I could see you were besotted with the woman, but I didn't think you'd go as far as getting in her knickers. Haven't you always told us not to get involved with guests? Anyway, can't you see she's an emotional desert? That woman had never had a loving thought in her life.'

Ramon was angry now. He felt defensive; probably guilty.

'How can you say that? You can't possibly know.'

Jannine sneered.

'She's a man-hater. Why do you think she uses that ridiculous character, Sister Luke? She's writing about herself. Why else do you think she's so good at it? Haven't you read how the woman puts men down at every turn. She revels in being cleverer than them. She's cold and calculating and very superior. She's an iceberg!'

'That's ridiculous!'

Jannine shrugged.

'Read her books.'

The girl's words hit Ramon hard. She was right. Floy Pennington did write about herself. She wrote from her own experience, not, it seemed, from imagination. He had the evidence in his hands at that moment.

'Look. I think that's enough. Miss Pennington is a guest here. We should treat her with respect.'

'And fuck her when she calls – to order, like room service! Will you put it on her bill? Spicy, well seasoned sausage, ten pounds an inch?'

Ramon glowered.

'You vulgar slut! Get out!'

'Don't worry, I'm going. I've got a job at the Red Lion in Stokey Magna. You can stick your job, and from now on you can stick your cock up Miss Pennington, not up me!'

As the angry maid reached the door, she put her hand into her pocket.

'Oh, I found the St Christopher I gave you. It was in her bed this morning. You'd better have it back. It might protect you on your journeys of delight between her legs.'

Chapter Six

*T*hat afternoon Ramon sat despondently in his office. He had several pieces of wrinkled paper on the desk, and his illicit copy of the manuscript of *A Mysterious Love Affair* by Floy Pennington. He had rescued the wrinkled papers from her waste basket and floor. Then he had cleaned the whole area and emptied the basket as if the maid had been in.

He scanned through the pages.

Lara van den Berg sat at her breakfast table. She felt isolated. Lonely.

Looking up she saw Pierre, the hotel manager. He wove his way expertly to her table across the busy room.

'Is everything in order, Miss Van den Berg?'

She smiled sweetly.

'Quite in order thank you, Pierre.'

Pierre stood back, at a respectful distance.

She studied him dreamily. His nearness made her stomach flutter. Unthinkingly the tip of her tongue slipped out and traversed her upper lip, licking away the white creaminess of yoghurt. Her mind was stripping him naked where he stood. If only the restaurant had been empty, she might have put out her hand and run her finger up the inside of his leg. She might have slipped down his zip and snaked her fingers inside his fly to feel the secret warmness there. Just the thought of it was driving her crazy, making her moist where she sat . . .

Ramon breathed heavily. Was that what had been going on in Floy Pennington's mind while he had spoken to her at breakfast? She hadn't shown a sign that she wanted to touch him. If so, she was more voracious than he had given her credit for. And if she had wanted him like Lara wanted Pierre, why had Floy Pennington berated him after he had made love to her?

He read on, scanning through the pages rapidly.

It was Lara's second night in the hotel. Most of the other guests were old, too old for her. And all the house-boys except one were too gauche. But even he did not seem forceful enough for her needs.

There was a young honeymoon couple in the room next door to hers. She had heard them making love night and day since her arrival. Through the communicating door between her suite and theirs, the unmistakable sounds of unbridled sex reached her ears. Her secret place wept tears of jealousy as she thought of the young bride having all the fun.

She was desperate. Perhaps she could lure the bridegroom away from his love. He might welcome an older and more experienced woman for a break.

Despite all her innuendo, all her subtle and not-so-subtle hints, Pierre Cocteau had steadfastly refused to make even the slightest move towards Lara. Perhaps he needed more obvious encouragement to make him come to her.

The windows of her suite looked out across the park, but the back window of her bedroom faced a small courtyard. By chance, the window of Pierre's bedroom was exactly opposite. She lay in bed, her finger deep between her legs.

The light went on in Pierre's room. He started to undress. Lara reached the window like a shot.

Pierre stripped down to his briefs, the triple bulge between his sleek thighs making her wet with excitement. Lara grabbed her reflex camera with a telephoto lens. She zoomed in on him.

He had an almost perfect body. The shoulders were broad,

muscular but not over-developed. His stomach, taut and spare, rippled as he stretched to take his vest slowly over his head.

The shutter clicked, the automatic wind-on whirring its way through several frames of high-speed colour film.

The brown of the Mediterranean races, his skin glowed as he stood, highlighted by a lamp. He was as smooth and perfect as any man she'd furtively viewed in raunchy magazines designed for women's eyes.

Was he aware that she was watching? She could not tell.

The shutter clicked again.

He posed briefly in front of a mirror. She homed in on the bulge between his taut legs, bringing it into sharp focus. The pants were cut away deeply at the sides, more like a posing pouch than normal briefs. The pouch hung provocatively full, prominently swelled with the alluring sexual anatomy of a well developed male. One long upright ridge was prominent, restrained only by the pouch. Was he thinking of her? Was he thinking of the way she had provoked him in the cocktail lounge, displaying herself to him in her cat-suit? Had she had an effect on him after all? Or was he thinking of that little trollop of a bar girl he had been touching up when he supposed that no-one could see?

As he shed his briefs, Lara gasped and pressed the trigger. He turned to draw the curtains. He was exquisite, his organ standing long and curved in its hardness, rearing like a cobra from its hood. Her knees trembled violently as she snapped more shots.

She sighed with frustration.

He went to draw the curtains.

Quickly, Lara reached out to switch on her dressing table lamp.

Still he closed his curtains. But she knew that he had seen her. She was convinced that he was aware that she had seen him naked.

Ramon took a deep breath. It was mostly true. It must have been the second night of Floy Pennington's stay. He had been foolish not to close his curtains before undressing. But her suite, his most expensive, had been

126

empty for some weeks before her arrival. For the moment he had forgotten it was let.

And Floy Pennington had guessed correctly about his erection. She had titillated him visually in the cocktail lounge. She had played with him, flaunting herself in that too-revealing cat-suit, which hugged the cleft between her legs and pointed her tits everywhere she went. Then she had ignored his every contact. He would have asked any other guest to leave. But Floy Pennington was a celebrity. She could get away with anything that she wished, and she knew it.

That little slut Jannine had seen him eyeing up Floy. She had unzipped him behind the bar while he served a guest. As he had poured the cocktail, she had sucked on his knob so wickedly that he had almost spurted in her mouth. Later she had feigned a headache. So in his room he had had to finish off the job himself. He had stood before the mirror, legs tensed outwards, rubbing himself until he had spurted across the mirror. But she had not put that in the book; it would have been too risqué for her readership.

Then he had seen Floy Pennington at her window, looking at him as he had stood naked, erect, his penis dripping. He had known that she had seen him. That whole night he had worried about what her reaction might be. Would she think him a flasher? Would she pack her bags and leave in disgust? He had imagined how she could have ruined his business by spreading salacious gossip. He had thought that she might even sue him for exposing himself to her.

Ramon returned to the manuscript. It spelled out clearly how Floy Pennington must have been feeling as she had written it. And he was clearly an essential part of it all. He skipped through; every detail making him more and more angry. He felt trapped. She was pulling him inexorably into her plot. What would she have him do next?

But, so far, there was no crime in these first manuscript pages. Surely that would come soon. After all,

Floy Pennington was a writer of murder mysteries.
Ramon read on.

*At breakfast the next morning Lara was excited. She had a
lever she could use on the desirable Monsieur Cocteau. If he
would not make a move on her, she would draw him to herself.
She would cast a noose in his direction and pull him in. Surely
no man as well endowed with virility as he was would resist
what she would do to entice him. And if that failed? There
was always blackmail. A subtle hint would do. A man in his
position would do much to avoid a scandal, an exposure of his
exposure.*

*Pierre Cocteau entered the room. Lara caught his eye. He
was clearly embarrassed, as well he might be. She would use
every ounce of that embarrassment to get what she wanted
from him.*

*With her gaze Lara drew her man across the room. He
arrived, his face flustered. Was he waiting for her to berate
him for his little misdemeanour? She would keep him on the
hook.*

*'Good morning, Miss van den Berg. Is everything all
right?'*

*'Everything is fine, Monsieur Cocteau, thank you. And
how are you this morning? I trust you had a relaxing night.
You looked so tense before I went to bed.'*

*Pierre stood before her, his normal calm ruffled by her
question.*

*This time she did not have to strip him naked with her
mind. It already held a perfect image. And today she would
have him send the film to be developed at a special place she
knew. It would be a great irony. He would be completely
unaware that it contained telephoto close-ups of his exposure.*

Ramon flung down the manuscript and thumped the
desk. So Floy Pennington had taken pictures of him.
He recalled how she had come into the office as bright
and smooth as polished brass and asked him to send a
film off for her by special messenger. He recalled the

name and address. DevelopeX, Amsterdam. He could guess what the X stood for.

Despite his anger and his overwhelming desire to get revenge on Miss Pennington, Ramon was drawn back to the pages of the manuscript.

Lara looked up at the man beside the table. He was waiting to be dismissed. She rose, wiped her mouth slowly with her napkin, and motioned it towards him, letting it dangle for a second before she dropped it. He caught the napkin and stepped back, bowing his head slightly as she passed.

'I'll need my pearls. Kindly have them removed from the safe immediately.'

With that, Lara flounced out. Purposely, she left it an hour before going for the pearls. Reaching his office door she swept in.

Pierre Cocteau stood with his arm around the bar girl. One hand gripped her neck, the other massaged her breast, naked with her blouse unbuttoned. They kissed voraciously.

Lara felt the rage rise in her like a tidal wave. But before it reached her face she iced it and packed it away. Even so, it took all her skill at poker to stop her anger showing.

Cocteau looked up and withdrew from the girl instantly. She curtseyed briefly, pulled her blouse together and fled, wide-eyed with terror.

'I'm sorry, Miss Van den Berg. I didn't hear you knock.'

He was flushed again with embarrassment, like some adolescent boy caught masturbating at his older sister's bedroom keyhole. Lara used his embarrassment to the full.

'I'm not surprised you didn't hear me knock. I've come for my necklace. Where is it?'

'I'll get it for you. Which one do you require?'

'The pearls.'

He opened the safe. Lara could see his hands shaking.

'Which box are the pearls in?'

'The white one, you stupid man! The pearls are in the white one, the diamonds in the blue and the emeralds the green!'

* * *

Ramon dropped the script again and stared. Floy Pennington had written, almost word for word, what had happened in the office that morning when she had caught him with Jannine. But she was not the author he had always believed her to be. She was a reporter. She was relating her own experience and feelings. And like many sensationalist journalists she was glossing the facts to suit her own purposes.

Jannine had said Floy was an emotional desert, that she didn't have any feeling. That was probably why she was still a virgin at thirty-one. He had not had a virgin since he was sixteen. This had been one reason why he had not taken Floy Pennington by storm. There had been a sense of sacredness about her that he had been unable to bring himself to violate. He must have been wrong to think that she had had a lover before coming down to the office.

So, since she was a maiden, she would have a hard time trying to relate the feelings of full-blown sexual relationships. As a reporter and not an imaginative writer, she would have to experience everything first before transferring it to the page.

Ramon continued with his reading.

'Will you put the pearls on for me, Monsieur Cocteau?' Lara gave Pierre a sweet smile, her anger at him well suppressed. She would teach him not to play with silly girls while she, a real woman, stood to one side.

Pierre took the string of pearls and went behind her. She bared her neck to him, lifting her black tresses so that he could fasten the clasp. As he wrapped the string around her, she made sure her hands touched his sensuously. When it was done, she turned to him, her eyelids fluttering just slightly.

Now his face was only inches from hers. His lips, so succulent and inviting, were poised, only tense moments from her own. As she moved towards them he swayed slightly, obviously affected by her closeness.

He smelt divine. She breathed him in deeply, a mixture of sweet perspiration and masculine after-shave.

As her lips touched his, he closed his eyes.

At that moment, she knew she had him.

The kiss was light and tender; not the passionate kind he had been receiving or giving with the maid. She stroked his cheek lightly with the tips of her fingers.

Whispering, she withdrew.

'Thank you Pierre. Perhaps I'll see you later.'

That night Lara waited for Pierre to go to his room. Her light was on. She sat by her window in underslip and bra, brushing her hair. She made certain she could see him and he her. Her reflection in the dressing table mirror showed her an image of his window. The same reflection would show him her bra as she sat sideways.

Now he was there. As he went to close his curtains, he saw her. His light went out.

Lara began her seduction. She stood, weighing her breasts in the cups of her hands.

Her pulse raced. Her fingers glided down her waist and shed the slip, slowly and provocatively. Now standing in bra and purposely skimpy panties, she felt wanton. Never in her life had she been more excited; more sexually aroused. Her pants were wet with the warm juice flowing from deep inside her, from inside the place where she wanted desperately to feel the hardened organ of Pierre Cocteau.

She drew a deep breath.

But she must goad him. She must not give him all his desire. It might take a night or two. Gradually she would increase her lascivious behaviour until he would burst, unstoppable, into her room. She must increase the pressure on him so that he would take her forcefully, for only then could she be fulfilled.

She undid the clasp of her bra and turned her back on Pierre Cocteau. Not yet would she show him her naked breasts. Her nipples hurt with the pressure of their erection, with their desire to be sucked by that broad-lipped mouth. But she held to her resolve. Perhaps tomorrow night?

Lara bent provocatively to pick up her slip. Then she switched out the light.

* * *

131

'The bitch! The bloody scheming cow!' Ramon's anger was increasing with each paragraph he read.

But there was still no crime. Did Floy Pennington plan to murder him and write about that? He shivered. Perhaps she planned to have Jannine done away with and have him accused of rape and strangulation. Floy Pennington had clearly been angry when she had seen Jannine and him together. Like Lara in her story, she had held her anger down well. Showing him only her icy face, she had snapped at him as he looked for her necklace of pearls. Then, like Lara, she had made him put them on her, knowing that he was shaking violently just by being near her.

The kiss between Lara and Pierre had been a invention. It was the first departure from what had really happened. But was that what Floy Pennington had wanted? Had she wanted him to kiss her?

And the striptease? She had been thrilled by what she had done to him, and could not have written it that way if she had not been. She had set out to arouse him and had ended up arousing herself. Or was it the other way around? Had his naked exposure at his window wound her up so much she had had her own sexuality triggered? Had she needed him?

Lara van den Berg was a libertine, but only because Floy Pennington was one too.

Ramon had come to the end of the manuscript. Only the crumpled papers remained. He scanned them. It seemed that they were several attempts at writing the same thing. None of them was finished.

Ramon read on.

The man stood by Lara's bed, her diamond necklace in his hand. His masked face, blue-grey in the moonlight, looked cold and hard. Had he come for her jewels and not realised she was in bed?

Slowly he began to slip down the zip of his trousers. Lara's heart missed a beat. At first, when he had crept silently in, she had thought him to be Pierre come in response to her erotic invitation.

Now she knew that he was someone else. He was taller, slimmer, more rangy in his build. At first Lara quaked with fear. Then, as the burglar stripped, her pulse began to beat to quite another stimulus.

Her titillation of Pierre had made her ravenous for a man.

Now he stood naked before her, his huge erection silhouetted against the light. Her stomach trembled uncontrollably. Her body thrilled with anticipation.

The writing on that sheet ended. Ramon's pulse was racing. This was racy stuff. It could have been written only by a woman who had experience of such things. Floy Pennington had related part of her experience when he had visited her the night before.

But the passage, and others like it, ended abruptly. In another version on another crinkled sheet, the burglar had a long stiletto knife. He had held it to Lara's throat. In yet another version he had tied her wrists to the rails of the Edwardian brass bed-head. Lara had struggled hard but had been unable to overcome the man.

None of the outlines solved the puzzle. Ramon could not tell whether the wayward Lara had met 'a fate worse than death' or not. Had she lain back resignedly to 'think of England'? He doubted it.

Had she succumbed to enforcement, revelling in having a man take her like that? Or, had she fought like a tigress, his cock inside her, his hand across her mouth to quell her screams?

None of the drafts had got further than the man menacing Lara. Why had she stopped there? Perhaps Floy Pennington needed the experience of that too.

Ramon scowled. What had Floy Pennington wanted?. Had she wanted love? Or had she wanted a strong hard fucking after all? She had been cold, disappointed in him, afterwards. Only when he had threatened her had her eyes lit up. What had she had been working him up to?

He recalled her words at the time. 'Are you going to ravish me?' It was a strange question for a woman who had enticed him to her bed.

Was that what Floy Pennington had needed for her book? Would that have been the crime? A burglary and a rape? Was that the sex she thought the publisher wanted so he could sell more books?

Ramon paced the office. When he had made love to Floy Pennington, instead of taking her by force, had he spoiled her plot? He smiled grimly. That was one thing he could soon put right. If that was what she truly wanted, he could don a mask and creep into her room that night. He could take her violently. Then she would really have a story.

One thing was clear. He would teach Floy Pennington a lesson she would not quickly forget. Ramon recalled his pledge to himself to tame her, and began to form a plan.

The switchboard in reception buzzed. The receptionist was on her break so Ramon took the call. He tensed as he saw the light on for Floy Pennington's extension.

'Hello Ramon. This is Floy.'

Her tone was husky, seductive and subdued. He wondered what her ploy was this time. She seemed to do nothing without a purpose.

'Yes, Miss Pennington. How can I be of service?'

Ramon's voice was sharp. Her deceit and her manipulation of him hurt. Inside, he was furious. But she was his guest. He calmed himself.

'I need to place a call to my publisher, Maxwell Bloomensteen.'

'I'll give you a line.'

'Your receptionist already has the number. Could you get it for me please?'

Ramon suppressed a frown. She was lazy. It was the kind of laziness which came with riches. Nevertheless she was a guest. He would pander to this whim. As for her other whims, only time would tell.

'I'll call you back, Miss Pennington.'

He switched the key. Her light went off on the old-fashioned key-and-lamp system. He cursed her laziness and dialled. When he called her back, she took time to answer. He tapped his foot with annoyance.

'Miss Pennington? I have your publisher on the line. Go ahead please.'

Ramon did not clear his line. With such a system it was possible for the operator to listen in without the other parties knowing.

'Hello sweetie. How's the new book plotting?' It was a deep American voice, full of false charm.

'Hello Max.'

'What gives, sweetheart?'

'I can't do it.'

There was a tense pause.

'What can't you do, sweetie?'

'I can't do this book. I'm just not cut out to write that kind of thing!'

'Nonsense,' he drawled. 'You always say that at the beginning of a book.'

'This one's different. I don't have the experience it takes.'

'I won't take no for an answer, Floy.' Bloomensteen had turned hard now. Ramon could hear that he was not a man to cross, no matter how famous an author she was.

'I can't do the sex!'

'Oh come on now, honey. You must be joking me. You're not lacking in that department, are you?' He sniggered.

'I can't do it, Max!'

There was a poignant silence.

'You'll have to. Remember, you've been paid two million for the paperback, TV and film rights. That's a pretty good advance.'

135

Ramon whistled silently. That was a lot of money for something not even written.

'But I've told you. I can't write that kind of thing.'

She was getting very upset.

'Sorry Florence, but that's just not my problem. Give me an outline and three chapters by the end of the month or find a new publisher. Oh – and if you can't do the book, send back the cheque.'

The line went dead at the publisher's end. Ramon heard a sob, then a click.

So, Floy Pennington was in trouble. She could not handle the sexual ingredient her publisher wanted. She had been paid a fortune for something she could not produce.

Ramon gloated.

At eleven-thirty that evening, Ramon sat in his office, his door open as he waited for her. Only when she entered did he look up at her. She glided in, dressed in her white bath robe, like the spirit of a nun. Her pale, oval face and its doleful expression made her look like a marble Madonna. The sparkle which her eyes had contained the night before was missing. Instead, her eyes were wet with tears. Had she been crying?

Floy took a deep breath. This was difficult for her. Ramon DuPrey's expression appeared hard. It was not anger she thought she saw, but resignation. Even so, she still felt an emanation from him. There was a light in his eyes as he studied her. Instinctively she could tell that he was still excited by her, even though he tried to hold it down.

Knowing the pattern of her movements, he went to the safe.

'I've brought the pearls, Ramon. Could you take them off please?'

'Take them off yourself. You know you can.'

She complied. He was clearly not going to play that game again. She unclasped the string of pearls.

'Will you put them away please?' She walked to the safe and handed them to him. He held out his hand silently.

As she trickled the pearls into his palm, her hand touched his. She felt a thrill. Pictures in her mind recalled the intimate caresses of the night before, the taste of his lips, the thrill of his head between her legs, his tongue working her towards that explosive tension.

She watched him silently as he put the pearls away and banged the safe shut. He stood up and turned. As before, his face was close to hers. Her breath short and sharp now, she swayed towards him.

Ramon's heart raced. The scent of the incredible woman was pumping him up harder with every second she stood beside her. How did the temptress do this to him? What was it about her that had him raging at her one minute, a trembling idiot at the next?

'I'm sorry about the bruise, Miss Pennington.'

She put her hand to her cheek and smiled with resignation.

'Don't be. Perhaps I deserved it.'

Ramon stood transfixed by her beauty and her allure. Even in her subdued state, there was that inner fire about her that excited lust in him, mixed with love. One part of him wanted to push her away, to tell her to get out of his life and to stop her tricks. Another part, the stronger of the two, wanted to take her wildly. It wanted to vent the pressure which the seduction of her presence was building in him.

Her bath robe hung loose as always, but more open than usual. She wore no bra. The deep valley between her breasts was exposed to his gaze. This aroused him more and he suspected that this was her intention. She wanted him, even though she did not say so openly with words. But no woman he had ever known had spoken openly of her deepest desire.

Never had he had a woman who had voiced her needs. Jannine was the most forward, but even she never said, 'Fuck me. I want your cock.' No, even Jannine made him guess exactly what she wanted and was peevish if he got it wrong. She would touch him up so he would know that she was hot. But even then she'd go cold on him if she thought he was taking her for granted.

Other women would be more oblique. 'Would you like a nightcap? Would you like to come up to see my snaps?' meant 'Do you want to come to bed? Would you like to see something more of me?' But they never said it in so many words.

As far as the women he had bedded had been concerned, he had had to be a mind-reader. And woe betide him if he misread the signs. 'You filthy bastard! What do you think I am?'

The problem was, half the time they did not realise they were giving out the message 'Fuck me.' And they would deny it if he went too fast, or too far too soon.

And with Floy Pennington he had got it totally wrong, but the opposite way to usual. She had wanted to be ravished. No lead up. No warm up. No introductory 'Let me get to know you before I go too far.'

Floy Pennington swayed towards him and closed her eyes. Ramon wavered. He almost took her in his arms. He almost tore aside the robe to bare her where she stood. He almost laid her across the desk, lifted up her robe to expose her, to sink himself deep between the luscious lips of the hair-fringed delight which she had displayed to him last night.

She let out a small sigh.

Ramon steeled himself.

'I think you ought to go, Miss Pennington.'

The words stung Floy. They were the same words she had said to him as she had banished him from her bed. When she opened her eyes they filled quickly with tears. But why shouldn't he reject her? Why should he take her after all that she had done to him?

Sedately she went, not running like a slighted adolescent. She held her head high and mounted the staircase as nobly as a queen with an audience of hundreds. Without looking back, she turned into the corridor above. Had she looked round, she would have seen Ramon DuPrey standing angrily at the office door.

Ramon paced up and down the foyer, unable to dispel his anger. He was mad at himself. He should have taken her, if only to vent his anger on her. But she was still a virgin. And she was naïve. Although she seemed to have set out to achieve a particular end, he sensed that she did not understand the havoc she was creating around herself. She had been treating him like an experiment. She had toyed with John. The boy had confessed when he had dared to return. John had pleaded to be taken off public duties until Floy Pennington had gone.

Damn her. Why should she get away with it? Just because she was rich and influential did not mean she could play with the fragile emotions of others.

Ramon went to his room. Her curtains were closed. He closed his own. He stripped and went into the shower. Usually the hot water running over his body made him relax, but not tonight. He was half hard, his member springing as he towelled himself between the legs, only needing a whiff of a woman or a mental picture of that tantalising triangle of curls to harden him fully at once. The continual stimulus of having Floy Pennington around, the constant erections she had aroused in him had made him like a tom cat on heat. He needed relief.

He had come when he had licked her. That had been joyous even though his member had not felt the heat of her velvet walls.

Ramon lay in the semi-darkness, thumbing at the web of his penis. Each stroke made it jump a little, made it harden some more. But what for? Just another jerk off? Just another waste of vital energy?

Pictures of those lush, pink lips flooded into his mind.

Pictures of her pouting nipples set in perfect mounds made his mouth go wet. His tongue wiped his lips as he rubbed himself, remembering her taste. His nose conjured up her scent. His hand increased its speed. His balls were tight now, his erection blown up full. The speed of his hand increased, the strokes became shorter. He began to pant. He pressed his fingers of his free hand hard between his navel and his matt of hair, to increase the pain of near-ejaculation.

He stopped the masturbation.

He needed Floy Pennington. Nothing else would be enough to douse his anger now. But if he did, if he went in now and fucked her hard, it would be what she had wanted all along. Damn her. He would not please her like that. He would take her in his own time and his own way. He would tease her mercilessly like she had teased him; stringing her along until she screamed for him to screw her. Then, and only then, would he give her the hardest ride she would ever have. Despite the fact that she was a virgin.

Floy awoke when the wall clock in her sitting room struck two. The room was hot, the heating turned up against the chill night. In her fitful sleep she had sloughed off her bedclothes and lay naked, watching a cavalcade of regrets file past in her mind.

It was a movement by the door which turned her attention. The door was open, not closed as she had left it. A man stood silently, silhouetted against the greyness of the sitting room beyond.

She took a sharp breath.

He moved towards her.

She recoiled. Then she relaxed. It was a dream, of course.

He held out her diamonds, just as the burglar she had written into the book had held out Lara's. But she could not see the long stiletto knife. Sure that it was there, her heart began to race.

140

He was close now, but she could not see his face. He was wreathed in black, a mask over his eyes.

Letting the diamonds trickle to the bedside table, he unclasped his belt. He slipped down his zip.

By now Floy's body was shaking violently, with fear and with elation. He was a dream. A dream to be enjoyed as well as to be feared.

Naked now, he stood over her. Reflexively she put up warding arms. He took her wrists and bore down, pinning them behind her head. Strongly, without violence, his pressure fixed her to the bed. Now he straddled her body, his knees outside her thighs.

Floy panted with the excitement of the totally unstoppable act. There was no struggle, no outrage or cry for help. She abandoned herself to the dream.

As his lips met hers, she shuddered. Unlike the loving lips of Ramon DuPrey, this dream burglar's lips were hard and demanding. Working widely over hers, she found herself responding to their touch. She found herself panting, dragging breath through her nose in order to breathe against the relentless onslaught of his mouth on hers.

Without withdrawing his mouth he lowered himself onto her, his whole body hot and hard and tense; as hard and tense as his penis. Her stomach tightened and loosened and tightened again, in waves. He forced her legs open with his own. Between her legs she could feel the heat, the strength of his erection, rhythmically working over her clitoris, slippery with the juice of her excitement.

Now she struggled. Her body began to writhe. Wildly she fought. But she did not fight to free herself. She fought to capture him, to make him penetrate her deeply. Desperately now, she needed to know what it was like. She needed to leave her maidenhood behind for ever. She craved release from the nagging tension which had been building in her hour by hour.

He refused her hungry demand. She fought more, the need for him lending strength to her arms so that

141

she could rip them free. Now one arm clasped behind his neck, pulling his mouth to her voracious lips. The other clawed at his back.

With his arms free, he hooked them under her knees, doubling her legs back, her knees almost to touch her breasts. Irresistible, he pulled her taut and open, more sensitised than ever to every stroking touch.

Still he did not enter her.

Wildly now she struggled, winding her legs around his rhythmic pelvis. He stroked long and hard from her upturned anus, sliding through her slippery purse, to rub her nubbin upwards before receding for the next thrust. Then it came again, angry and unstoppable. Rigid, it drove against her. Ploughing through the yawning furrow to her hardened nub, he pressed for a moment, his sac rasping at her. Then he pulled back again.

Again and again he ploughed; forceful and un-relenting.

As her head arched backwards her breasts thrust upwards, nipples rigid with the need for a sucking mouth; he sank his teeth into her neck. She gasped and cried out with pleasure-pain. Where he rubbed his hardness on her she was on fire.

The bite triggered an explosion in her.

A concentric wave of sensation ripped through her body, setting up a paroxysm of contractions in her abdomen. Against her, she felt him tauten and slide one last time through her valley to her mound. She felt fluid warmth, then a steady beat against her belly.

Suddenly it was over. Together they lay, both shuddering ecstatically from the experience.

After some minutes, Floy became calm. The tension of years had left her. She floated as if in a void.

And she knew what was to come next in the dream. The knife across her throat. The sharp pain. Then the warm wetness of blood.

She was not afraid.

It was several seconds before she realised her burglar-lover was gone. When and how he went she could not recall. Floating in bliss she had not felt her body lighten. Even now she might be dead.

She felt her pulse. It ticked steadily. Her hand went to her neck, just as she had planned for Lara van den Berg's to do. There was no blood. The gushing jugular which Lara's hand would find was quite intact, even though her neck stung. Floy did not have the awful realisation which Lara would have, that death was only a few heartbeats away. There was no rapist-murderer standing by her bed, gloating with bloody, dripping knife and dripping cock.

Floy sprang up and switched on the light. The bedroom door was shut. She looked down at her nakedness among the crumpled bed sheets. Now she grabbed a hand mirror from the bedside table. Her throat stung. It was not cut, but the marks of teeth were plainly there to see. Something fluid on her abdomen, opaque and warm and thick, caught her attention. Floy stared. She touched it. She smelled the unmistakable smell which had tainted her hand as she had milked Jay Polland, and young John too. That sweet and rancid smell was real!

Floy turned her head to the pillow and began to weep with emotions she had never felt before.

Breakfast was fraught with uncertainty. Floy had no appetite. She waited for Ramon DuPrey, but he did not come. Neither was he in his office when she called.

She tried to work but could not. Only pictures of the last night's sensual scene would come. She walked in the grounds but the feelings would not leave her. They haunted her all day.

The dream had been so real, but it had not followed the plot. If it had done he would have raped her. She would have had her throat cut, or been strangled at the least. But he had not even entered her. Despite her struggle to swallow his rigid organ with her sexual mouth, he had steadfastly refused to let her feast.

But had it been a dream, there would not have been a love bite on her neck and semen on her stomach when she had woken.

Ramon had kept himself very busy all day. He had several long local calls on the phone and had occupied himself with making a dozen different arrangements, delegating tasks and generally giving instructions.

He was clearing out the store room next to his bedroom when Floy Pennington found him. The corridor was piled with rubbish, an old mattress and a large pile of boxes.

'Hello Ramon. I'm glad I've found you. I asked for you in reception but no-one seemed to know where you were.'

Ramon spun round when he heard her voice. He quickly shut the door to the store room, embarrassed at finding Floy Pennington in the staff quarters.

Looking down at his ragged working jeans, he dusted his hands.

'I'm sorry, Miss Pennington, you have me at a disadvantage.'

She smiled, but it was not that superior smile she had used before. He thought how sad she looked, how wan. The bruise he had made in his rage still showed on her cheekbone. One part of him wanted to put his hand out and caress it, to put right the hurt with a loving touch. Another part of him wanted to jeer.

And although she wore the collar of her white blouse up, he could see his teeth marks on her neck. He was half glad and half sad.

'I need a favour, Ramon.'

She seemed nervous. Standing away from him, she fingered dust from the frame of a faded print of *The Sunflowers* by Van Gogh. The picture hung crookedly opposite the store room door. She tried to straighten it. It swung back, crooked again.

Ramon raised an eyebrow. He did not hide the sharpness in his reply.

'What kind of favour do you want this time, Miss Pennington?'

She blanched and put her eyes down for a second. When she looked at him again, tears were plainly visible.

'I need a signature on a contract. A witness for my own signature. Will you do it for me please?'

The voice was so plaintive that he could not refuse. And she was still a guest in his hotel.

'Very well.'

She moved down the corridor.

'Will you come now?'

This was a surprise to Ramon. Was she asking him to go to her rooms? Was this a 'Would you like to come in for coffee' invitation? Dusting off his clothes he fetched a packet from his own room and followed her warily. She stood with the door open.

Gingerly he went inside.

The word processor was off. The original manuscript lay on the table where he had left it. So she had not written any more of her story.

Floy Pennington moved to the desk. She picked up a gold fountain pen and signed the last page of a thick document.

Ramon had to stand close so that he could witness her writing.

She handed him the pen.

It was warm from the heat of her hand. His fingers tingled just to hold it.

He countersigned, dated the signature and pushed the paper aside.

When he looked up she was close, her face only inches from his. She swayed towards him, her eyes searching his. He thought he saw longing there, followed by uncertainty.

Ramon pulled back and pushed her away.

'Oh no, Miss Pennington. You're not getting me that way again.'

Sorrow filled her eyes.

'I'm sorry.' She sniffed. 'But I need your help, Ramon.'

He backed away and held up a hand defensively.

'Oh no. Not this time. Anyway, what makes you think I can help you?'

For a moment she looked lost. She looked uncomfortable. The wildly successful Floy Pennington had taken on more than she could handle with the new book. And she expected him to help.

'I'm out of my depth, Ramon.'

At last she was being honest. He fixed her eyes with his and said nothing.

'I don't have the experience to write what the publisher wants.'

He snorted.

'It seems to me that you're a fast learner.'

That appeared to hurt her. She flinched, stiffened herself and went on.

'I understand why you're angry. It was unforgiveable of me to do what I did to you.'

'You're damned right it was!'

He would not suppress his anger. Why should he? He was talking to her as one human being to another; not as a guest in his hotel.

'You're right. You see . . .' She was obviously having difficulties with a confession. He let her stew.

'You see. Before I came here I'd never had any sexual experience with men.'

Ramon was astounded. A sensual, stunning woman like Floy Pennington had not experienced any men in her life? He recalled what Jannine had said about her being an iceberg. The Sister Luke character she had invented had been manless too. He knew Floy was a virgin, but that did not preclude oral or manual sex. He knew that a woman could be touched and licked and sucked and come explosively without a cock. Without a man.

'No, it's not what you're thinking. I'm not lesbian. Mind you, I don't condemn them.'

Ramon was nonplussed. This conversation was taking a surprising turn. She sat down. The effort of making her confession seemed to drain her.

'I never gave men a chance. I was always too busy with more pressing things. After I wrote my first best seller at the age of twenty-four, there was no time. I've been buried in my work for the past seven years, Ramon. Life, in the way of sex, has passed me by.'

He stood rigid, his legs braced. Staring down on her, he felt severe. She had chosen her way and she had made a lot of money.

He still found it hard to forgive her for the way she had used him. Apart from that, he had something in his pocket which was hers and it made him very angry.

A long silence followed. Ramon could not go. He could see that Floy Pennington was struggling with something she needed to say.

Eventually she looked at him directly.

'It was you who was the burglar last night, wasn't it?'

He said nothing, trying to gauge if she was angry or not.

'How did you know, Ramon? How did you know that was supposed to happen?'

'I read the manuscript.'

He blurted it out. Why should he deceive her like she had deceived him? She raised an eyebrow.

'I don't apologise for reading it, Miss Pennington. In a way I feel I had a right to. I can't deny that I was shocked. Not at what you wrote. It was the way you did your research that made me sick.'

She smiled thinly.

'I'm sorry. I didn't mean to hurt you like that.'

Ramon turned half away from her, his arms stiffly folded. Floy continued.

'I had to act out the emotions. I didn't have any experience to draw on.'

He spun on her, growling.

'You could have asked, damn you!'

Floy Pennington blanched. Then she seemed to collect herself. Standing up, she went to him and touched his arm, speaking softly.

'But that's just what I couldn't do, Ramon. It had to be like that or it wouldn't have worked. It needed spontaneity. If it had been agreed or planned it wouldn't have held the tension or the emotion that it did. I'm an inexperienced and unemotional person, I'm afraid. I can't write about sensations which I've never felt.'

He threw his head back with a sharp 'Huh!'

She stroked his arm.

'I always use live situations before I write. That's why the books are so successful. If they were staged, they wouldn't be the same. It's the true emotion, the element of surprise, the unpredictable situations which give a book its spark.'

Ramon shook her hand off his arm.

'So what happens next? You have me killed? Or do you plan to have Jannine's throat cut and me accused of raping and murdering her?'

Floy Pennington looked hurtfully into his eyes.

'Of course not.' She looked away. 'To tell you the truth I'm in trouble. I can't go on with the sex. I just don't have the experience.'

'Too bad.' He laughed in her face. 'I suppose you want me to fill in more detail? Do you want me to fuck you now? Six different ways so you can choose the best?'

She lowered her eyes. Ramon glared and grabbed her chin to make her face him.

'You wanted me to ravish you didn't you? Just like you planned to have the burglar do to Lara. Well, when I came to do it, I couldn't. I'm not like that. If you thought I was, you picked the wrong man. But I'll tell you one thing, Miss Pennington. You don't deserve to be made love to. I'm sick of your acting; of your playing with people's emotions and feelings. Why for God's sake can't you be honest and do things openly?'

Tears welled in her eyes. One made a track down her cheeks.

'Ramon?' She touched his arm again. 'Ramon, you're right. But I was desperate. If I don't do this book, I'm ruined. If I don't honour the contract I'll have to refund the advance. I've been paid two million dollars.'

'Oh dear. How sad.'

'I don't have it. I've already spent most of it.'

He grinned cruelly.

'Then you'll have to find a way of finishing the book, won't you? But don't expect any help from me.'

'Of course. I won't bother you any further. I'll leave first thing in the morning. But I'll pay the month that we agreed for the suite and the Pollands' bill.'

'Pay for what you've had. That's all I ask. And you're damned lucky I don't charge you for the experiences I gave you, whether you liked them or not.'

'Ramon, I'm sorry.'

He moved towards the door. Damn. Despite everything that had happened between them, the thought of Floy Pennington leaving in the morning made him feel sick.

But how could he stop her leaving.?

What would be the point of her staying?

These were questions which could not be answered. It was a matter of the heart, not of logic. All he knew was that for some insane reason, he still loved and wanted Floy Pennington. Perhaps this was what had made him so angry with her. There had hardly been a time since her arrival when she had not occupied his thoughts, sometimes beautiful and loving thoughts, and at times very angry ones.

Even if she had not played her sexual tricks on him, she would have driven him mad with desire. Perhaps, in an ironic way, those tricks had given him the only chances he would ever have of making love to her. Before she had thrown him out of her bedroom, it had been a memorable sexual and emotional experience. And last night more so. Although he had purposely refused to screw her, the whole thing had been exhilarating. He had had control of her. She had screamed and bucked and desperately sought to capture him so she could spike herself on him.

Now, she looked so pathetic; so lonely standing in the centre of the room. Tears tracked down her beautiful face. Ramon knew that he was looking at Floy Pennington the woman, not Floy Pennington the famous writer. Perhaps for the first time she was feeling like a woman, not the rich bitch her success had turned her into.

Ramon's hand was on the door handle when he remembered the packet in his back pocket. A surge of anger welled again.

He threw the packet to her. Its contents strewed over the floor. Pictures of a naked, rampant male standing in his lighted bedroom looked up at them both. A close-up of his phallus, purple head swollen glossily, twin lobes up tight in their sac, ready for action, lay on the carpet for their eyes to see.

'Those came for you by special courier this morning. Have them as keepsakes of your stay here.'

At eleven-thirty Floy put on her bath robe and left her room as usual. She was, by her own admission, a creature of habit. The story she had written about a burglar coming to steal her necklace was too vivid. She would not risk losing one of the most valuable things she still possessed. The pearls must go in the safe, even if it meant facing Ramon DuPrey's wrath again.

The office light was on. She knocked timidly. There was no reply. Was he in there with that girl Jannine? A cavalcade of vivid scenes filed through her imagination. Jannine naked, bent across the desk with Ramon's mouth buried between her legs, licking at her blonde-fringed lips? DuPrey's member driven deep between the girl's tight buttocks? His trouser belt like a bridle around her pretty neck while he rode her like his steed, she whinnying and bucking on his pumping cock with every thrust?

Floy knocked again. Still there was no reply. She hesitated. At least she would give them time to dress.

A minute later, she plucked up courage. Tentatively she turned the door handle and entered.

Ramon sat at his desk looking pale and frightened. Had he been expecting someone else?

'Ramon? Ramon it's only me. Are you alright?'

'Come in, Miss Pennington.'

His manner was wooden. Something was wrong with him.

She flung open the door and rushed to the desk. Only then did she realise that he was not alone after all.

There was someone behind her. She would have turned but something hard and cold touched her temple.

A brief glance in a mirror on the wall showed a picture of herself, her face white with terror, the black snub nose of a pistol pressed tightly to her head.

Chapter Seven

Floy froze as the gun nuzzled her.

She felt her face drain of all colour. Another quick glance in the mirror confirmed it. It also showed an image of an unsavoury looking man. A florid, round face peered over her shoulder, its nose red, its hair unkempt. Attached to an overweight body, it had little eyes deeply set in puckered skin.

The gun was gripped in a podgy hand. This shook as if the man was as nervous as she. She hoped that his tremor would not set the thing off and blow her brains over the wallpaper.

Garlic breath wheezed over her shoulder. Floy turned her face away with a bad-smell expression. Ramon stared at her, his face grey, his mouth opening and closing. Nothing came out.

Floy snapped her head round to face the man, pushing the gun away.

'What the hell's going on!'

It was a spontaneous reaction, but she thought that anyway attack was probably the best form of defence.

He levelled the gun at her again.

'Take off the pearls!'

At this, Floy spun round to face him fully. She

glowered. Gun or no gun she was not going to give up her pearls easily.

This sudden movement seemed to take the man by surprise. He stood back. Then he pointed the pistol at her chest, his gaze flicking nervously around her face.

'You don't move. You give trouble and I am shooting. *Verstehen?*'

Floy frowned. So he was German.

She shot a mouthful of vernacular German at him.

'Piss off, you fat bastard! You'll get my knee in your balls if you don't put that toy gun down. And you'll have to shoot me before you get my pearls.'

The man was clearly shocked. He had not thought that such a genteel lady would speak so crudely, and in his own tongue. Then he pulled himself together, retaliating in thick Bavarian German.

'That's enough! You shut your mouth, and do not move. You tell me where are the diamonds or I shoot you. *Verstehen?*'

She ignored him and stuck out her hand.

'Give me that gun, Dumkopf!'

The man wavered, his face rucked into puzzlement. He looked past Floy at Ramon. Floy took a quick glance over her shoulder.

Ramon sat with his hands up, a bewildered look on his ghostly face.

'For God's sake, Miss Pennington! Don't fool with the man. Can't you see he's dangerous!'

By this time the gunman had recovered his composure and was snarling.

This didn't put Floy off.

'Don't you tell me what to do, Ramon DuPrey! Call yourself a man!' She turned to her assailant, her hand still outstretched. She barked in German, 'Now, are you going to give me that gun, or am I going to have to take it?'

She swept forward, her left hand coming down hard on the man's gun arm to sweep it away. At the same time, she side-stepped.

'Floy! No!'

There was a loud crack. Everything went black.

When Floy opened her eyes, everything was still black.
Her body was cold and stiff but she seemed to have no
pain. She tried to move. Her wrists were tied behind
her back. A blindfold around her eyes cut into her face.
She groaned.

There was the steady drumming of an engine and a
bumping sensation. They were in a vehicle.

'Floy! Floy, are you alright?'

She raised her head. She could see nothing but she
felt the warmth of breath fan around her mouth.

'Ramon?'

'Yes. Don't try to sit up. Are you in any pain?

She sank back onto something soft under her head.

'Are we dead?'

She heard the escape of the breath of an almost silent
laugh.

'No, we're not dead. Though we're damned lucky
not to be.'

'What happened?'

'The gun went off as you tried to knock it away. God
knows how the bullet missed you. It made a huge
furrow in the top of my desk and ricocheted past my
ear.'

'Didn't he shoot me?'

'No. You fainted.'

She felt stupid. It would have been better in a way to
have been shot. But to faint in the face of the enemy
was humiliating.

'What happened then?'

'They blindfolded us and dragged us both into this
van.'

'They? What do you mean, they?'

'There are two of them. The other one's a mean
looking creature, as long as a bean pole and only half as
skinny.'

'Why have they kidnapped us, Ramon?'

154

'I heard them talking about a ransom. I think they're going to try to get money from your publisher. They think he'll pay to get you back.'

'Huh! We'll rot in hell before Bloomensteen coughs up anything! What do you think they'll do to us if he doesn't pay?'

'I heard the fat one say that if no-one would pay a ransom for you he'd take you home, tie you up and use you until he was tired of you. Then he'd rent you out to his friends. The thin one had a hard time stopping him screwing you over my desk there and then. When you fainted, your robe was open.'

'And what did you do?'

'He had the gun. There was nothing I could do to stop him.'

Floy shuddered.

'Where are they taking us, do you know?'

'How the hell would I know?'

'Three's no need to be so bitchy!'

At that moment the van stopped. Doors slammed and opened. Floy felt a cold draught. They were pulled out roughly. She felt herself lifted over a shoulder, her head down. She tried to struggle, but the grip on her legs was too strong.

The sound of a door creaking and several echoing footfalls preceded being dumped on something hard.

The door creaked again and slammed. A bolt scraped. Then the doors of the van clanged. It revved and left.

Floy sat up.

'Where are we?'

'It's like a dungeon. The roof is curved and the walls are damp. You're lying on a wooden bench.'

'How the hell do you know?'

'My blindfold's slipped off.'

'Can't you get mine off.'

'Sorry, my hands are tied.'

'Can't you work yourself free?'

'I'm trying.'

Floy shivered.

She did a mental exploration of herself. She still wore the bath robe and had slippers on her feet. It was no wonder she was cold. Otherwise she felt intact. It didn't feel as if she had any bullet wounds. Neither did she feel that she had been sexually interfered with, even if they had had a good gawp at her. She didn't mind about Duprey; he'd licked her intimately the night before so she could hardly be coy with him. It was the other two that she was scared of. What if they should decide to sample what they'd seen?

She shuddered and shook herself. The familiar weight of pearls around her neck was not there. She groaned.

'Where are my pearls? You didn't let them take them, did you!'

He hissed at her.

'What could I do? They had that gun. You were lucky they were only interested in your jewels. If they had been like the burglar you wrote into your book, they would have stripped you and fucked you too.'

'There's no need to be so crude.'

'Huh! Rape is crude, Floy. You might think it's alright for you to write it in a book, but it's different when it happens for real. Perhaps if you were to be raped you'd realise that. But just keep going the way you are: it won't be long before you goad a man into screwing you without asking nicely.'

'It did happen to me for real! You came into my room and – and violated me.'

'No, I didn't.'

'Yes you did. You told me it was you!'

Floy sat upright indignantly, aiming her rebuttal at his voice in the darkness.

'I came into your room. I didn't have you.'

'But I . . .'

'There's a difference, you know, between what I did and what I could have done.'

Floy folded her arms across her chest. She knew he could see her and it made her feel better.

'Whatever it was, you needn't be so damned sanctimonious about it. And there's no need to be so aggressive, either.'

'Wouldn't you be aggressive if someone came into your place and held you at gunpoint, then tied you up and threw you into the back of a van?'

'All right! But just because some local hoodlums decide to rob your hotel, there's no need to take it out on me!'

'They weren't there to rob the hotel. They were only there for your jewellery.'

'Huh! Who told them it was there?'

'You did, you silly woman. You've pranced around in those jewels for a week. Half the county must know about your baubles.'

'Don't you call me silly!'

'Why not? That's what you are. That was a pretty stupid stunt you tried to pull with the gun.'

She hurrumped at him in the darkness.

'I'm not the sort to be pushed around by morons like that. I'd rather die than give in to force.'

'You nearly did die. I think they would have been mad enough at you to shoot you if I hadn't opened the safe.'

'You didn't give them my diamonds and emeralds as well?'

Floy sprang up, dropping her feet to the floor. Bumping full into Ramon, she pushed at him. He caught her by the shoulders gripped her hard.

She struggled. He held her tight.

'Of course I gave them the jewels. Did you expect me to die too? I might be your faithful servant, Miss Pennington, but I'm not that much of a slave.'

'You fool! Don't you realise how much that jewellery was worth?'

'I don't care how much it's bloody worth.'

'You would if you knew how much it would buy.'

'Is that all you think of?'

'Of course it's all I think of. Money is very important

to me. Anyway, how the hell did you get your hands free?'

'I worked them loose.'

'Good. So now you can untie mine.'

'Not while you're in such a bitchy mood, I won't. Anybody would think that losing a few jewels was the end of the world.'

'It could be.'

'Look, all I care about right now is that you're alive.'

'I don't believe that. I don't believe you care about me at all. All you care about is what you can do to me with your – your . . .'

'My cock? What the hell is that supposed to mean?'

'You know very well. You've wanted sex with me ever since you saw me. Well, you got what you wanted, and now I suppose you'll just want more.'

'My God. I just don't believe this. I wanted sex with you? Who the hell was it who did a striptease in front of my window night after night? Who flashed her tits and spread her legs and then complained that I hadn't rushed in like that charging bull?'

'Don't tell me you didn't enjoy ogling me through your binoculars each night. And don't tell me you didn't enjoy sucking my breasts and licking my – '

She cut the word. She could not bring herself to say it aloud. It was a word she knew well but had never used before. It was a word she had spent most of her life dissociating herself from. Until the last week, that part of her anatomy had been put into isolation, not to be felt, or touched or referred to, let alone used for its sexual purpose.

Only when she had looked at Ramon DuPrey's sexual organs through her zoom lens had sensations begun to stir in her own.

Then, when she had stripped in front of him, something had happened down there which had both shocked and elated her. At first she had been horrified when strange thrills had run through her, starting on the inner surfaces of her thighs and running up deep into the cavity between her legs. Then as she had learned to be more and more provocative in her tease, the lips of her vagina had become engorged. Her clitoris had begun to stand up on its own, thrilling to the feelings which ran through her.

As she had lifted her breasts, her nipples had hardened too. They had become so hard that they had been almost painful with the pleasure.

As she had gone on with the temptation, she had felt like Salome dancing erotically before Herod. She had begun to pant with the excitement of what she was doing, not only to Ramon DuPrey, but to herself.

Then she had become wet. It had happened on the first night as she had turned her back on Ramon. She had bent down, trying hard to stop herself from baring her vaginal lips to him. For an instant she had wanted to rip off her knickers and widen her stance. She had wanted to stretch herself, fantasising that he would put his incredibly swollen organ into her. At that moment, a shudder of sensation had run through her. She had become warm and slippery, and deliciously alive with tingling energy.

From that moment, she had wanted to feel Ramon Dupry's phallus deep inside her.

When he had come to her suite at last, her heart had pumped with excitement at the thought of swallowing that long, stiff shaft of flesh. Then he had cheated her. He had brought her to a climax, but he had not fu – he had not penetrated her to achieve it.

'Of course I enjoyed what I did,' Ramon shouted at her, 'but it would have been a damned sight more enjoyable if you'd participated, instead of lying there like some goddamned nun being raped, forgiving me for every fucking stroke!'

His words ripped through Floy like a chain-saw. Blinded by anger as well as the blindfold, she lashed out with her foot again and again.

* * *

Ramon sidestepped after several kicks had caught him on the shins. Instinctively he pushed Floy. She fell back on the wooden bench behind her. Conscious that she might bring up an emasculating knee at any moment, he spreadeagled her on the bench and threw himself on top of her.

With her arms tied behind her, she was helpless.

Trapped in his jeans, his cock came up against the hard bone of her pubis. His lips hit her lips full on.

She gasped and struggled. But he was heavier than she and she was at a disadvantage as her legs were splayed each side of him so that she could not kick.

He pressed her shoulders to the bench.

In the struggle, his shirt had ripped open; her robe too. The coolness of her skin met his, the softness of her breasts cushioning him as he pressed down on her. When she had come into the office, he had suspected that she was naked under the robe. When she had fainted he had laid her on the floor, her beautiful breasts spilling out and her smooth dense mat of black pubic hair drawing three pairs of male eyes to the succulent lips not quite hidden between her legs.

Ramon growled.

'I'm sick to death of your petulance. It's time you learned what playing with a real man can get you into.' He thrust himself hard against her pubis, splaying her legs even wider with his own.

'Pervert! Let me go!'

'Me a pervert? Isn't this what you wanted? Isn't this what you set out to get, right from the start? Isn't this what you wanted the burglar to do? Didn't the burglar tie Lara to the bed-head in one version of your story? And didn't you shut your curtains after flashing your tits and arse at me so that I would get so frustrated I would storm in and do this to you?'

She thrashed her head from side to side, but still he captured her mouth. She twisted again. He moved to match her. He pressed his lips to hers, even more uncompromisingly than he had as the 'burglar'. She stopped thrashing and succumbed to his demand for her mouth. Then she began to work her lips against his.

Floy Pennington was a mystery to Ramon. At one time she was fiery to the point of being irrational in the face of danger. In another moment she would become a temptress. But when he had responded to her temptation and loved her, she had turned into an iceberg and had thrown him out.

Now, as she panted under the pressure of his kiss, she began to move her pelvis. The movements were small at first. Then as the kiss went on, her tongue darted out to fence with his. Her hips began to gyrate.

Through his trousers he could feel the hardness of her pubis, grinding on his rapidly hardening rod. He moaned.

This served to increase her fervour. She shifted and wound her legs round him so that she could rub her clitoris on his bulge.

Now she was panting deeply. Her head went back for him to access her neck with his teeth, just as he had done in his burglar's guise.

In his anger at her, Ramon bit her hard. He needed to revenge himself for the cruelty she had handed out to him.

She cried out ecstatically.

He brought his mouth down on hers again, his lips working over hers in hungry circular motions. This time she responded avidly, eating at him, her mouth sideways on to his.

Ramon groaned again. Could he stop himself from having her this time? Probably not. But why should he? This was what he had set out to do. He had sworn to tame Floy Pennington. He had sworn to make her crave him; to make her get down on her knees and beg for him.

So first he would get some sweet revenge. He'd made her implore him for his prick. He thrust it hard against her. She opened wider and wound her legs more tightly round his thighs, clamping him to herself.

'Tell me why I should screw you. Why should I give you any more pleasure after the way you treated me?'

She locked her mouth on his, straining upwards blindly to capture his lips.

He pulled away.

She panted and moaned.

'Don't, Ramon. Please don't tease me.'

'But you teased me, Miss Pennington. You teased me mercilessly and then you threw me out of your bed.'

'Don't call me Miss Pennington. It sounds so hard. Please call me Floy.'

'You didn't answer my question. Why should I give you any more pleasure?'

She sighed deeply.

'Because I want you. I want to feel your . . .'

'Yes?'

'I want to feel the strength of it pushing into me. I want to feel the heat as it bursts. I want to feel it beating inside me just as the burglar's beat on my stomach, leaving behind that warm thick pool.'

Ramon sighed, took a deep breath and closed his eyes. She whispered, straining up to his ear.

'I need you, Ramon. I want to know what it's like to be – to be fucked. I need to get rid of this awful tension which wracks me.'

He rubbed himself against her a couple of times, the warm wetness from her soaking through his jeans. She moaned. He hardened and strained in his trousers. But he knew that once he let it loose, he would come in a couple of seconds. Just having her tied up, and lying between her legs, and denying her pleas for him to take her, was bringing him to such a height of stimulation that he was almost coming already. And he could sense it was having the same effect on her.

He sneered.

'You need to know what it's like to be fucked so you can write it into your damned book.'

'No, it's not that. That's finished with. I need you, Ramon.'

'I don't believe you. You need the experience, you bitch; so that you can know what Lara feels like when the burglar rapes her. So that when you write about it in all its graphic detail, people will pat you on the back and tell you what a marvellous author you are. So that you can make millions, or keep the millions you have already had in advances. So that you can spend it on more jewels and a bigger, more expensive car, you snooty bitch!'

He put his mouth to hers, grinding down angrily on her, thrusting his tongue into her mouth. While his hands clamped her shoulders, his imprisoned erection rode in the warm softness between her legs.

She writhed under him.

This was too much. He had never held back this long before, particularly when his partner was so eager. He pulled back.

'All right, Miss Pennington, I'll ravish you. Then you can feel what Lara will feel when the burglar takes her.'

Ramon was angry now. He could not recall when he had been so angry with a woman. She had used him from the beginning and still she was using him. He was still convinced that all she wanted, despite their precarious situation, was to have the experience of violent sex. She was still regarding him as a tool for her work.

He slid downwards. His mouth found her breasts. He took a nipple and sank his teeth into the nimbus, just hard enough to make her squeal. Then he slid further down. His mouth found her clitoris. He lip-chewed at it. She writhed.

He undid his belt, slipped down his zip and shed his jeans. He had no pants on. Apart from his shirt he was naked. He raised his head.

'And shall I tell you something else, Miss bloody Pennington? When you first did your striptease and froze me out the next morning, I swore I would tame you. And I will, make no mistake about that.'

He shifted up her so his erection was ploughing

through her ravening lips again, ready to change angle and plunge its head deep inside her.

His words stung Floy deeply. But despite the fire he had stoked in her, despite being trussed up and at his mercy, her mind was thinking clearly. Her temper flared. She would not be tamed.

'Technically, you can't ravish me.'

'Of course I can ravish you! I'm stronger than you. Your hands are tied and I've got you where I want you. Feel how hard and ready I am.' He pushed hard. 'There's nothing you can do to stop me, Florence Pennington.' Again, he slid himself between her engorged leaves of flesh.

'But you can't ravish me, DuPrey.'

He forced her legs back so that she was stretched open to him, his swollen hardness poised at the entrance of her maidenhead.

'How much do you want to bet I can't?'

'You can't ravish me because I consent to anything you want to do to me. If you want to – to fuck me, I agree. If you want to beat me, to assuage your anger at me, then that is what you must do. If you want to bugger me, I will not object. So, DuPrey, no matter what you do, I remain in control. It is I who have you where I want you. You cannot tame me because I consent to everything you want to do to me. You cannot tame an already submissive creature.'

Ramon eased his pressure on her thighs and got off her. He sat with his legs dangling over the edge of the bench.

'Damn you to hell, Pennington. You're a witch.'

Five minutes passed. The only sounds were of their laboured breathing.

Floy swung herself round to sit beside him. She sensed where he was and moved close to him. She spoke softly.

'But aren't we forgetting something, Ramon? Neither of us is in any position to control the other while those thieves have us holed up here. We might be dead before morning. Shouldn't we forget our anger at each other and think of a way out of this?'

She sensed him turn away from her. She snuggled closer.

'Ramon. I'm cold. And your anger makes me colder. Please can we forget our differences. I need you for more than just sex. I'm as scared as hell, if you want to know. I might have put on a brave face in front of that gunman but I've never been more terrified in my life. Perhaps that's why I blacked out.'

She could sense him turn to her, his breath hot on her face. He put his arm around her shoulders.

'Here's an old blanket they threw in with us.' He draped it over their shoulders and tucked her robe around her.

As they leaned back against the wall behind the bench, she put her face on his shoulder and whispered.

'What are we going to do, Ram?'

Ramon relaxed. As his anger had drained away, his penis had softened too. It just sat squashed between his legs, defeated in its quest.

She had been right when she had said he could not ravish her if she consented, if she offered no resistance. However hard he drove into her, it would be just what she wanted.

She had done the same to him when she had lain in her bed. She had allowed him to kiss and caress her. She had opened to him when he had licked the insides of her thighs, when his tongue had migrated to her nubbin.

Now she had called him Ram. No-one had ever coined a pet name for him. And Ram, whether she had intended it or not, felt right to him. He supposed he was a ram. He had served many young women since the age of sixteen, building up considerable experience of their foibles, their likes and dislikes.

He had had women who were coy, who wanted sex

but pretended that was the last thing on their minds. He had had ones who had pretended that they wanted it, who had let him work their nipples, and touch them intimately and then had shut their legs and shouted at him for being a horny bastard.

He had had those who had touched him up, who had slipped their delicate fingers inside his fly as they had pressed him to some wall. They had gasped at the size and length of what they found there and then fled as soon as he had put his hand inside their knickers.

When he had been twenty, he had had an older woman who had been desperate for a man. 'Would you like to come up for coffee,' she had asked innocently. He'd gone up. When she had come back from the kitchen, carrying a tray and wearing nothing but black stockings, he had nearly bolted. She had calmly opened up his fly, pushing him back into the settee when he had tried to rise. She had licked his balls and made him hard in seconds. Then, without a word, she had stripped him naked before he could take one sip of coffee. Then she had taken him in her mouth to make him harder. He had come profusely, sending a fountain high into the air. To her annoyance he could not get a hard-on again. So she had pushed him out into the garden, naked, his clothes thrown in a heap after him. It had been that incident which had made him vow never to let a woman dominate him again.

Before he had encountered Floy Pennington, he had thought that he had known all about women. She was the biggest mystery and the greatest challenge yet.

Floy felt repentant.

'Ramon. I'm sorry I got you into this mess. Believe me, I didn't think it would end like this. I came to your hotel to get away from everything so that I could write my book.'

'But I thought you were looking for a man. That's what Lara was looking for.'

'That's true. I was looking for a man I could base my

main character on. I hadn't thought about what he would be required to do. I was so naïve, I thought I could work it out without having any personal experience to go on. I was wrong.'

'That's the part which baffles me.' He turned to her and placed his lips in the hair of her scalp. He kissed her thoughtfully. 'I don't understand how such a beautiful woman, such an extraordinarily sensual creature as you, could get to thirty and never have any experience with men.'

'It sounds ridiculous, doesn't it? But that's how it is, though don't get the wrong picture. I've had plenty of experience of men. I just haven't any experience with them.'

'I don't get it. Anyway, that's all water under the bridge. Another thing I don't understand is why such an intelligent, exciting woman as you should resort to subterfuge to get me interested.'

'I didn't plan it, Ram. Honestly. It just happened. I was appalled at myself at first. Then I began to enjoy it.'

'There's nothing wrong with enjoying love and sex, Floy.' He kissed her hair again.

'I know. I'm learning that fast. I just had the idea that it was wrong, that's all. I had the idea that it was sinful to flirt openly with a man in public.'

'Wasn't dressing in that revealing cat-suit flirting?'

'I suppose it was. But I didn't do any verbal flirting.'

'You didn't have to. But you could have. In this modern age, women can express their needs to men.'

'Ah, but I'm not of this age, Ramon. I'm like someone who has just arrived from another planet and is quickly having to learn the rules on this one. I'm like someone who arrived with no feelings and suddenly found so many things getting turned on that I became intoxicated by it all. Until I saw you standing naked at your window, masturbating, I had no idea what an erection really looked like. Neither had I realised what the sight of a man's erect organ would do to me.'

* * *

Ramon stroked her cheek with his thumb. She was talking like a little girl who had grown up overnight. This puzzled him, but he let it go because she was talking to him. That was very important. And she had lost that hard, aristocratic air she had used when she had first come to the hotel. In the dimness of the cellar, he could see that her face was sad. It made him sad too.

'When I arrived at the DuPrey Hotel, things started happening to me. Some kind of chemistry started working as soon as I met you.'

'What kind of chemistry?'

She snuggled up to his shoulder.

'I don't know. It was very strange at first. When our eyes met there was a sort of electric shock. It seemed to jump across the desk between us. It hit me so hard that I nearly reeled backwards. Then I collected myself and shut it out.'

'I noticed.' His voice was hard. Ramon knew it but did not hide it. He had been hurt by the way she had shut him out immediately that spark had jumped between them. In that moment he could have vaulted the reception desk, swept her into his arms and held her for ever. But the shutters had come down in her eyes and he had been chilled by the coldness of her manner. Also she had been a very important guest.

Floy turned her head and kissed the thumb stroking her cheek.

'Even though I shut you out, my heart was thrashing. When you took me to show me the suite, I don't know how I managed to get through without throwing myself at you. I've never felt like that about anyone, especially a man. I've always held my emotions down tight. Nothing ever got out.'

'I felt the same about you. I wanted to hold you in my arms too.'

Ramon thought how he had been so captivated by the sensual allure of his guest that he had hardly been coherent. He had babbled his way through the interview, almost unable to take his eyes off her. He had immediately wanted her sexually. But if that had not been possible he had wanted at the least to be close to her; to touch her skin; to run his fingers through the glossiness of her black hair.

She rested her head on his shoulder.

'Aren't we silly. Why can't people say how they feel, instead of holding it all in?'

'That's what society does to us, Floy. It takes a natural thing and makes it into such a hotchpotch of contradicting feelings, we don't know where we are with them.'

Ramon gasped as she slid her mouth around his face to find his lips. He turned to meet her lips and kissed her tenderly.

'I think we should start to be more honest, Ram.'

He shrugged.

'I will, if you will.'

'All right. Where shall I begin?'

'Tell me what happened to make you start to tease me each night.'

She found the crook of his neck with her lips.

'It was the excitement of seeing you naked that started me off. I watched you through my camera lens. It brought you right into my bedroom. As you played with yourself my clitoris started feeling funny. I put my finger down there for the very first time. Then, when you strained your erection and it spurted out over your dressing table, my vaginal walls began to contract. It was so marvellous, but so wicked.' He kissed her tenderly. She sighed. 'I knew you'd seen me watching you masturbating. I wondered what that might have done to you. I knew what it had done to me. I lay nearly all night working my clitoris with my finger until the excitement built up to such a pitch that something like a bolt of lightning shot through me. I was exhilarated and exhausted at the same time.'

'Your first solo orgasm?'

'I suppose so. At breakfast the next morning I think I over reacted. I thought what I had started might get out of hand. I was afraid I wouldn't be able to control what

169

might happen. I was scared, Ram. Then I realised that Lara would behave like that. Remember, she was a bitch, and a nymphomaniac. So I became a bitch. I played the part. I suppose I've become something of a nymphomaniac too.'

She dipped her head and found his nipple, mouthing it lightly into hardness. He shivered with the sensation.

This woman was amazing. Although she said she was frightened, she had shown no fear. She had gone about getting what she had considered she needed, even if she had done it in a strange way. Now as she nibbled at his chest, he was getting hard again. Was she acting the temptress for her purpose, or was she making love to him spontaneously?

'When I came to you for my necklace and asked you to put it on, it was not because I couldn't do it myself.'

'I guessed that.'

'It was because it gave me an excuse to be near you. It gave me a reason to have you touch me. It made my stomach go to jelly while you stood behind me with the necklace. When you touched me, I wanted to put my hands up to yours and capture them, to hold them tight and not let them go.'

'Like Lara did?'

'Yes. Lara did the things I wanted to do, but had dared not to.'

'And the striptease? You gave me the impression you were a seasoned performer.'

'Did I?' She laughed.

'Yes, you did.'

She pecked him on the cheek.

'I got carried away. As soon as I began to undress, I felt the incredible feelings I'd had while I'd masturbated. I'm afraid I became addicted to it.'

'There's nothing wrong with that. I masturbate when I need to. It relieves the frustration. A lot of women have told me that they do the same thing.'

'That's interesting.'

'Is it?'

'Yes. Now do you see how really naïve I am?'

Ramon ignored the remark. He did see how naïve she was, but there was little to be gained in telling her so. She was clearly a virgin in her mind as well as in her body. He was glad in a way that he had not fucked her. On the other hand he was more determined than ever to be her first. He would make it an occasion she would remember all her life. With some luck and a deal of skill, he would make her want him addictively just as he had set out to do. At the moment, she thought that he could not tame her. She was wrong. First, he would turn her into a wild beast, ravening for him. Then he would tame the beast.

'Why did you drag in John?'

'I thought that making you angry or jealous would spur you on. Then I found that I was fascinated by his beautiful young body. I was exhilarated as I held his penis and it started to rise up in my hand. When I worked it gently, he moaned. Then as it went so hard I got carried away. Before I knew where I was, it was gushing in my hand. His semen spurted out all over my face. I found I wanted to lick it off and spread it all over my body. It was alive and sensuous and erotic. I loved it.'

'You scared him.'

'I know. Poor boy. I thought every young man would jump at the chance to have sex with an attractive woman. I was devastated when he ran. I thought there was something dreadful wrong with me.'

'It wasn't that. You picked the wrong boy.'

Floy turned her head to him, her brow rucked under the blindfold.

'What do you mean?'

'John's gay. He's having an affair with my groom. I caught them in the hay loft.'

'Oh dear. How strange. I didn't think of that.'

'You didn't think of many things.'

'So it seems.'

'What happened after John rejected you?'

'I went for sex lessons.'

'You what?'

'I went for lessons with Jay and Prissy. They said they'd teach me. Prissy said Jay would have sex with me if I wanted, just so I could feel what it was like. She said she wouldn't let him hurt me for my first time.'

'I don't believe this.'

'It's true.'

'I would have done that for you if you'd not been so damned stand-offish.'

She kissed his cheek.

'I know, sweet Ram. But all of you were too gentle, too kind. I would have loved to feel Jay inside me, and you. But I wanted to feel the fear and the violence that Lara would invoke with her teasing. Remember, I'm still so innocent. I'm only just beginning to feel emotions. It scared me at first. But what I did to you frightened me more.' She kissed his cheek again. 'It made me realise how dangerous it was to have no feelings. That leads a person into hurting others and herself.'

'I know it does. I was on the receiving end of that.'

'I'm truly sorry.'

He sighed.

'Did Jay screw you?'

'No, I just watched him kiss and lick Prissy.'

'You mean, all over?'

'Yes. Then I held Jay while he drove his manimal into her.'

'Manimal?'

She laughed. 'Yes, that's a word I coined. A penis looks just like an animal when it rears up out of its sleep.'

Ramon gave her a squeeze around the shoulders.

'And what did Polland do with his manimal?'

'It made him groan with pleasure when I touched it. I enjoyed giving so much pleasure. It was very exciting.'

'You talk about it as if it was a spectator sport.'

'Do I?'

'Yes you do.'

'I'm sorry.'

'That's all right. What happened then?'

'Prissy and I lay dreaming while we massaged each other. I went to sleep.'

'Not a very attentive pupil, were you.'

She laughed.

'When they woke me up by sucking on my nipples, Jay touching me between the legs – it was time to come down to you.'

'Why did you still do that?'

'I was addicted. Each night I became more stimulated by my own performance.'

'And each night you became more frustrated that I didn't come to you?'

'Yes. And when you stripped naked and started doing those exercises in front of your window, I was so wet. When you started thrusting your erection out and pumping it up so hard that it took on a long curve, I couldn't stand it any longer. I just had to shut my curtains.'

'That made me really mad, I can tell you. That was the straw that broke the back of my reticence.'

She giggled and bit him under the chin.

'I'm glad. I was so wound up I would have come round and broken your door down if you hadn't come to me first.'

'Why didn't you?'

She pushed against him.

'That wouldn't have been proper!'

'My God! The woman displays herself to me night after night and then thinks it's not proper to come to my room to have her hole filled.'

'That's vulgar.'

'Is it? Isn't it just erotic? You want your hole filled, don't you? You want to feel me inside you?'

In the dimness she put her lips lightly to his and left them there in a long tender kiss.

Ramon half turned to her. Under the blanket he took

173

her in his arms, one hand around her back, the other smoothing at her cheek. As the kiss lingered, his hand slipped down and found her breast, its nipple already erect.

Floy breathed deeply. The explicitness of their words and the openness of their talk had made her quiver with excitement. The tension which had been stirred by his earlier assault had become even more unbearable. If he didn't take her soon, she would go mad and end up begging him to take her.

As Ramon's fingers took her nipple, she wanted his hand there. She wanted it to weigh her breast, then to slip down to find her clitoris, just as he had on that first night in her bed.

'Ram? Will you untie me now?'

He bent into her neck, bit her and let out an animal growl.

'Not yet. I like having you tied up.'

'You're an animal.'

'Grrrhhh. A manimal?' He bit her again.

She put her head back and laughed aloud.

'But that isn't fair.'

'What isn't?'

'With my hands tied, I can't hold your . . .'

'My cock. Go on. It's what you want to say, isn't it?'

'I want to hold your cock. There, I've said it. But why should you be able to do anything you want to with me, while I can only kiss you? I can't even see you with this blindfold over my eyes!'

He laughed.

'Then you'll have to learn to use your mouth, not your hands. And you'll have to learn to work by touch, won't you.'

She pouted.

'But I wanted to hold it that first time I saw it at the window. I want to strip you naked and watch it grow. I want to se how it stiffens into that rigid curve. I want to see it discharge like it did over me when you burgled

174

me. And I want to feel it beat like it did that night on my stomach.'

'You, Floy Pennington, are a libertine.'

She giggled.

'And it feels marvellous. For the first time in my life I feel strangely free. Even with this blindfold and my hands tied, I feel freer than I've ever felt before. I feel that I can say and do anything I need to do with you. I can be an animal woman. I want to mate with you; to experience you, Ramon and,' she set her head down momentarily, then raised it proudly, 'I want to fuck you with total abandon until I shudder. I want to feel you come inside me.'

Ramon thrilled at the thought of the sensual creature mating with him. But the way she was talking meant that she still wanted to keep control. She wanted to fuck him, and in the way she wanted to do it.

'I want to make you feel just like you made me feel on that first night, Ramon. Will you let me?'

He let out a small laugh.

'Can I stop you?'

Chapter Eight

Floy laughed lightly.

'I suppose you could stop me making love to you. But will you?'

She slipped out of the blanket. Kneeling on the floor between Ramon's legs as they hung over the edge of the bench, she snuggled her face between them. She forced them open. He leaned back to allow her access.

Blind, she felt his knees touch her shoulders. Bending her head, her lips found his inner thigh. She worked up it, just as he had done to hers the first time he had come to her bed.

As the thigh became thicker and warmer, she began to lap in little cat-licks.

He trembled.

Floy's mouth was within inches of his genitals. She breathed deeply, taking in the scent of him, comparing it with Jay's. This made her mouth lips tingle as her vulval lips got hot. She could sense them swelling, her clitoris becoming engorged.

He widened his position and thrust himself forward to the edge of the bench to give her full access to himself.

When her lips found his sac, he let out a long sigh.

Floy breathed deeply again. She licked, outlining the

heavy ovals with her tongue. They retracted. Finding the drooping head of his penis, she kissed it tenderly. It jumped. Now she ran a line of little kisses over the top of the large but flaccid organ. Slowly, it began to swell. She could sense it with her lips.

In the darkness of her blindfold, she was fascinated to feel the way it did this. How could a penis be soft one minute, then so rod-hard the next? This was something she would have to find out more about.

Ramon groaned ecstatically.

'You know what'll happen if you do this, don't you? You wanton creature.'

She kissed the rising member again.

'Are you threatening me, DuPrey?'

'Yes I am.'

'But wouldn't that be pandering to my wicked motives? I might write about it afterwards.'

'Just you try it. If I see a wrong description of my dick in your book, I'll screw you for defamation of its character.'

She giggled.

'Don't you mean sue me?'

'I know what I mean.'

'But won't you let me make you come like you made me? I don't quite know how I'll do it, but I want to try.'

'I'm sure you'll work it out. You seem to be a fast learner. I'm sure you'll be a real expert with penises after a bit more practice.'

'And of course, you won't mind how much I practice on yours.' She laughed.

'As long as you let me practice making it come inside you.'

'You'll have to wait. I'm busy right now. I need to start learning.' She licked his sac again. 'Perhaps doing it in the dark will spare my blushes.'

'I can't imagine you being embarrassed at anything.'

'I was too embarrassed to show you my breasts until the last night of my striptease.'

'But you enjoyed it when you did show them to me.'

He bent and put his mouth to her head. 'You've got the most perfect tits I've ever had the pleasure of fondling. The most exquisite nipples I've ever sucked. Why should you be ashamed of them?'

She took the velvety warm head of his penis in her mouth and suckled on it gently a couple of times.

'I admit it gave me pleasure to have you look at them. When you caressed them I went hot all over.'

'I'm glad. I thought, when I made love to you the first time, that you didn't enjoy it very much.'

She ran the tip of her tongue from the groove under the glans right down to the hanging ovoids. Then she set her head in his direction.

'I enjoyed it too much. I liked it so much that I was scared that I would lose control of myself. I wanted to throw myself at you, to swallow your beautiful cock as you stood over me so angrily. Your anger made me thrill. Then you hit me.'

'I was mad at you.'

'I know. I said I was sorry.'

He grunted.

She licked around the sensitive edges of the head, sensing the helmet shape with her tongue. The flaccid thing of a moment ago was standing upright now but not as hard as she wanted. She had to rise up on her knees to bear down on it with her mouth. Then she drew her mouth off it tantalisingly slowly.

'That next morning as you stood in your office, I wanted to slip my hand inside your trousers and find it. I wanted to make it hard like I'm making it now.'

'I guessed that you wanted to touch me.'

'How did you guess?'

'Because that's what you made Lara want to do in the book.'

Floy had the irresistible urge to extend her exploration of his growing erection with her mouth. She slipped down the length of the deeply-grooved shaft and licked the loosely wrinkled sac again, bobbling his testes from underneath. Again, they retracted.

'Why do they do that?'

'Do what?'

'Why do these go up when I lick them?' She licked again.

'For protection I suppose.'

'When Jay was making love to Prissy, his testes disappeared altogether.'

'Oh? You must have been very close.'

'I was. I held them in my hand while he thrust into her.'

'You randy little – '

She moved her mouth to his groin and nipped at the muscle, tensioned as he widened his legs for her.

'Stop that, you she-devil!'

She licked his testicles again.

Ramon moaned as he stiffened to her teasing.

Floy Pennington was working him with her mouth like a seasoned pro. Surely she had done this before. It didn't seem possible that she was the inexperienced virgin she claimed to be, even though her intact maidenhead showed that she was.

Now she had her mouth over his fast hardening shaft. Her tongue lapped down the underside.

He slipped off the bench and stood with his buttocks against the edge, his feet splayed outwards, straining backwards so that his pelvis was thrust forward, his erection as hard as he could make it.

Ramon groaned once more as Floy Pennington slipped her mouth up and down the swollen ram, taking it deep each time. Working her lips, she sucked up the foreskin and then plunged it tight down again.

'Mmmm,' she moaned, not taking her mouth away for conversation now.

Ramon began to pant. This was getting too much. A few more thrusts and he would shoot. For a second, he thought of pulling her up, and stretching her out on the bench like he had before. He thought of sinking himself deep into her, mingling his heat with hers.

But he stopped himself.

If he was going to train her to be a wild animal before he tamed her, he should let her have her head. He should let her get the taste of him, the taste of his juice. Once she had tasted it, she might want to do it again.

'You're a tease, Floy Pennington. I'll come in your mouth if you go on.'

'Mmmmmm,' was all he got back from her.

He tensed his legs wider, thrusting harder into her mouth. She was tenacious. She would not relinquish the hold she had on him.

So he began to move in her mouth. As she knelt before him, her hands tied behind her back still, he held her head, and thrust his shaft between her lips. Then he withdrew, her lips dragging his foreskin over the swollen purple knob. Then he plunged, and withdrew again. His legs began to tremble, the pressure of his climax building.

She sucked as he thrust with long regular movements, plunging the sheathed tip until his glans nearly touched the back of her throat.

Now Ramon groaned and thrust into her rapidly. The heat of her mouth made him strain. Pressing his fingertips into his bladder area, he came with a deep shudder, pumping violently. He could not withdraw. She held him fast, sucking on him gently. He took a deep breath and shuddered again, beating steadily in her mouth.

Still she didn't let go. Instead, she swallowed and sucked on him as if she wanted to milk him of every last drop of fluid he could produce.

Panting, Ramon leaned back on the edge of the bench, his excitement spent, his penis ticking rhythmically in her mouth. She clamped it tightly in her lips, keeping on the pressure. This kept him hard while she sucked, pulling at the foreskin gently.

Gradually he softened.

They stayed still in the darkness for several minutes. When Ramon looked down at her, Floy had his pride and joy between her lips, suckling it as a baby would suck a dummy for comfort.

He ran his fingers lovingly through her hair, smoothing at it; calming her. She was sobbing. But still she sucked on him.

He sighed.

Floy Pennington was the most amazing woman he had ever met. She would be the most exquisite, the most voracious lover he could ever wish for.

Floy sobbed as she suckled at Ramon DuPrey. Her tongue kept working at the little hole in the centre of the helmet, trying to coax the last salty drops of nectar out. The experience of taking him in her mouth and bringing him to a shuddering ejaculation had made her knees quiver. She had nearly orgasmed, but not quite. This left her wanting more, wanting not to let go. She wanted to work him up to hardness again, and to have him put this most wonderful of organs deep between her legs next time.

Strangely now she felt a bond between them. It had been the most personal thing any woman could do with a man. And she had been the closest to this wonderful man that she might ever get. Between her legs or in her mouth, he could not have been closer. Bringing him hard with her tongue and lips, making him yearn for release in her mouth, had been a triumph for her. He had been right to refuse to untie her. Had he done so she would have used her hands to make him come. That would not have been the same for her.

Now, as she knelt between his muscular legs, the salty taste of his juice on her lips, made her sob with a mixture of joy and sadness. She had become a lover. In that one simple act she had left behind for ever that chaste existence she had so tenaciously held on to for the whole of her adult life.

He had been right to be angry with her after she had spurned him that first night. But now she had redressed the balance. She had sacrificed herself to his orgasm now just as he had foregone the sensuality of coming inside her in her bed.

Floy moved underneath Ramon, her head bent back as he towered above her. A memory of Jay's sexual equipment hanging over her as she lay under the bed was the only image she could draw on in the darkness.

She extended her tongue. Finding the crease between his legs, she lapped forward. His testes hung loosely now, the left one larger and lower than the right. She smiled to herself. He might be a wonderful man, but, like Jay, he was no genius either.

Her mouth wide, she drew the weighty ovals in one at a time. Gently she held him. She knew how much trust he must be placing in her. No man would give those most prized, those most delicate of organs to any woman he could not trust.

One bite, one squeeze and he would writhe in agony of the floor. She knew; she had seen men kicked there, or gripped with wicked hands.

Releasing his precious eggs, she licked at the weeping tip of his shaft-head, still salty. He did not move. She sensed that he was allowing her her exploration, but his member's interest in her was at a low ebb.

She was frustrated.

She still craved to feel him inside her, but for now she would have to deny her need for him. There were more urgent things to think of. They had argued and fought and titillated and goaded one another for too long. It was time to end her loving of Ramon DuPrey and to escape this dungeon. Being thrown together with him had taken away all her inhibitions. The peril they were in had been drowned in a sea of sensuality.

She had had him close to her, just as she had craved to do from the time her eyes had met his. The danger had given her an excuse to snuggle up to him, to be intimate with him without any subterfuge.

Still in the darkness of the blindfold, the unreality of the situation had enabled her to do things to him which,

182

a day ago, she would have found impossible. Some acts seemed to require darkness to carry them through.

Now, as she knelt before the gorgeous male, her nose hard pressed into his black matt of wiry pubic hair, tears ran down her cheeks from underneath the blindfold. For the first time in her life, she had made love to a man.

Ramon gently eased out of Floy's mouth. He put his hands around her face and drew her upwards until her lips were within reach of his.

'That was beautiful, Floy.'

He kissed her tenderly, his own lips exploring her semen-moistened mouth. He didn't care that he was tasting his own juice on her lips. It made the kiss all the more intimate. For a moment he withdrew and looked down on her.

It had been right to keep her blindfolded. He sensed that in that darkness she had been able to feel a sensuality which would otherwise have eluded her.

It had been right to keep her tied. Her own spark of fierce independence had driven her to find a way of doing what her instincts drove her to, despite the bonds around her wrists. In the darkness, she had achieved more as a lover with her mouth than ever she would have with her hands in the harsh light of day.

'I love you, Floy Pennington. I think I've been in love with you since the moment you flounced across my foyer.'

She came to him again, hardening her kiss, pushing her tongue deep into his mouth. Ramon withdrew gently again.

'At first I thought it was just infatuation. I thought that it was just your exquisite body my own body lusted after. But then I began to realise there was more between us than sexual attraction.'

As she kissed him, Ramon carefully untied the blindfold.

Floy blinked tears away from her eyes. She whispered.

'Are you going to untie my wrists now, Ram?'

He smiled.

'Will I be safe?'

'Quite safe. But be warned: next time I'll make love to your majestic creature with my hands. If you found that beautiful, you haven't felt anything yet!'

He laughed and whispered as he kissed her tenderly on the tip of her nose, his breath mingling with hers.

'Hold me, Ram. Now my fire's gone down, I'm chilly again.'

He stood against her, feeling the warmth of her velvet skin on his. He took her round the waist, smoothing down towards the marvellous swells of her bottom with his open-fingered hands.

He knelt, his mouth coming right to her breast. He found the nipple with his tongue and brought it into life. As he sucked lovingly, his hands slipped round her, found her bonds and slowly untied them.

Without moving from her nipple, he clasped her hands in his, pushing his thumbs through the ovals she formed between her own thumbs and her palms. He worked them steadily, sensuously in and out.

In turn, her thumbs gripped his coitally, easing off and squeezing, each like a little sex mouth.

Still he sucked her breast.

At last he rose, leaving her nipple like a lover would leave his love-mate, sadly and alone.

As they stood, together, bush to bush, breast to breast, she looked into his eyes lovingly. He loved her eyes with his. They breathed each other's breath.

Then for some time they sat on the bench with the blanket wrapped around them, Ramon's hand on her breast, her hand warm between his legs.

With the blindfold off and the bonds untied from her wrists, Floy snuggled tightly up to Ramon. Gently she massaged the limp tube which came to her hand. It would not come up. She judged that she had done too good a job on it. It was fully satisfied. It might be some time before it became hungry for her again.

She was still frustrated, her sex-lips still swollen and hot. But that manimal would have to wait. With patience and the right opportunity, it would have its time.

She looked around their prison in the dimness of moonlight striking through a glass roof-light.

The chamber was of brick, vaulted like a tunnel. About four paces wide, but twenty or more long, it had wooden benches down each side. One had rotted away, the brick piers which had supported it lying loosely on the stone floor. The shelving smelled of rotting apples.

At one end was a door. Floy got up and walked to it. Hinged to open outwards, it was firmly shut. She walked to the other end of the vault.

There was a small truck, iron framed with wooden sides. She presumed it was for transporting goods, probably apples, which had been stored there.

Ramon watched her with interest. She turned to him with shining eyes.

'Shall we escape?'

He frowned.

'How do you plan to do that?'

'Come on. I'll show you. Bring some of those loose bricks.'

In a few minutes of carrying bricks, the truck was full.

'I don't see how loading up a truck with bricks is going to get us out of here, Miss Pennington.'

She grinned.

'Easy, DuPrey. The door opens outwards.'

'And?'

'Have you seen those sports programmes where people go down an appalling ice slope on a kind of sledge?'

'Yes.'

'And have you seen how they get behind the thing and push to get the speed up before they jump on.'

Ramon scratched his head.

'Yes.'

'Well, we're going to do the same. But when the truck gets to the door we aren't going to jump on. We're going to let go. Got it?'

He grinned at her.

'Got it!'

They got behind the truck and pushed with all their strength. It was very heavy and started slowly. But as they neared the door it was going fast. At the last moment they let go.

The truck smashed with a deafening crash. The door fell outwards, steam-rollered by the truck.

Floy flung her arms round Ramon's neck and kissed him wildly. She jumped up and wound her legs around him like a young girl might greet her doting father.

He hugged her, holding her around her naked bottom, then set her down and stood back, beaming.

'Clever girl. Where did you learn a trick like that?'

She smirked.

'I used it in one of my books when Sister Luke was shut in a cold store. She had a truckful of meat, but the result was the same!'

The night was misty, although a half moon gave enough blue-white light to see for thirty or forty paces. They peered out of their prison warily. The apple store stood half buried in the ground, half covered with turf. There was a slope up to ground level.

Floy crept upwards and scanned the surroundings. They were on the edge of an orchard. Trees marched away from them in ranks. In front of them lay a lake, a boat drawn up on the shore. Although moonlight shimmered on the water, she could not see the far shore through a haze.

A rough track led away and disappeared into the orchard.

A glimmer of light through the trees and the sound of an engine made Floy grab Ramon's arm.

'They're coming back for us, Ram! Come on!'

The van was out of the trees now and heading for them. Bending low, they skirted around the mound of the apple store and made for the trees, but too late to escape detection. The van's lights went up as it began to speed across the grass towards them.

They sprinted.

As she fled, Ramon in front of her, Floy's bathrobe flowed behind her, leaving her half naked in the moonlight. The train of white was caught in the van's headlights.

The van skidded to a halt just as they made the treeline. Doors slammed and angry voices shouted after them.

They tore between low-growing trees, the branches swiping at Floy's bare flesh, clawing at her robe as they wove and dodged, leaving the lights behind them.

Her heart drumming in her chest, Floy heard an ominous sound. She stopped momentarily to check. Her spirits sank. Yes, it was the bark of a dog.

'Ramon, hurry! They've set a dog loose on us!'

Ramon stopped and turned. His heart pounded at the sight of Floy Pennington standing almost naked in the moonlight. His mind snapped a picture of the beautiful breasts, highlighted with a glow of blue. The blackness of the triangle of hair accentuated the deep vee between her long and shapely legs. Her flat stomach heaved with exertion, her navel pumping in and out, making his solar plexus tremble.

That all took place in a second. Now his mind snapped off the Venus of the Woods and on to the problem at hand.

What would the men in the van do? He knew that the dog would track them unerringly through the trees. It would only be a matter of time – their stamina against the dog's – before they were caught.

'Make for the lake again, Floy.' Grabbing her hand, he pulled her. 'We'll go round in a big arc. They won't expect us to make back towards the lake shore and the van.'

They crashed on, the dog's barking nearer now. Once again the lights of the van were visible. Then Ramon saw the glint of moonlight on water.

They sprinted out of the trees, the van thirty paces to their right, the dog's bark very close.

'Make for the punt, Floy! I'll hold the beast off!' He picked up a dead branch and started walking backwards.

Floy watched as a large Rottweiler shot out of the trees and made straight for Ramon. She pushed the punt into the water and jumped in. The dog stopped a couple of yards away as Ramon began to sweep the branch in front of him. It barked loudly. Then it grabbed the branch and began to tussle with Ramon.

At the edge of the water now, Ramon glanced behind him to see where the punt was. Floy had it in deeper water, her hands paddling in lieu of a pole.

Ramon thrust his branch at the startled dog. He turned and splashed up to his waist through the water.

The dog bounded after him. Ramon hit the end of the boat and heaved himself in, pushing it forward with one last kick on the bottom of the lake.

Floy gasped as the Rottweiler, nearly at the boat, barked at Ramon's receding ankle. She leaned forward and dragged him in.

They both paddled for their lives, the dog keeping pace at the stern, still barking loudly. But it could do no more than bark now. Soon it was left behind as the punt floated forward under its own momentum. Floy took a deep breath and sank onto the flat bottom of the punt.

Ramon grinned.

'Whew! That was close.'

'Are we safe?'
'For a while, I think.'

Ramon leaned forward and kissed her. Then, as he paddled with his hands, he studied her. The robe was wide open. Her breasts heaved with exertion. She was aroused, he could tell by the way she was lying with her legs carelessly open and her nipples pointing towards him in the moonlight. He wanted to lean forward and take each rampant protrusion in his mouth.

Her eyes lit up, shining in the moonlight, shining unmistakably with lust.

'Do you want me, Ram?'

He shot her a puzzled look.

'Of course I do. But not now. We've got to get away.'

She smiled and spread her legs wider, drawing up her knees as if unaware that this would display and stretch her long lips. To Ramon it seemed like a hungry, furry animal, its mouth opening and closing slowly as she tensed and relaxed it provocatively. It was a trigger for his own response.

'Take me now, Ram. Fuck me!'

'You must be mad!'

'Of course I'm mad. I'm mad for you. Can't you see? I think it's the danger; the excitement of nearly getting caught. And the fear of one of those men having me before you do. I'm soaking. Look.' She dipped her hand between her legs and brought it up wet. It was an unnecessary ploy, with her plump labia glistening in the bluish light.

She reached forward and tugged his hair, pulling his head towards her open legs.

'Floy!'

She leaned back, pulling his hair so hard that it hurt him. She pulled his face into her waiting chasm.

The musky smell drove him wild. He managed to glance over his shoulder. The van lights shone distantly

189

in the mist, two men and a dog silhouetted in a halo of brightness.

'Floy, this is crazy!'

'I know it is. I'm crazy for you, you beautiful man. Fuck me, Ram!' She panted. 'Put your cock into me now! I don't want to be caught by those creatures before I've been had by you. And I don't think I can stand any more of this stimulation without coming soon. Please, Ram! Please!'

Ramon was dazed. It was what he had planned. She was pleading to be fucked. He had never had a woman this crazy before. It was the thing all his fantasies were made of, being commanded to shaft a beautiful woman in a dangerous situation, with the danger of being caught or discovered.

Pulling his hair hard, she dragged his nose deep between her legs again. She rubbed him into the furrow between her legs, his mouth forced to taste the salty sweetness of her juice. By his hair, she dragged him up her body, his face grazing her breasts until it reached her mouth. She took his mouth with hers, voraciously. Her free hand clawed at the shirt flapping loosely about his back.

Suddenly she turned, putting him under her in a wrestling hold, her hand still pulling at his hair to hold him down. The punt rocked. Her other hand found his buckle. It was undone. She ran his zip down. Now the hand was inside his fly, her fingers probing. She gripped his hardness. Her mouth bore down on his lips, locked on to his mouth. Her hand worked at his now straining shaft, massaging; running down to the root and up again. He stiffened to the touch.

Now she was on her knees, dragging wildly at his wet jeans. She got them halfway down his legs, letting him spring free. He felt cold air as he waited for her enveloping heat. Panting, she sat astride him, lowering herself onto him. Rubbing slickly back and forward, clutching at his waist with her fingers, giving out little cries of frustration, she was unable to capture him yet.

190

His stem lay too flat against his stomach. She let go with one hand to grab it and thrust it into herself.

Suddenly, Ramon reacted. She was going to ravish him! It was getting out of control. He would not be taken by her. He would not let her control him in sex. He would tame her, not she him.

Ramon rolled her off him, and was on her in a flash, her legs frogged wide apart. With one thrust he was in her.

She screamed out and flung her head back, her finger-nails tearing at his arms.

Then, instead of heat between her legs, Ramon felt coldness. There was a gurgling sound. An awful realisation hit him.

The punt had sprung a leak. It was sinking.

The next seconds for Floy were a nightmare. She had hardly felt the heat of Ramon inside her when he had withdrawn again. She felt rejected. He had taken her virginity with one violent thrust and then abandoned her. She grabbed for his hair to try to pull him back on her. But he was on his knees, pulling his jeans up and fastening them.

Then she realised that the punt was sinking.

She panicked.

'Ramon! I can't swim!'

Water was halfway up the sides of the punt in seconds. Ramon reached out and grabbed her.

'Hang on to me. You'll be alright.'

In ten more seconds, they were up to their necks in very cold water. Floy felt Ramon's arms under her armpits, his hands on her breasts. He swam with her on her back, towards the lights of the van. Why was he swimming towards their pursuers?

Ramon was a strong swimmer, so they made steady progress. She glimpsed the shore, the men close now, the barking dog clearly heard.

Floy became hysterical. She began to fight. Breaking away from Ramon she floundered, lashing out at him with her fists. In her frenzy she began to sink. Her head went under; her arms went up. She felt a hand grappling her hair. It pulled her up to the surface again. She gasped. She flailed at him again.

Then he hit her hard on the chin.

Everything went black.

It was the drumming of the engine and the bumping of the van which brought Floy to her senses. Everything was black again, just as it had been in the vault. Again she was blindfolded, her hands tied behind her back, the robe wet and cold around her. She could feel that it hung open at the front.

She moaned. A lot of good that escapade had been.

Then she heard a panting sound only a few feet from her ear. There came a low growl as she moved.

She froze.

'Don't move suddenly, Floy. The Rottweiler is only waiting for the slightest excuse to turn us into dinner.'

She moved her head in the direction of Ramon's voice.

'You hit me, you lousy – !'

'I hit you because you would have drowned us both if I hadn't.'

'I wasn't going to be taken back into the clutches of those morons!'

'There was no other choice. I couldn't have swum to the other side of the lake. I had to go to the nearest shore.'

'You're a coward!'

'I'm practical. I could have let you drown.'

'I'd rather you had!'

'Don't be stupid!'

'Don't you call me stupid!'

'I'll call you what I like, you silly bitch!'

Floy turned away from him. The dog growled. She snapped at it.

'And you can shut up too, dog!'

192

The journey seemed to last for hours before they stopped. The door opened.

'Get out, and no funny business. If you make one false move, I'll let the dog rip you apart, understand?'

It was a mean sounding voice. Floy shivered.

Acutely aware of the wet robe flapping around her and showing her nudity to the man at the van door, Floy scowled under the blindfold. She fervently hoped that he didn't get any ideas about taking her home and using her for sex. She had written a thief into the book, and had revelled in having sex with him when she had thought it was a dream. But this was all so cold and real and frightening. She could not bear to be raped by a man like this. Nor by the German-speaking moron who had held a gun to her head.

Angry still from the thought that Ramon had taken her virginity and then abandoned her, Floy felt deeply hurt. She had so much wanted her de-flowering to be a more memorable event. It had been memorable, but not in the way she had wanted.

Had he taken her in her frenzy in the bottom of the boat, had he fucked her hard in her bed instead of making love to her, that would have been enough. She would at least have known what it felt like to be taken by a man.

She would have preferred to have had Ramon take her in the comfort of her own bed. But, had all this not happened, she would probably have left The DuPrey Country House Hotel after he had berated her over her behaviour. Her photographs of him naked at his window had finished him off.

Had this abduction and robbery not taken place, she might never have been close to Ramon DuPrey again. She might never had had the exhilaration of having him come in her mouth. She might have left with her tail between her legs, instead of having him between them, even with just one violent thrust. She might never have had the courage to have sex with a man again. God only knew what she had gone through to do what she had done. Had it not been for the money, she would never have entertained the idea.

A hard hand in the small of her back brought Floy back from her reverie.

There were steps, some doors and then a rush of warmth. She was pushed roughly along for some minutes. A door opened. She was pushed again and fell on her face, landing on something soft.

Then she heard a scuffle. It was Ramon.

'Get off me you bastards,' he growled. The dog growled too somewhere close. She heard struggling, then a dull thump and the sound of air leaving someone's lungs forcibly.

They had hit Ramon in the stomach. One part of her cried out in horror. A harder part of her said, serves him right.

Someone grabbed her from behind. She started to fight but he was too strong for her. Suddenly, her hands were free. He let her go.

A door slammed. There was the sound of heavy feet and then all went quiet.

Floy lay listening for the sound of the dog panting. There was none. Cautiously she put her hands up to her blindfold and pulled it off her. She lay on a mattress on a bare floor, the dim light in the room coming from a shadeless lamp hanging in the centre of a brown-stained ceiling.

It was a small room, three paces wide, four or five long. A radiator under a blanked-off window pumped out heat to make it pleasantly hot. An inner door stood open, showing a toilet and shower within.

She swivelled round, gasping with surprise. An upholstered single-bed base leaned at a slight angle against the wall. On it, Ramon DuPrey was spread-eagled like a man on a rack. His arms, spread out above his head, were tightly tied with rope. His ankles were tied likewise at the bottom. He looked like a large figure X, his naked abdomen heaving in the centre.

His torn shirt hung wetly, loose at the sides of his

194

smooth, bronzed chest, streaked with pond weed strands. He panted in an effort to get his breath, looked at her and scowled.

'Well, don't just stand there! Untie me!'

Floy stood in front of him, her robe open, her legs apart. She clamped her fists on her hips and shook her head defiantly.

'I said untie me, you stupid bitch!'

'Don't you call me a stupid bitch! If you hadn't swum into their arms we wouldn't be here now!'

'No, you stupid woman, we'd be at the bottom of the lake!'

'Don't you call me a stupid woman, either!'

'Why shouldn't I call you stupid? You're all tits and no brain!'

Without thinking, Floy's arm lashed out. She caught him a swingeing blow across the face. It was so hard it swung his head round. Her hand stung with the force of the contact.

She watched, horrified, as the whiteness of the cheek turned red in the shape of five long-fingered weals. Ramon's eyes filled with tears.

Ramon could feel tears running down his cheek. She would think they were tears brought on by the force of her blow. But she would have been wrong. The fact that she had hit him in anger cut him deeply. This was the last thing that he had wanted. In the coldness of the vault, they had become so close. He had told her that he loved her.

In the boat, the force of her passion had unbalanced him. The last thing he had wanted was her demand to fuck her there, while they were fleeing.

He had planned to take her in his own time; slowly and seductively, with her clamouring for him, not in the bottom of some rotten punt.

Everything seemed to have gone wrong. But there was nothing he could do about it. Only time would tell if Florence Pennington would relent in her anger at him. If she didn't, he was determined never to touch any woman again.

Floy turned away from Ramon. She couldn't bear to look at him. He seemed so hurt. She cursed her temper. Wasn't it that which had always got her into trouble? How many times had she been told that her fire would consume her one day?

She made a decision. Turning to Ramon, she stepped up close and tenderly kissed the weal on his face.

'I'm sorry, Ram. That was a bitchy thing to do after you saved me from drowning.'

She put her lips to his and held them there, the heat of his chest radiating to her bare breasts. As she stood in front of him, she wanted to lean on him, to feel the heat of his body against hers. She did not have the courage. That sexual fire which had raged through her in the boat had been quenched by the subsequent near-drowning. She wondered if it would ever return so strongly.

'Please forgive me.'

He smiled thinly.

'Only if you untie me.'

A surge of energy went through Floy. He had kept her tied up while he had dallied with her. He had made her make love to him with her hands tied behind her back. Now she had him where she wanted him. Now she could get her revenge. She could do anything to him that she wanted. There was no fear of retaliation from him. He might curse her, he might struggle, but while he was securely trussed to the bed frame she could play out some fantasies which had been churning in her mind for the past days.

Chapter Nine

Ramon gaped as Floy stripped off her dripping robe, greened with pond weed. As she stood naked in front of him she lifted her breasts seductively. He stared at her with disbelief. Surely she was not still fired up, not after her ducking and near-drowning. As she went to the radiator and draped the robe over it, he took a deep breath. The sight of her perfect bottom bending and the two plump black-furred lips pursed between her legs made him tremble.

She rose and came back to him, standing in front of him, her legs splayed, her pubis thrust out. Putting her arms up behind her head, she combed through her tangled hair with her fingers. Her breasts tightened into perfectly symmetrical tear-drops, inviting to his mouth. She had done this in her room on the last night of her titillation. Within an arm's length of her, he was help-less to do anything about it, just as he had been then.

He cursed his swelling bulge in the tight vee of his shrinking jeans.

She looked at it and smirked.

'It's no good getting excited, DuPrey. There's nothing you can do about it while you're tied up.'

'You minx! You're doing this on purpose!'

'I'm getting myself tidied up and my robe dried, that's all.'

He snorted. She was playing the temptress again, but this time she was doing it with him in the room. She knew full well that she was stimulating him to hardness and that he could do nothing about it. What was she doing it for this time?

'That's enough of that, Floy Pennington! Now just come here and untie me!'

Smirking again, she went to the open door of the toilet.

'I won't untie you unless you're a good boy!'

'Look, don't play those bloody games with me, woman! Just damned well take these ropes off!'

She threw her head back in a silent laugh.

'Why? So that you can finish what you started?'

'Isn't that what you want?'

She gave him a coy look.

'You had your chances, Ram, and you flunked them. You took my virginity with one selfish thrust and then withdrew!'

Ramon exhaled with exasperation.

'The bloody boat was sinking, you silly woman!'

She gave him a 'huh' and slitted her eyes.

'That was your hard luck, wasn't it?'

Ramon took a deep breath, shook his head and closed his eyes.

'I don't believe this is happening!' He opened his eyes again, glowering at her.

'Stop playing games, Floy. If you don't, I swear when I get free I'll put you over my knee and give you the hardest spanking you've ever had.'

She lowered her eyes, looking at him coyly from under the long black lashes.

'Promises like that will get you nowhere, DuPrey!'

Ramon could see it was a game for her. She had him where she wanted him and was clearly going to do whatever she liked with him. His heart pattered. All the signs were good. She was getting so aroused that she would be begging him to have her soon. What a contrast from the cold, aloof Florence Pennington who had flounced through his hotel only days before.

'Don't be so grouchy, Ramon. I'm going to see if the shower and toilet work.'

Frustrated, he groaned and threw his head back. Then he heard a tinkling sound. She was having a pee! The cistern flushed. Then she turned on the shower. He had not realised how much he wanted a piss until then. He pulled at his bonds but they were too strong. So, no matter how he had got himself into this, he would have to go along with it as best he could.

She shouted from the shower.

'The shower works. And there are towels. At least they've put us somewhere where we've got the rudiments of civilised life.'

He shouted back.

'It's all right for you. Don't forget I'm tied to this damned bed frame and I need a piss too!'

She walked out in front of him, her body lathered in soap, her sensual curves and hollows highlighted by the glossy wetness. He gulped. Water streamed from the black diammond of her pubis as if she was having a pee in the room. This made his need even more urgent.

'You can have a wee in a minute. Can you hang on until I finish showering?'

He tried not to listen to the sound of the shower. He would just have to wait. But at least he would get untied. When he had had his pee, he would be back in control over her. He would finish what she had begged him to start in the boat. That had been madness, but he still had the urge to carry on.

He had heard about women under threat of death who became as horny as hell. It seemed to have happened to her. He supposed that it was some primeval instinct to reproduce while the going was good. That way, if the male was killed, there was at least a chance that the female would carry a child to replace him.

And he recalled how his cock had shot up when she

had rejected him after he had made love to her the first time. He had been angry then. Perhaps that was a similar response. But the anger had swept away the emotion of love he had felt for her as she had lain haughtily in her bed. The exhilaration of bringing her to a climax had changed into blind hatred. It had taken all his willpower to stop himself stripping off the covers she had coyly held up to her tits, and fucking her unfeelingly.

That was not in his nature. He was not a violent man, though something in Floy Pennington made him at times so angry that he could strike her.

She also stimulated him to a point of sexual pleasure-pain that he had never felt before. He wished that it was she who was tied to this damned bed frame. He'd give her something to write about. He'd lick her to within a millimetre of coming, and keep her there on a knife-edge for hours, until she cried out for him to bring her to a conclusion.

He'd suck her tits and lick her beautiful thighs in an orgy of exploration until she shuddered uncontrollably. And when he cut her down, he'd refuse to screw her until she begged at his feet in tears.

Yes, he wished that he had Floy Pennington tied up like she had him.

But being in bondage to her was making him as horny as hell anyway. Right now, stretched out with his legs open to her, his swelling interest was outlined clearly in his jeans.

In a minute she would release him. He would relieve himself and then he would get his revenge on her in a prolonged orgy of fornication.

Floy felt clean and relaxed after her shower. She turned off the water and flung a large towel around herself. She smelled good too. The soap and the shampoo which had been left in a bathroom cabinet, had made all the difference to her imprisonment.

She and Ramon might be kept here for a long time. If

the villains thought they would screw any ransom out of Bloomensteen, they were all in for a long wait.

In a warm room with a toilet and shower, a long internment would be tolerable, especially when she had the Ram to service her fast developing sexual needs. A couple of days earlier, she would not have dreamed how these needs would explode into a whole spectrum of erotic desires. Her body was still aching for something she had not yet properly experienced. It was still aching for fulfilment. She assumed that this would only come in all its glory of relief when he brought her to climax with the exquisite manimal she had sucked on. She wanted to feel it spurting again, but this time inside her.

She had never imagined, from the sterile drawings she had seen, that such a flaccid, sluggish thing as a penis could grow into such a muscular limb as did Ramon DuPrey's. When she had gazed for the first time on his erection through the telephoto lens of her camera, it had been the first male organ she had seen blown up in lust. When he strained it, and the veins had stood out around its shaft, it looked for all the world as if it was a permanent arm growing from between his athletic legs.

Ramon's erect member was longer than Jay's, but Jay's had been just that bit thicker. Not having managed to get Jay's between her secret lips, she would not know which created the better sensations – thickness or length? Perhaps they both had their merits.

When she had gone down on Ramon with her mouth, she had marvelled at how solid it had felt. It had gone right to the back of her throat and almost choked her as he had driven it in.

Then it had gushed. It had spurted the warm thickness of his nectar into her, salty and clinging in her throat. And it had throbbed with a steady beat in her mouth, making her run with love juice until she had nearly come spontaneously with him.

Then she had kept it, not wanting to relinquish it

from her mouth. But gradually it had lost its hardness and reverted to its former sluggish self.

'When the hell are you going to untie me so that I can have a piss!'

Ramon's shout brought Floy's attention back to the shower room. Rubbing her hair, she went to him, leaving on the bathroom light. She switched off the room light. Now the dimly lit scene was far more seductive.

'What's the noise about?'

'Don't mess about. When are you going to let me go? I need a leak.'

She smirked.

'Who said I was going to let you go?'

He scowled.

'Look, if you don't untie me soon, I'll wet myself!'

She tut-tutted at him, and stood in front of him, drawing the towel provocatively through her legs.

'And you can stop that, you bloody witch!'

Only a couple of feet from Ramon, Floy stopped rubbing her vaginal lips, dropped the towel and stood with her legs apart, her fists parked on the curves of her hips, her taut stomach emphasising the triangular prominence of her svelte-haired mound.

'I said you can have a pee. I didn't say I would untie you.' She wagged a long forefinger at him.

His face turned thunderous.

'Ha, bloody ha! I suppose you think that's funny.'

'Not at all. I said I would untie you if you were a good boy. So far I don't think you qualify.' She grinned.

Ramon pleaded. His need was getting desperate now. And he was damned if he would wet himself in front of her.

'Look, I'm sorry I shouted. But you make me so bloody mad at times, for Christ's sake.'

She gave him a stern school-marm look.

'Don't blaspheme. Wait there.'

'I can't bloody well do anything else, stupid!'

Floy went into the toilet and came out with a plastic bucket. She smiled at him sweetly.

'Here you are.'

Ramon growled.

'How the hell do you expect me to use that with my hands tied!'

To Ramon's horror, Floy put the bucket down. She undid his belt. Then she unzipped his fly. A thrill went through him. The wanton hussy. She was going to get him out and make him piss.

He kept up the pretence of anger.

'What the hell do you think you're doing now?'

'You want to urinate, don't you?'

'Not with you watching me, I don't.'

'Come, come, Ramon,' she chided, 'I've held it before. And I've suckled it and licked it, remember. Surely you don't mind if I hold it while you pee?' She smiled coyly.

Ramon looked at her and scowled. He looked down at himself. She had bared him by spreading his fly as wide open as it would go. Long but flaccid now, all his hardness had ebbed away with the tension of the situation.

'You hussy, you're revelling in this, aren't you?'

She grinned.

'I must admit it's interesting.' She lifted the bucket and took hold of his penis. 'Now, are you going to be a good boy or not?'

That was too much for Ramon. He peed into the bucket while she held him. The relief was enormous.

To his surprise, she squeezed it to expel the last drop and shook it twice before she put the bucket down.

'You've done this before, haven't you, you bloody tease?'

'What makes you say that?'

'The way you squeezed it and shook it. Usually, only a man knows how to do that.'

'Shake it once, maybe twice, but the third time is playing with it, eh?' She gave him a mischievous grin, her eyes alight with fun. 'I've had plenty of practice. I used to be a nurse. I've nursed dozens of young men back to health. I've bathed them and toileted them and seen to nearly all their needs.'

Ramon studied her with open eyes. Her face was serious. The glint of mischief which had been there a moment before was gone. He could see tears in her eyes, as if she was remembering emotional times. Floy Pennington had a new surprise for every hour of the day.

'You amaze me, Florence Pennington. Or should I say Florence Nightingale?'

'There's no need to make fun of me. I was a good nurse. Some say I was the best.'

He whispered.

'I'm sure you were. I think you would be the best at anything you tried.'

'I am. When I put my mind to something, I do it thoroughly.'

'I know. I've experienced some of that. Come here.' He gestured with his head. She came, obediently. She was cowed now, a sadness in her eyes still.

'Kiss me, Floy.'

She obeyed. Putting her lips lightly to his, she held them there. Her eyes closed.

Ramon closed his eyes too. He savoured her. He drew her warm breath into his mouth, holding it before releasing it. Her body radiated to him, its naked heat warming his bare chest, her pubic mound touching lightly on his member.

He withdrew from her and buried his mouth into her hair close to her ear as she leaned forward onto him. Her breasts touched him warmly, soft and elastic against the hardness of his torso.

He whispered.

'I love you, Floy Pennington. You are the most beautiful, the most seductive, the most fuckable, the most infuriating female I have ever come across and I'm wildly and insanely in love with you.'

* * *

Floy let herself sag against Ramon. She said nothing to his eulogy. Instead, she snuggled her face into his neck. Her breasts pushed hard against his strong chest, her nipples matching his, kissing them.

He smelled of man. He smelled of perspiration, and a curiously musky scent which permeated upwards from his penis. She had smelled it as she had made love to him. It made her clitoris thrill, her vaginal lips engorge with anticipation.

Her hands came forward to find his penis, hanging where she had left it, open to her touch. With both hands, she cradled it, her palms making a nest for it. Her fingers around his testicles, the soft shaft nestled between the heels of her hands. It began to swell.

She closed her eyes and breathed deeply.

She felt secure. She had her man, strong and vibrant against her, and she was in a position of power over him. This made one part of her thrill. Another part of her was reverent. He was beautiful and kind and loving. He was romantic and caring. But beyond that, he was virile, and as horny as a stallion, whenever she desired to make him be.

She revelled in the power she had to make him hard. She thrilled at the way she was able to galvanise him into action with provocative use of her body. When she had opened her legs to him on the boat, a thrill had shot through her. It had been so wanton, so unspeakably erotic in the face of danger. She had teased him into action despite his awareness of the threat they had been under.

In a trice she had had him hard. To her frustration, she had become too slippery, too excited at the feeling of sliding her lips over the springing shaft of flesh. Then she had had him tight in her hand, forcing that glorious nine inches of heated manhood upwards, pressing into the tightness of the membrane of her maidenhead. All she had needed to do was to sink herself onto it, and the deed would have been done. But he had rolled her and been on top of her in a second, in control.

The he had thrust.

The pain had been excruciating. Her hymen had been tough, kept strongly protected to ward off lust. She had never been allowed to ride a bike or sit astride a horse. She had never been able to run and jump like other girls. The main command of those who had tutored her, those who had sought to mould her every thought and to suppress her every physical desire, had been to keep her legs shut tight.

She had been forced to walk with her legs together, clothed secretly in long man-proof skirts and undergarments. She had been forbidden to sit in any way other than with her feet planted firmly on the ground. Her maidenhead had never been touched. It had never been stretched. It had never been looked at or referred to. She had been a virgin in thought and deed and had been totally and thoughly intact when the gorgeous Ramon DuPrey had thrust his rigidness through the small hole in the membrane and cut her adrift for ever from her past. Her future was irrevocably cast now, in a direction away from that former life. There was no going back, and she was glad.

His thrust had hurt like hell.

It had hurt her both physically and emotionally. But, angry as she had been at him for withdrawing, she still craved for him to finish the deed – though not yet. She would hold herself in check until she had experienced from Ramon DuPrey those things which she might never ever have an opportunity to experience again.

And now, he said he loved her.

She wept.

Ramon pulled back from her as far as he could.

'What's wrong, sweetheart?'

She withdrew her face from his neck and faced him, her lips only inches from his. Tears streamed down her face. He bent his head forward and licked them off. Tears came to his own eyes. She looked so beautiful, yet so sad.

'Floy. Tell me why you're crying.'

She set her head back, her chin up, and sniffed. She smiled thinly.

'I'm crying for my lost youth, Ramon. I'm crying for the years of my twenties. I'm crying for the young men who wanted me to love them in their dying moments. I refused to hold them like I'm holding you. I'm crying for those like me, still trapped in the life I used to lead, oblivious of what men and women have to give each other.

'I'm crying because I've uncovered in these last few days with you sensations, needs and desires which I never knew I had, which I don't know how to control and which I'm desperately afraid of.'

She wound her arms around his neck and held him close.

'What kind of fears are they, kitten? Tell me.'

Ramon felt helpless. Tied like a crucified saint, he could not hold her. If she would not untie him, he could only comfort her with words and lips. For some reason she wanted to keep him like this. Perhaps, after all that had happened between them, she was afraid of him, afraid of what it would do to her if he was free to overpower her. Clearly, Floy Pennington did not want to be controlled by anyone. He would not press her. He was not in any position to do anything except to accede to her will. He would have to let her work out her needs and fantasies on him and hope that he would not come to any harm.

'I fear what might happen if I let you love me, Ram. I fear losing my independence. I'm afraid of being dominated by another human being. My past is full of domination, of suppression and of cruelty done for "my good". I was twenty six before I even started to fight back. I have no experience of loving others. Any physical or emotional love that I ever felt for other human beings was ruthlessly stamped out. I don't know even if I can love anyone.'

Ramon thought deeply. He had known that Floy

Pennington was inexperienced. Jannine had called her an emotional desert who would suck him dry. But he could see that Floy knew it too, and she was struggling to come to terms with it. She was having to fight with her sensuality too. No matter how suppressed she had been by someone, the libido which coursed through her was formidable. He had picked up on her sexual energy in the first second of their contact. It was like a ravening dragon inside her, hot and fiery and roaring to escape. He guessed that she had spent her life battling to keep it imprisoned. Equally, he suspected that she had lost the battle now.

Exposing himself to her at his window seemed to have triggered in her sensations which she had been unable to stop. Now she was trying to exercise some control over him while she worked out her feelings and desires. She was afraid of herself, not him.

He whispered.

'There are only two ways to find out anything in life, Floy. One is to be told by others. The other is to experience it yourself. The problem with the first is that others only tell you what they want you to know. Their experiences can never match one's own.'

'What are you saying?'

'I'm saying that unless you experience making love with someone, you will never know how it feels. You know that's true. Isn't that what all your strip shows were about? Isn't that why you lured me to your room? Wasn't that so you could experience sex?'

'Of course it was. But I made a serious mistake. I didn't know the difference between having sex and making love. And you blew the whole plan.' She smiled coyly.

He was relieved. At least she was smiling now.

'I spoiled your plan because I made love to you instead of giving you the good hard fucking that you thought you wanted? The fucking that Lara was after?'

She nodded into his neck.

'I became confused. You got under my protection as

208

well as between my legs. I had to withdraw from you, I didn't know what else to do.'

'And you crucified me, just like you're doing now.'

'I'm sorry, Ram. I didn't understand that either. I didn't know what I was doing to you. And as for crucifying you now, it wasn't me who tied you up here. It was those men who stole my jewellery.'

'That's true. But you could untie me.'

She pulled back and smirked at him.

'I like you like this. It gives me a tremendous sense of power.'

'You're a libertine, do you know that?'

'You've told me that before. But it doesn't make any difference. I won't let you go, just as you wouldn't untie me in that vault. But I won't hurt you either, Ram. I might whip you just a bit to make you yelp and to teach you a lesson for keeping me tied up. I'm going to keep you tied up now because I need to experience you safely. I need to feel my way around your body without any fear of retaliation.'

'I wouldn't retaliate against you.'

'You did in the boat. I was going to ride you. I was going to ravish you. I was going to swallow this beautiful manimal into myself.'

She worked his foreskin, skinning it down tight so that he hardened in her palm.

'I was just about to do that for you.'

'You refused to! I was going crazy for it. I wouldn't be denied it a moment more. Then you rolled me over and took control.'

'But you were going to let me ravish you in the vault. Wouldn't that have been a loss of control?'

'No, because I would have allowed it. Allowing someone to do something is not the same as them taking it.'

'Then I allow you to do anything with me that you need to do; except inflicting actual bodily harm, that is. I value my equipment. I don't want it damaged, if you don't mind.'

'I wouldn't hurt it. I think it's marvellous. I've gone to sleep each night with it in my mind.'

'You could have gone to sleep with it inside you if you'd played your cards differently.'

She gave him a playful push.

'Let's forget that. It's water under the bridge.'

'Well you can do anything you like with it now, within reason.'

She leaned forward and kissed him tenderly.

'Anything?'

'Anything.'

'Can I lick it all over?'

He laughed.

'If that's what you want to do.'

'Can I suck it again and make it fountain like it did before, and drink your spunk from the tip?'

'You shock me, Flo.'

'Do I. Why?'

'It's not a word a lady uses.'

She laughed.

'It's exciting. Bawdy. Don't you like it?'

'Of course I do.'

'Well, don't be such a prig then.'

'Me a prig?'

'Can I suck your balls?'

'As long as you don't squeeze or bite them.'

'Can I fuck your cock?' She whispered it and shivered.

He bit her neck.

'If that would please you, bawd.'

'Can I stick my finger up your arse? I understand it's wickedly exciting.'

He laughed aloud. She was talking like a little girl, excited at having a new doll to play with. And she was using words like a well brought up child would pick up from an urchin in the street, revelling in their naughtiness, not fully understanding their social taboos.

'I suppose you can stick your finger up my arse, if

that's what you really want to do. Feel free to do what you like with your dutiful servant, Miss Pennington.'

She wound her arms tightly round his shoulders, burying her head in his neck again.

'Ramon DuPrey, I think you must be the most incredible man in the world.' She pulled back from him again, a slight query on her face, thoughtfully rubbing the pond weed from his chest with her fingertips. 'Why did you call me Flo, just now?'

'It just slipped out.'

'It's nice. I like it.'

'Don't you like Floy?'

She licked her fingers and removed green stains from his cheek.

'It's all right. It's short for Florence shortened to Floey. I thought Floey was childish. Floy is a more sophisticated name.'

'For a more sophisticated lady?'

'Sophisticated in the true sense of the word now: "corrupted, adulterated, tampered with".'

'But you've enjoyed being tampered with.'

She giggled.

'I've enjoyed every minute of it. But I wish you would have tampered with me more. I still desperately need you, Ram, deep inside me.'

'You can have me deep inside you. All you have to do is let me go.'

She grinned.

'Not until I've enjoyed you mercilessly.'

'Harlot!'

She pouted at him girlishly.

He smiled at her. She was so beguiling when she was in a playful mood.

'And why do you call me Ram?'

She giggled and kissed his cheek.

'Because you are one. You are my own beautiful ram. You are my stud and I'm going to ride you – until those men come back, anyway. Then I'll probably throw myself on their guns and end it all. But at least I'll have made love to one man in my short and turbulent sex life.'

'You're very melodramatic.'

She frowned.

'Mother always used to say that. She was always trying to knock it out of me. She said I was a tomboy, a rebel.'

'It sounds as if she was a bitch.'

Floy suddenly felt sadness. So many people in her life had meant well. But their well-meaning had suppressed the spirit which had always surged in her.

'Mother meant well. But right to the end, she couldn't control me. She used to despair. She used to say, "You are the scourge of your mentors and your peers. I can never understand your rebelliousness, Florence".'

'If my short experience of you is anything to go on, I think your mother was right.'

Floy nipped his neck.

'I shouldn't be too critical, if I were you, DuPrey. Remember you're my prisoner. I might decide to tickle you to death instead of fucking you to within an inch of your life.'

'Where did you learn such ideas? You're the most outrageous woman I've ever known!'

'Why do you say that?'

'Because you seem to take a delight in talking crudely and telling me what you want to do to me.'

'It was you who taught me to say cock.'

He smiled.

'But I didn't teach you those other words.'

'Isn't that how all lovers talk? Jay and Prissy did.'

'I don't think everyone does.'

'Anyway, DuPrey, we agreed to be honest with each other. You didn't like it when I lured you to my boudoir under false pretences.'

'I know we agreed to be honest, but aren't you taking it a bit too literally?'

She drew back and pouted at him. Then she slipped

her hand under his testes and palmed them. The other hand wrung his shaft gently.

'You forget that I'm like a person from another planet. All this is entirely new to me. It's as if I lived in a desert all my life. Then one morning I opened a window to find that an oasis full of new and exciting life had sprung up overnight.' She started to work the shaft with her fingers, stripping the foreskin back then pulling it over the head again, rubbing the web under the head with her palm. Each time it jumped a little and stiffened more. This made her tingle between the legs.

Her heart beat furiously.

'Anyway, DuPrey, don't be so stuffy about crude words. They hold more excitement than their medical equivalents. Do you become stimulated when I ask if you want coital intercourse with your erect penis penetratng my vaginal canal?'

'You're just a harlot deep inside. I think you're a nympho. But I love it. Sex words on your sweet lips make me go weak at the knees. You look so pure and elegant, so butter-wouldn't-melt-in-your-mouth. It gives even those words an extra erotic edge.'

She put her lips to his and thrust her tongue deep into his mouth. It fenced with his. He gasped.

She pulled back again.

'I am a wanton hussy, Ram. Don't forget I've got at least fifteen years of catching up to do in the sexual intercourse department. When you stood at the window with this manimal at full attention, you released the harlot in me.' She pulled and squeezed him gently. 'It's something which I can't control. I doubt if I shall rest until it's run its course.'

'You're doing very well as far as I can see.'

'Yes, but there's a long way to go yet. Don't forget, I haven't had this inside me properly yet.' She pumped it up and down sensuously. 'And I'm told there's more than one way of doing that.'

He laughed again.

'At least a half dozen that I can think of.'

She was working the length of his erection now, her thumb and forefinger making a circle, ringing it and moving rhythmically.

'Will you show me every way of fucking that you know?'

'If you'll let me.'

'Of course I will. But not yet. And anyway, don't forget we might both be dead by dawn with bullets through our heads.'

'I doubt it. They've probably scarpered with the jewels by now.'

'What makes you think that?'

'I don't know. That big fellow looked nervous. They were both very shifty. It seemed as if this was the first time they'd robbed anyone.'

She laughed.

'Just like me. Virgins at the stick-up game. Perhaps they'll leave us here to rot.'

'They'll probably tip the police off to come and find us in a couple of days.'

She giggled, and worked him with long slow strokes, his tip rigid against the inside of her wrist. The sensation was making her wet between the legs again.

'Do you mean I've got a couple of days to experiment with you, DuPrey?'

'I shall be dead from thirst and hunger by then.'

'Or from fucking me?'

'From loving you, perhaps. Or from lack of sleep. Do you intend keeping me trussed up like this all night?'

'I don't know. What time is it, do you think?'

'I haven't a clue. But if you don't start your experiments soon, I shall fall asleep out of boredom.'

'Is that a hint?'

'You could say that.'

Floy thrilled. He wanted her to start on him. But she would not be hurried. She would take him in her own time. She would savour every part of his body and work him up to a pitch where he cried out for her to relieve him of the pressure she was building in him.

214

But first she must strip him naked. She could not do anything worthwhile with his shirt and jeans on.

She went into the bathroom. In the cabinet she had been surprised to find a pair of surgical scissors and a bottle of baby oil. There were also some sticking plasters, and some small silver foil packs. To her, they looked like packs of surgical blades.

She took them all into the other room.

'Look what I've found.'

'What are you going to do with those?'

She grinned.

'You'll see.' She took the scissors and started to run them up his shirt sleeve.

'Floy! Do you mind! You'll slice me open if you don't watch out!'

'Nonsense. I was a nurse, remember. I've cut shirts off many an injured man.'

'I'll be an injured man if those scissors slip.'

'Don't be a baby.'

Within a couple of minutes she had his shirt in tatters on the floor. He was naked to the waist now, his trousers open to the crotch, his pride and joy sticking upwards like a ram, his testes hanging over the bottom of his fly.

She stood back and studied her prize. His bronzed arms were taut as they splayed upwards to the bonds at his wrists. Under his arms, wisps of black hair lay neatly upwards; not like her hair which grew in a fuzz if she let it.

His torso was smooth and tight and muscular. There was not an ounce of spare flesh on it. His navel dimpled in his heaving abdomen, panting in and out rhythmically. She could see that he was excited; perhaps as excited as she was. Good, that would keep him hard and make him spurt strongly when she made him.

When he had kept her tied up, and had made her make love to him with her mouth, she had been exhilarated. She expected that he felt the same now.

Floy felt lightheaded. The sense of control over this

powerful man was intoxicating. Adrenalin ran through her, making her heart patter. Her breath panted with anticipation. Her mind raced with technicolour pictures of all the possibilities at hand. At hand? She smiled to herself.

Now she put her lips to his chest.

He groaned.

She moved them upwards in little teasing bites until her face forced his head back so she could access his neck. She bit him hard, just as the 'burglar' had bitten her.

He let out a gasp.

'Vampire!'

Her heart thrashed in her chest. Her solar plexus tightened.

Now she moved downwards slowly and inexorably, her mouth moving round to bite him in the waist. He gasped and tightened the whole of his body, unable to move away from her, his erection springing with the added tension.

She worked her tongue in his navel. He shuddered, waves of muscular contractions rippling through his torso. At the same time the long stiff shaft came up and caught her under the chin.

Now she bent and took the rosy knob in her lips, running her tongue down the centre groove and the web of skin on the underside.

He shuddered and strained it up into her mouth.

She resisted and withdrew. She would not bring him yet.

Now she took the scissors and ran the blades down the inside legs of his jeans, taking care to avoid his testicles. With both sides slit down a foot or more she was able to strip the trousers downwards, baring his male equipment entirely.

She knelt in front of him and looked.

'Who's the voyeur now, Flo Pennington?'

'Voyeuse, you mean. Not me. Voyeurism is mostly a secret thing. I'm not being underhand. I'm looking at your beautiful male anatomy.' She ran a finger down the centre seam of his rock-hard penis. It stood harder still.

'I think this is the most exciting thing I've ever seen in my life. What makes me marvel is how you make it stand so hard when it starts out so soft. How do you do that, Ram?'

'I don't do it, silly. Cocks have a mind and a life of their own.'

She put her tongue to the shaft and licked it sensuously. Then she licked the heavy ovals, her tongue resting tightly in his scrotum.

'Well, however you do it, I think it's gorgeous. Do you like it when I lick it?'

'It drives me mad. You're a real pro at this.'

She sat back and frowned up at him.

'I hope you don't think I'm doing this for money!'

'I didn't mean it that way. Anyway, aren't you doing it to learn about sex for your books? Don't you write for money?'

'Of course I do; for as much money as I can get. But I'm doing this because I like it! And because you're a wonderful specimen of masculinity. I'm doing it because the smell of your scent drives me wild. And I'm doing it because I love your cock. So don't be such a prig!'

'Sorry, I'm sure. I only meant that you're good at what you're doing. I find it hard to believe that you've never done anything like this in your life before.'

Floy sat back on her haunches, her fists turned inwards on her hips.

'You better believe that I've never done anything like this before!'

'All right! Don't get on your high horse again. But since we're being honest, tell me how come sexual intercourse passed you by until the ripe old age of thirty?'

'Thirty-one!'

He grinned.

217

'Don't split pubic hairs. How is it that you've only just found your sexuality?'

'I told you. After my first best-seller, I didn't have time for men. I was too busy writing the next seven books.'

'Okay, but that takes care of only the last six or seven years. So what were you doing before that? If you were a nurse, surely you were propositioned a dozen times a week?'

'Of course I wasn't!'

Ramon shook his head.

'I don't believe you. A sensuous woman like you draws horny men like a magnet draws tin tacks.'

Floy stiffened. He was getting onto tricky ground. She slitted her eyes.

'Just shut up about my past, will you? It's none of your business.'

'I'm making it my business. I'm letting you use my body freely and without protest for your experiment, Miss Pennington. The least you can do in return is tell the truth about your curious lack of carnal knowledge.'

Floy scowled. She suddenly felt guilty. Pictures from the past days of debauchery with the Pollands and Ramon DuPrey crowded in on her. She thrust the thoughts aside. But some deep-down mechanism in her wanted to confess.

She glared at him.

'All right! I'll tell you. Though God know why I should.' Tears flooded into her eyes. She was aware of Ramon studying her as she knelt between his spread legs, his hairy testes hanging inches from her face, his veined member still straining upwards, the velvet head bulging prominently. She kissed it, savoured it, drew a deep breath of its scent while she plucked up courage to reply.

He spoke softly.

'Well then, Flo? Why?'

'Because I was a nun, stupid! Why else would I be so naïve!'

Chapter Ten

Ramon's mouth dropped open.

'A nun? Bloody hell!'

Floy looked up at him, her eyes streaming with tears.

'I wish I hadn't told you now!'

Ramon shook his head.

'I'm sorry. It was a bit of a shock, that's all. But it makes sense of everything.'

'What kind of sense does it make? All it's done for me is make me feel ashamed of myself.' She put her face in her hands.

'Come here, Flo.'

She looked up, her face blotchy.

'What are you going to do?'

'What the hell can I do to you while I'm tied up? Just come here, will you! I swear I'll rip this bed apart if you don't.'

She stood up, but away from him.

'It's no good you backing off now. Just come and snuggle up to me.'

'Why? So you can gloat over having a nun?'

'Now you're being paranoid. Nothing's changed between us as far as I'm concerned.'

Floy leant against him tentatively, her hands hanging by her sides.

'That's no good. Put your arms around my neck like you did before.'

She did as he commanded.

'Now kiss me like you have been doing.'

She pressed her lips to his.

Ramon moved his lips gently in a loving kiss. There was nothing else he could do to comfort her, to reassure her that her confession meant little to him.

Of course it had been a surprise. The way she had behaved was not what he would have expected of an ex-nun. But it explained so much. It told him why she was so naïve. It told him why she had never had any sexual experience. He could see why she had been so aloof, so superior in her manner. She had walked like a nun; glided across the foyer of the hotel like a nun. She had held her head high, even after he had made love to her the first night and almost ravished her on the second.

But she used sexually explicit slang as if it was the accepted currency of any relationship. And where had she learnt about such things as anal stimulation? He had thought that Florence Pennington was a surprise an hour, but this was the biggest surprise of all.

Another thing puzzled him. Why had she left her Order? Had she been slung out for un-sisterly behaviour? Had she, after all, been caught with her hand comforting some young man in his dying moments?

And then there was the money. By her own admission, she was voracious for it. Her jewels and the money she earned from writing seemed to be the things she cared about most. When she found that she could not write the sex into her book she had been devastated. He had seen fear in her eyes as she had talked about having to return the two million dollars advance. It had been sad to see, even though he had been angry with her at the time.

Clearly she had been a rebel. The 'mother' she had referred to earlier had most likely been a Mother Superior.

Her considerable libido would have been her biggest

enemy in a convent. But she might have been unaware of its true nature until he had unwittingly triggered the libertine in her. It would probably have surfaced in her adolescence as rebelliousness.

But she had come to the DuPrey Country House Hotel to work out the content for the book. She had specifically set out to gain sexual experience. Then she had become caught in its emotional nets. She had not reckoned on the need to be loved as well as to be fucked. She had thought she could just lie there and allow him to screw her without getting involved. She had been wrong. And she had been angry when she had found that out. Now, caught on the hook of lust she had cast at him, she was ashamed.

Ramon pulled back gently from her mouth. He licked her cheeks of salty water and kissed the tip of her nose.

'I think you're incredible, Flo Pennington. I don't care about your past. I don't care about why you did what you did. All I care about is that you're here with me. Despite the circumstances and how we lured each other into them, I thank God that I've had an opportunity to hold you and taste you and caress your beautiful body and to fence with your formidable intellect. All I ask now is that you let me show you fully what a man and women can experience together.'

'If we get out alive, Ram.' She snuggled into his neck.

'We will. We'll fight the bastards tooth and nail if they show their ugly faces in here.'

Leaning back, her arms still around his shoulders, her pubis pressed hard against his erection, she smiled up at him. Her eyes watered with admiration.

'And what then, beautiful Ram? What if we do get out of here? After the initial excitement is over, after I've experienced everything about your body that I can, what then?'

'After you've done all that, we could start loving one another seriously. I love you already and that's all that matters to me. But do you love me?'

* * *

Floy pressed her breasts against him again, tucking her face into the crook of his neck so he could not read her expression. That was a hard question to answer.

Did she love Ramon DuPrey? She loved his body. She loved his manimal, and how the great purple knob had stood proud in her mouth. She loved how his plum-like testes hung heavily in his sac. She loved the tautness of his stomach, the way it heaved when she sucked at his rearing shaft. She loved the mouth which sucked and teased and ate at the soft fleshy lips between her legs; the tongue which darted and fenced and toyed with her tongue, sending lines of tingling energy down into her clitoris. She loved the rich Mediterranean brownness of his smooth, elastic skin. She loved his hairless chest and abdomen which made her tongue want to lick every inch of it until it glistened with her saliva.

She loved his legs, long and muscular and smooth. She wanted to slide herself up and down them and leave them slick with her juice.

She loved his sense of humour. Little things, like the way he had told her not to split pubic hairs, and that he'd screw her and not sue her for defamation of his cock, had made her laugh inside. He seemed to take all this so lightly, even though she had seen from the outset how scared he had been at gun point.

She had loved the feel of him, hot and rigid inside her for that one second, and she had been devastated when he had ripped himself out. She had writhed when he had tongued her inner secret lips, when he had licked her clitoris after creeping into her room. She still thrilled when she recalled how he had made her orgasm with his burglar's flashy tool which had refused to prise her open, even though it had left her gasping to be filled.

Yes, she loved every bit of Ramon's male body. But did she love Ramon?

'Ram?'

'Yes, kitten.'

'Ram, I need you still.'

'That's okay. I need you too, Flo.'

'I want to make love to you, Ram.'

'Then love me, Flo.'

'You won't think I'm a tart?'

'Of course I won't. What makes you think that?'

She pulled back and looked into his eyes, breathing his breath.

'I've been talking and behaving like a tart, haven't I?'

He grinned at her.

'Yes you have. But I've loved every minute of it. A tart in a nun's body must be just about the most erotic combination any man could experience.'

'I learned well then?'

'It seems so.'

'Do you want to know how I learned?'

'If you want to tell me.'

'I learned some things from Prissy and Jay, but most from prostitutes. They used to be brought in to the Missions I worked at in London and in Hamburg. Some of them had been beaten up by their pimps, some were down on their luck. We nursed them back to health. They were amused at how innocent we were. Some of them used to tell me all about what they did with men and what men wanted to do with them. They told me things to make me blush. And they talked in sex language all the time. I learned it well although, until I came to the Duprey, not a word of it had ever escaped my lips. I thought that when men and women had sex, they always spoke like that. Jay and Prissy did.'

'It seems you had a good education for what you set out to do.'

'The best,' she smiled thinly, 'or the worst, depending how you look at it.'

'And the striptease? How did you learn that?'

She put her eyes down for a moment. When she looked up again, her face was defiant.

'One of the women was a stripper. She told me how

223

to turn men on, although I think she had learned the art too thoroughly.'

'It seems she did.'

'The first time I stripped for you I was surprised how sexually excited it made me. I followed her directions to the letter, although I think she would be very surprised that I ever took any notice.'

'You're a good learner.'

'Not really. She said there's a stripper in every woman if she would only dare to look.'

'I can imagine.'

'She told me never to let the man see everything; to keep them on the edge of their seats.'

'You did that alright.'

'But I broke that rule at the end.'

'What do you mean.'

'I let you see my – '

'Your what?'

'Prissy called it her quim. I think it's a lovely word, don't you?'

'Stimulating.'

'But I did show you more than I was supposed to. I wanted you to see it. I was so stimulated, I wanted you to rush round to my suite and drive your gorgeous shaft deep into me.'

'I did rush round to your suite.'

'I know. But by that time I was scared.'

'It was a dangerous thing to do, Flo.'

'I know that now. But you see, Lara didn't know how dangerous it was either. That was important.'

Her hands slipped to his chest and smoothed at his skin, her fingertips kneading it lightly. Just touching him still made her tremble.

'What happened to Lara?'

'The burglar ravished her. Then she had her throat cut.'

'Ughh! By the burglar?'

'No. That was the mystery.'

'I thought you didn't have a plot.'

She smiled.

'That was just to lead you on. I thought that by telling you that I didn't know what to do, sexually, with Lara, you might provide me with a few more experiences without me asking you directly.'

Ramon whistled through his teeth. So the famous Miss Floy Pennington had not been stumped for a plot after all. Her cries for help had been just another subterfuge.

'So who did it?'

'You don't expect me to tell you that, do you?'

'I've learned not to expect anything where you're concerned, Flo Pennington.'

She smiled at him broadly.

'Then you won't be expecting this, will you?'

Suddenly she was full of energy. The confessions of the past ten minutes seemed to have unburdened her soul. He drew a deep breath as she slid down his chest and stomach, her lips kissing avidly all the way. When she reached his member, she licked it like a lollipop until its veins stood out.

Then she took the scissors.

'What are you doing?!'

She snipped. He drew a sharp breath of alarm.

'Floy!'

Grinning, she rose again with a curl of black pubic hair between her fingers.

Calmly, she took a sticking plaster, put the curl of hair in it, and stuck it to her groin.

Ramon relaxed.

'What the hell was that for?'

'I want a little bit of you between my legs, DuPrey. If we never see each other again when we get out of here, I shall always have you there to remind me of this time.'

'You, Florence Pennington are a – '

'Libertine? I know. And I'm loving every minute of it. I think my confession to you has got rid of my remaining inhibitions and those last regrets about leaving the Order.'

'Why did you leave your Order?'

'I didn't fit in.'

'I can imagine.'

'I wrote my first book while I was still in holy orders. That was *Murder in the Cloister*. A priest was found with his throat cut in our convent. The police didn't have a clue who did it. I took an interest in it.'

'And you solved the case?'

She grinned.

'Of course. One of the nuns did it. The priest had been taking her confession and taking liberties with her at the same time. When she found he was doing it to others as well, she thought that it would be best for the convent to remove him from the scene. I wrote it up as a thriller and the publisher was interested. He used to come to the convent posing as my uncle. He gave me a dictation machine and I used to slip him tapes of my drafts.'

'And what did the Mother Superior think of that?'

'She didn't know until the first book became a best-seller. Then she said I had to choose between my calling and the writing. I started getting such a lot of money. The money was the more important to me. So I left.'

'What do you do with the money? How do you manage to spend it all?'

Floy looked at him sternly.

'I give it away, of course. I maintain thousands of deprived children all round the world. I educate them and support their families. What did you think I did with the money?'

Ramon put his eyes down.

'I misjudged you, Flo. I'm sorry.'

'I forgive you. Apart from my clothes and a few sticks of furniture in a poky flat in London, those jewels and the car are my only possessions. They're for show, to support the image of a successful writer. It's part of the contract.'

'I can see why you were devastated at the idea of having to return the advance if you didn't do the book.'

226

Tears came to her eyes.

'I was forced to do it, Ram. I detested the idea of sex in my books. What I did with you, I did for the children. But now I've started something I can't easily stop.'

'Do you regret it?'

'Of course not. It's added a new dimension to my life. And now, dear Ram, that's enough of my confessions. I've got the most beautiful man in the world tied up in front of me and it's time I did something with him. But first . . .' She knelt with the scissors.

Ramon groaned.

'Oh my god! What's the woman up to now?'

'I'm cutting the rest of your trousers off. I want you absolutely naked when I make love to you.'

'Floy.'

'Yes?'

'Before you do that, I've got a confession to make, too.'

She stood up, a query in her eyes.

'If you're going to tell me that you're married, leave it until I've made love to you.'

'No, I'm not married.'

'You're gay?'

'Hardly! No, it's something worse than that. I think you'll be very angry with me.'

Putting a long forefinger over his mouth, she whispered.

'Leave it until I've made love to you. Then you can tell me. Who knows, when I've had you inside me, I might be in a good mood to hear your confession.' She bent with the scissors again.

Ramon could do nothing. He was completely at her mercy. He just hoped that she wouldn't decide to snip something more fleshy for a souvenir. But she was having some trouble with the scissors on the tough denim of his jeans.

He looked down.

She had a foil packet in her hands. She ripped it open and held up the contents to him.

'I thought it contained surgical blades. What's this?'

'You don't know?'

She frowned.

'Would I ask if I did?'

'It's a condom.'

'This is a condom? Fascinating. I've never seen one before. Can I try it?' She was grinning widely.

He rolled his eyes upwards and sighed with mock exasperation.

'Go on! Get it out of your system.'

Ramon thought again how much like a child she was. Here she was, a woman of thirty-one playing doctors and nurses – or was it cowboys and indians? She had him trussed up like one. Now that Floy Pennington the Iceberg had melted, she was a delightful, simplistic creature; nymph-like in her body and in her naughtiness.

She finished cutting off his jeans and stuck the scissors into the bed cover near his head.

Now she placed the rubber sheath on the pulsing red knob before her. He smiled as she rolled it down carefully, her attention glued to getting it on right. When she had it stretched out fully, she sat back on her haunches and admired her work.

The tightness of the sheath made Ramon harder. Condoms always seemed to do that to him, even though he hated wearing them.

She began to snigger.

'What the hell's so funny?'

'I think that little blip on the tip looks ridiculous. I suppose it's to catch your spurt.'

'That's the general idea.'

'It isn't very big.'

'I think it's big enough.'

'Can I try it?'

'What do you mean?'

'Can I masturbate you until you fountain and see if you can fill it?'

'Floy! You're the bloody limit.'

She pouted.

'I think you're a prig.'

'So you said before.'

Before Ramon could remonstrate further, she had leaned forward and taken his erection in her mouth. She quickly withdrew, making a face.

'Uggh. That tastes vile.'

'You're not supposed to suck these ordinary ones. You need flavoured ones for that.'

She grinned.

'You're joking!'

'No I'm not. You can buy fruit-flavoured ones.'

Her grin widened.

'If we get out of here alive, will you get me some banana flavoured ones?' She made her thumb and forefinger into a circle and ran it down the sheath. 'I love bananas, don't you?'

'Floy, I'm getting tired. My arms have gone to sleep and I need to rest. Are you ready to cut me down?'

Floy did not reply. Instead, she took the top off the baby oil and filled her palms. The flats of her hands slid up his legs, over his stomach and to his chest, leaving a glistening trail behind them. Then she rose with them until her lips were opposite his and whispered.

'I'll cut you down after I've made love to you.' She kissed him tenderly, and worked the oil sensuously into his skin.

Ramon breathed deeply, his pulse beating in his temple and his straining member.

With more oil on her hands Floy cupped his testicles and began to work it in. Then she massaged his shaft until it shone. Sliding her hands slowly, her fingertips delved between his legs, kneading at the insides of his thighs. Her fingers swept out, over his testes and up to the tip of his penis. Then down again they went, dragging his foreskin tight, tensioning the loose scrotal skin as they swept under him again. This plunge-and-pull movement was repeated several times until she had Ramon panting deeply, rigid and pulsing, she judged, with the need to climax in her hand.

Without another word, Floy rose on the balls of her feet and slipped herself over his stem. She shuddered as she lowered herself on to it, her engorged lips already richly lubricated so that he slid into her deeply. So deeply did she sink that her clitoris rested on the root of his shaft sending thrilling sensations racing to her panting solar plexus.

He felt incredible inside her, hot and hard and huge.

Ramon whispered.

'Floy, I can't withdraw from you, tied up like this.'

She kissed him tenderly.

'I know. Why do you think I've kept you tied up? I'm not risking you pulling out again. I'm going to work it until I explode. I want my first true fucking with you to be under my control, DuPrey.'

'But I'm close to coming, Flo. I'll come inside you if you're not careful.'

'But that's what I want, Ram. I want to feel the heat of you inside me. I want to feel it running down the insides of my legs. I need to know that I've fucked you to completion and that I have been properly fucked in return.'

She spread her arms up over his, her legs against his too, her breasts supple on his oil-slick breasts. They were like two human X's, one against the other. At the centre she was impaled on his erection.

Their stomachs heaved in unison, slippery with the oil. Their chests heaved together, her breasts tight against him, her hardened nipples lapping at his. She put her mouth to his lips and breathed him in, whispering.

'I love you, Ram. I think you're wonderful the way you pander to my fantasies.'

'I love you too, Flo.'

Floy was content. She was exhilarated. She was tingling from her finger tips where they touched Ramon's, to her teats as they contacted his nipples, to where she held his hardness, to the tips of her toes against his toes. She had captured her man and she was not about to let him go.

They stayed there, connected for some time without moving.

The room was hot. The light was dim. His heart beat with hers, lulling her into delicious sleep. All her sensations were concentrated on the hardness between her legs and the hairy root of it nuzzling on her prominent nub. She could feel the little hairs of his sac, prickling on the supersensitive surfaces of her inner thighs.

She began to move with the heaving of his diaphragm. As she did so her clitoris came down hard on the root of his cockstem.

Gradually she increased her gyrations. He began to moan and to move counter to her, increasing the sensations as much as his bondage would allow.

Floy began to pant. She began to lift herself on the balls of her feet and then drop herself down hard onto him, rasping the centre of her sensation in his mat of hair. Each time, her clitoris thrilled.

She began to grind as she lifted and lowered herself, her legs spread widely over his.

He was thrusting into her now every time she dropped, his pelvis pushed out against hers. She turned her feet outwards and began to flex her knees to widen her stance every time she came down on him. The inner surfaces of her thighs slid on his legs.

Ramon began to shudder. His head lolled from side to side. His tongue came out.

She took the tongue in her mouth and sucked.

Her palms rubbed his palms, her breasts rode over his chest, slippery now with perspiration as well as with the oil.

Floy could feel her own skin slick with sweat. This increased the sensation of contact between them until she cried out with ecstasy, writhing on him, working herself into a frenzy of desire to release her tension.

That desire rose like a tide and she clenched her muscles about his thrusting stem to bring herself to a climax.

Ramon cried out. He gasped. His chest inflated and collapsed. Floy felt a hot surge.

She sensed his rich seed burning deep inside her. Then she felt a trickle down her loins, her love-syrup mixed with his. The heightened sensation his fluid created on her inner lips drove her into paroxysms, tightening and loosening rhythmically on the rigid limb. Her body began to shudder uncontrollably.

She let out a long and agonised cry, like the final cry of a mother giving birth to her baby. Then she shuddered deeply as wave after wave of energy gushed from her focus of exquisite senses, burst up through her stomach, through her navel to her breasts, then upwards, engulfing her face and burning her lips.

She panted, breathless as the waves of sensation washed over her, slowly easing to ripples and then to a gentle swell.

'Ramon, that's incredible! I love you! I love you!'

She locked her mouth on to his and hung there as he pumped inside her.

After minutes and in a half daze, she took the scissors from where she had impaled them in the bed near his head and cut the bonds at his wrists.

Ramon enfolded her in an iron-hard hug. Their legs were still splayed against one another. She held him inside herself tightly, tensing her muscles so as not to let him go, springing on her toes so that her legs frogged open and closed, working herself gently over his root.

When eventually he slipped away, she cut the bonds on his ankles. Then she switched out the bathroom light.

In the darkness, hot and sweaty, slippery and tired, they curled up together on the mattress. Ramon slid his thigh between her legs so that it was in contact with the fleshy mouth there, so that it sucked at his own taut flesh each time he moved. He wound his arms tightly around her, pulling her to himself.

Floy kissed him long and tenderly.
Then she slept.

Ramon lay in the darkness, the heat of his lover's sexual lips burning his leg. But his unheard confession burned him more. How could he tell her his secret? It would have to be soon. There was no way he could keep it from her for much longer.

Her confession about writing to earn money to support thousands of children and destitute families had driven a knife of remorse into his heart. He had been angry at her for the way she had appeared to be so fixated on money. She had appeared to be prepared to do anything to get it. He had thought of her as a literary prostitute and he had ridiculed her for it. At least prostitutes were honest in what they did for money. Floy Pennington had been so devious.

But right now, there was no point in worrying about it. In the morning, things might look different.

Floy was hungry when she awoke. A crack high up in the boarded window let in enough light for her to see Ramon. He slept deeply beside her, his leg still between hers.

Her rumbling stomach and the light said morning. She began to plan.

If either of those villains came back now they would get a nasty surprise. She would show them that Sister Luke was not one to be abducted without a fuss.

Slipping out of Ramon's leggy grip, she went to the loo. Closing the door she put the light on and ran the shower. But first she addressed herself to a loose towel rail. A couple of good heaves and it came off the wall. It was heavy: solid metal. She tip-toed to the other room and leaned it by the door. Now she had a weapon.

The bathroom was hot. The water too. She thanked God for that at least. Now all they needed was for someone to bring food. That would be her main chance to use the weapon so they could escape. Of course, they would need to find clothes. She had destroyed Ramon's in her lust to strip him naked. And she would not be able to go about in the bathrobe for long.

This morning she felt strong and alert. She felt fulfilled. She felt like a real woman at last. It had taken thirty-one fraught years of life to get to this point. There was no turning back now. There was no way she was going to have her life cut short by petty criminals.

The water running over her breasts felt delicious. It streamed down her stomach and ran off her pubic hair in a little tickling river.

She soaped herself, quivering at the heightening of sensation the lubrication brought to her skin.

As she shampooed her hair, two large brown hands slipped under her arms and cupped her breasts. Taking the nipples between thumb and forefinger they plucked as a mouth closed on her neck.

She would have recognised those wonderful long-fingered hands anywhere.

'Good morning, you beautiful creature. What a pleasant surprise to find a water nymph in my bathroom.'

She turned her head to him and caught his lips as he peered over her shoulder, breathing deeply as his hands slipped through the suds to her mount of Venus.

'Don't you ever stop wanting sex, DuPrey?'

'Not while you're nearby, Flo Pennington. I've wanted sex with you since the moment I saw you.'

'Even as you stood in Reception?'

'Even as I stood in Reception.'

He took the shower-head off its hook and ran hot water over her breasts. She trembled. He ran it down her stomach and over her pubic mound. Slowly, as the needles of the spray tickled on her clitoris, she began to quiver. She widened her stance to allow the instrument of delight access to her secret lips. Still behind her, he worked the spray up tight so that the pressure of the water penetrated into the cavern of delight he had explored the night before. She frogged her legs to give the spray deeper intrusion, opening herself wider as

Ramon kept the jetting head close to the lips, swollen now with the sensation.

As the hot water played in the tingling hollows each side of her leaves of distended flesh, Floy began to tremble violently. Teasingly, he removed the shower-head and hung it up.

She moaned and stood up, turning to face him.

'Why did you do that? I was just about to shatter into a million pieces.'

He bit her neck.

'Why should the shower head have all the fun? I want you to shatter with my cock inside you and my finger deep in your arse.' He bit her nipple playfully.

'Torturer!'

Her hands found his testicles and cupped them. He was already hard, rearing in the hot stream between them. Floy threw her head back into the spray, closed her eyes and sighed.

'You arouse fast.'

'I woke with a terrific horn. I think it must be your pheromones.'

'My furry what?'

'The scent of your body and your sex. It drives me wild.'

'You're just an animal.'

'Grrrrr!' He bit her shoulder. 'And you like it.'

Ramon looked down on her. She was radiant. Her eyes shone with life and with mischief. He kissed her tenderly on the lips, water streaming off their mouths.

She reached for the soap and began to lather him. Ramon relished every second as her hands slipped seductively over his chest and legs. She left his genitals until last.

'Why are you so brown-skinned, Ram?'

'My father was from Southern France. My mother was English. We lived in England at what is now the DuPrey Hotel.'

He moved his legs wide apart.

Now she lathered his sac and the upstanding limb growing tautly out of it. She tensioned the hood back and worked the head delicately with the tips of her fingers, her thumb massaging the web of skin in its prominent purple valley.

'Is that why the house is so French in style?'

She rinsed him off and slipped the foreskin over the glans. Then she kissed it. It was so hard the foreskin slid down again.

'Yes. My grandfather built it in the French style of the time.'

She slipped her hand between his legs and ran them inside the crease between his buttocks.

'My parents inherited the estate and turned the house into a hotel. When they died in a plane crash, I had to take over the running of it.'

Her forefinger found his anus and began to massage it.

'I wondered how you came to be the proprietor at such a young age.'

He groaned and thrust himself forward as she massaged him with her finger.

'I think that's the most erotic thing I've done to you so far, Ram.'

'Don't think it'll get you anywhere. I'm not that easily seduced.'

She grinned and went down on her knees and kissed the tip of his proud mushroom.

'What do I have to say to seduce you? Do I have to say, Ram, please fuck me.' She grinned and took him in her mouth, giving a couple of hard sucks. 'I want this to be strong and hard. I don't want you to stop until I scream for mercy.'

She slid up his body and slipped her arms around his shoulders, spray bouncing off her head. She kissed him again, closing her eyes.

Ramon shut off the water, took her with one arm around the shoulders, the other between her legs, lifted her off her feet and swung her out of the shower. His inner elbow in her expectant crevice, his hand in the small of her back, he swept her up. As they left the shower streaming with water, bubbles of remaining lather broke in little pin-pricks all over their skin.

In the other room, he dropped her onto the mattress and stood over her, glistening; the pillar of his penis straining to stand out from his body.

His erection pulsed at the woman beneath him. He could see she was already slick with the expectation of his first thrust. Her eyes shone with mischief and with that same sexual energy which she had shot out at him and captivated him from the first day.

At that moment, Ramon thought that he had Floy Pennington well and truly tamed. He had turned her into a ravenous creature, begging now to be taken.

He decided that he would leave his confession until he had enjoyed her prodigious sexuality just one more time.

Sinking to his knees between her back-stretched legs, his cockstem came to rest in her labial groove, its tip on her swollen clitoris. He ploughed through it as he had done in her bed, her lubrication sensitising him to hurting pitch.

'You're the most incredible, the most tantalising, the most erotic creature I have ever known, Flo Pennington.'

She grinned.

'And the most fuckable?'

'Definitely the most fuckable.'

Her grin widened.

'Then fuck me, DuPrey. Fuck me mercilessly and don't stop until I say you can.'

With one determined thrust, Ramon changed angle and drove into her. She cried out, straining her head backwards.

He fucked again, deeper and harder, right up to the hilt.

She shuddered; her tight, syrupy lips sucking noisily

as his nine pink inches disappeared from sight, pulled right out and plunged again.

Voices outside the door sounded agitated. There was a bark. Floy sprang from Ramon's impaling stem. Her eyes were alight with the fire of anger now.

She vaulted to the door. Ramon shot out a hand but could not stop her.

'Floy!'

Wielding a length of chromed pipe, she raised it just as the door opened.

Ramon cried out, but too late.

Held above her in both hands like an axe held by an executioner, the bar scythed down at the florid-faced man halfway through the door with a tray.

'Franz! Look out!'

The bar crashed down on the man's shoulder. The tray went clattering; toast, tea and cups and sugar splattering walls and floor.

Between his legs shot a smooth black and brown streak of dog-flesh. It bounded at Ramon. He turned to ward it off. The dog was on him in a second.

Floy screamed. To his horror, Ramon saw a flash of chrome aimed at the dog's head.

'No, Floy!'

He rolled to protect the dog, its tongue lathering his face with loving licks.

The bar came down across his back. He yelped and sprang up. The dog bounded up at him.

'Heel! Sally! Good girl! Down girl, down!'

Floy stood dumbounded. Her mind raced as she took in the scene. The big German had his mouth open as he stared at her glistening nakedness. Ramon stood grasping an energetic Rottweiler by its collar, his glistening erection springing with the motion of tugging at the dog. His face was wracked with remorse.

In the open doorway stood a tall thin man, an expression of bewilderment on his face. Hanging crookedly on the wall behind the man was a faded print of *The Sunflowers* by Van Gogh.

Rage sprang into Floy's face. It took no time to gather before it exploded.

'You lousy scheming bastard!' She raised the bar at Ramon. He put a hand up defensively. The dog growled and strained at its collar.

The two men slunk away, leaving hot tea steaming on the floor, shards of crockery in its midst.

'You set me up, you louse!' Floy glowered at the man standing dejectedly before her, his penis now drooping rapidly.

'I tried to explain, Floy, honestly I did. You wouldn't hear my confession.'

Floy felt betrayed. It was beyond belief that a man could sink to such a low trick and still say he loved her.

'You said yourself that you wanted more sexual experience. And I thought you didn't have a plot for your book.'

He looked unconvinced as he said it.

'And I suppose you thought you'd invent a plot for me, did you?'

Ramon lowered his head. The dog whined.

'Something like that. It was the only way I could think of to stop you leaving.'

'Stop me leaving? And getting your revenge on me for using you, don't you mean!'

'I was angry with you at the time, Flo.'

She snarled.

'Don't you ever use that ridiculous name on me again! Do you hear?'

Floy marched past him, grabbed her robe from the radiator and swept out without putting it on. She turned in the doorway, naked and defiant.

'And I don't want to see you ever again, Ramon DuPrey! And you can forget my hotel bill! Regard it as my fee for my services as your prostitute!'

Chapter Eleven

The wall clock showed eight when Ramon strode into the hotel kitchen. A large, florid-faced man wearing a chef's hat stood frying eggs. A tall seedy looking man was making toast. They both glanced at Ramon sheepishly as he entered.

Ramon smiled thinly and handed them each a brown envelope.

'Thanks for your help, fellows. The Stokey Magna Amateur Dramatic Society would have been proud of you.' They both smiled at the compliment. Ramon grinned. 'But I think perhaps you overdid it when you tied me so tightly to the bed base. I know I said you should truss me up, but I thought I would be able to get free when I needed to.'

'Very sorry, Herr DuPrey,' the German said, his eyes looking down at his frying pan.

'That's all right, Franz. I've paid you both double the fees we agreed. It was worth every penny of it. But not a word to the other staff, okay?'

'Sure, boss,' the seedy man echoed.

Franz coughed nervously. 'Has the beautiful lady departed?'

'I'm afraid so, Franz. She dressed and left without a word.' He turned to go. 'By the way, put the starting pistol in the centre drawer of my desk, will you. I'll take it back to the Athletics Club tomorrow. I'm going to get some sleep now. I'll see you later to discuss the evening menu.'

Not a day passed without Ramon thinking of Floy Pennington. There had been no word from her. But he had kept track of her in the papers. She had hit the book-buying public's interest with the sexual content of her book, renamed *A Murderous Affair*. According to the trade press, people were buying Floy Pennington who had never read her before. She had been on television and on radio.

It was mid-afternoon on a day five months after Floy had stormed out. With lunch over, Ramon was taking his break. He sat in his office reading *A Murderous Affair* for a third time. It had been out for only a week when it had entered the best-sellers' lists. Now two companies were vying for the film rights.

Ramon was unable to leave the book alone for long. He could not stop seeing himself as the suave Pierre Cocteau. He could not help seeing John, Jannine, the Pollands, an elderly colonel and his wife, a dapper business man and several other of his guests all portrayed as potential suspects in the bloody demise of Miss van den Berg.

Floy Pennington had used much from her experiences in the apple store and in the prison room at the hotel. She had built their adventures into the plot for Lara van den Berg to act out.

Lara had had her throat cut eventually. Sister Luke had happened to be visiting in the nearby village and had come hotfoot to solve the crime.

He put down the book wearily and stared out across the park. The driveway was shrouded with mist rising in the warm late autumn afternoon. The great iron gates were only just visible.

A large red car, its beige hood down, swept into view. Ramon blinked. Was it a mirage?

The car stopped shimmering as it came closer to the hotel. His heart leapt as he sprang up and darted to the window.

As the burgundy Bentley Mulsanne hushed to a halt at the bottom of the steps, the jet black hair of its stunning female driver settled round her shoulders.

His heart thumped. He still could not believe he was awake.

John, his head bowed, was opening the car door to Floy Pennington now. She spoke to him briefly and swept up the steps. John was lifting luggage from the boot of the Bentley.

Ramon rushed into reception as Floy Pennington glided across the squared marble floor, a red tailored suit and white blouse setting off the blackness of her hair and the darkness of her eyes.

These eyes met his momentarily. As Ramon locked his gaze on to those of his unexpected guest, there was a flash of energy. He almost reeled. For an instant, he could see that it had hit her too. Then she blocked it and masked her response.

Her face was impassive when she reached the desk.

'Good afternoon, Mr DuPrey. I booked a suite in the name of Smith. Do you have it ready?'

Ramon was taken aback by her coolness, although she was not quite so aloof as Floy Pennington the Bitch had been on her first entrance. And she had booked a suite already? He flustered.

'We've put you in the suite you had last time, Flo. I mean, Miss Smith. Would you sign the register?'

He turned the hotel register towards her and handed her a pen.

She signed her name and returned the pen.

He took down a key.

'I'll show you up.'

She waved a dismissing hand.

'That will not be necessary. Have the boy bring my luggage up, will you?'

With that, she took the key and was gone.

Ramon stared after her. It was as if she had never been away. It was as if they had never been lovers or had never been on more than formal terms. She had left a cheque for the Pollands' bill but had never paid her own. Although, when word had got around that the famous Floy Pennington had set her latest success in the Duprey Country House Hotel, business had boomed. It had more than made up for the loss of revenue from her suite. Other people had wanted to stay in the suite, to sleep in the very bed in which Lara van den Berg had been murdered.

The pen Floy had returned to Ramon seemed to burn his hand. He put it carefully in his pocket so that no-one else should use it.

John refused to take up Floy Pennington's baggage. Neither did Ramon want to take it up himself. He called another boy.

As he was about to go back into the office, he glanced at the register. He took a second look.

It said Flo Pennington, not Smith. She had written it clearly. There was no mistake. Neither had she written Florence or Floy.

Ramon was in turmoil, the remainder of his afternoon a blur. He spent the evening either pacing his office or shouting at the staff for no good reason.

Floy Pennington did not come down. She ordered dinner in her suite. Ramon had been tempted to serve it himself but he resisted the impulse. Nothing would be worse than being close to her again and to have her ignore him just as she had before.

By eleven thirty he was a mass of jelly. His hands would not stop shaking. Eleven thirty was her time. Would she come down in a white robe and deposit her pearls? She had been a creature of habit. He smiled wryly at the pun now, imagining Floy Pennington in a nun's attire. Convent life would have been run to a strict schedule. That was probably why she had been as regular as a clock in her ways.

The next half hour passed painfully slowly. There

was no tentative knock on the office door. There was no ghostly-white figure on the stairs when he looked.

By midnight Ramon was frantic. When the telephone rang, he was so keyed-up that he nearly jumped out of his chair. He went to the reception desk to pick up the call. The indicator was lit for Floy Pennington's suite. He gulped.

'Yes, Miss Pennington. How may I be of service?'

Her voice was cool, detached.

'I have a technical problem, DuPrey.'

'What kind of technical problem?'

'I can't undo the fastening on my necklace. Could you possibly send someone up to assist?'

There was no way he was going to send anyone else to Floy Pennington's suite. Ramon shot up the stairs two at a time.

His knock on her door was tentative. There was no answer.

He knocked again. Still there was no answer. Was she playing a game with him?

He stood for several minutes debating with himself. She had called him to her room. It had not been his imagination. Neither had it been when she had lured him there before.

He took a deep breath and put his pass key in the lock. The door was not locked on the inside.

The sitting room was empty, the word processor standing on the table, its screen dead. Cautiously, Ramon took the few steps to the bedroom, lit by the dim light of the dressing table lamp. He could not see the dressing table from where he stood. The bed was empty.

He peeked nervously around the door.

Floy Pennington sat on the stool before the dressing table.

Ramon gulped.

She sat brushing out her gleaming hair as if he was not there. He watched her for more than a minute. She

244

didn't turn. He took all the courage he could muster and stepped into the room.

'So you've come at last, DuPrey.'

'Yes. I've come.'

'My necklace clasp is jammed.'

Ramon stepped up behind her. He took the clasp in trembling fingers. It was not stuck. It came open easily. He slowly drew off the necklace and settled the pearls onto the dressing table.

She said nothing. Getting up, she gestured to him to sit on the stool. He obeyed.

This time she wore sheer black stockings, two taut lines of elastic reaching upwards to a lacy belt around her otherwise naked waist. It formed an arch of black, framing a skimpy diamond of see-through black lace which just covered her prominent mound and dived enticingly between the long and shapely legs, parting the lips it was meant to cover.

She stood just three feet in front of him with her legs apart. Her hands went to her bra, lifting and cupping her breasts.

Ramon gulped again. He could see the nipples poking hard through the lacy material. She was aroused. Floy Pennington the libertine was aroused. His shaft began to stiffen.

Floy's pulse raced. This was the most risqué thing she had done with Ramon DuPrey, but it was already the most stimulating. He might reject her and walk out at any moment in disgust. He had probably been gravely hurt at the way she had left him in her anger. And she had lured him to her room before, only to refuff him after he had made love to her. This time she had been more direct in her invitation, but would he storm out before he got hurt again?

The tight string of lace between her legs thrilled her clitoris with every little move. She slipped her hands behind her back to unclip the bra strap. As it fell, she caught it and held it protectively in front of her.

Her nipples under the loose cups were rock hard. But they were yearning for his mouth to suck them harder. She was yearning for his lips on hers. But not yet. The stripper had tutored her well. She would string him along a while longer, praying that he would not leave. If he did, she would throw herself at him and physically stop him. But now he was quiet, bemused at her behaviour, but not showing signs of anger. There was no need to sacrifice herself to him just yet.

She turned her back and let the bra fall away. Holding it on one long forefinger, she suspended it in front of Ramon and then let it drop in his lap.

He picked it up and held it to his mouth.

Taking a hair band from around her wrist where she had placed it before he came, she raised her arms and started to put up her hair.

The warmth of a body on her back made her take a breath. Long-fingered brown hands slid under her arms and cupped her breasts. Fingers and thumbs took each nipple and gently tugged at them. Floy took a deeper breath and leaned her head backwards.

Ramon said nothing. Words would have been an intrusion in the scene. When Floy Pennington had undressed like this before, nothing had been possible in either words or deeds.

This time Ramon did not have to suffer the agony of separation. This time he would not just sit and watch. Neither, he could tell, did she want him to.

He put his mouth to her shoulder and kissed her heated skin. She shuddered slightly. Then she turned towards him, her breasts open to his gaze. With wonder, he stood back and looked on them. Then he knelt before her. One at a time he took a nipple in his lips and sucked, running his tongue around the nimbus until each stub of erectile tissue stood proud.

Floy put her hands around his face and gently lifted him. She said nothing either. Guiding him back to the stool she made him sit. Then she closed her eyes and massaged her breasts with her fingers. Her legs apart, nearly touching his knees, her black mount thrust forwards.

Confident, Ramon slid down his zip, releasing the pressure within his pouch, letting his hardness spring free.

Floy looked down on him through sultry eyes, her lips pouted. She ran her splayed fingers downwards, fanning them on her stomach and slipping them down the outside of her thighs. Then, tantalisingly slowly, she snapped off each suspender, undid the belt and let it drop silently to the carpet.

Ramon sloughed off his trousers. She opened her eyes but gave no sign that she had seen him undressing.

Ramon slowly removed his tie. She ran her fingertips under the elastic of her G-string, moving it down her hips until the black lace diamond was replaced by a black-haired one.

Floy felt the heat of the moisture of her own excitement. This tantalising of Ramon DuPrey was making her avid for the mushroom-headed column rearing now between his legs.

As Ramon slowly stripped off his shirt, she cupped her breasts again, watching him. Then as he pulled his vest over his head, his muscles bulged, making her quiver at the sight of the smooth brown expanse of chest. She wanted to sink her teeth into his pectorals; to feel their hardness with her mouth.

She resisted.

Now he was naked, now he was tantalising her. Although his face was impassive she could see his eyes gleaming with desire as he watched her finger sliding down inside the dark cleft between her legs.

The finger automatically found her clitoris. Her sexual mouth had had much sucking on this finger since they had parted, but never had it tasted a man. She worked the finger, plunging it in, drawing it slowly out to emulate what she needed from him. She knew he would become even more stimulated. The lasciviousness of the act made her pant. Her pulse hammered at her temple. Her mouth was dry.

As he stood, she shuddered as his silky, purple glans swelled, as the hard, veined shaft rose like some serpent rearing towards her.

She wanted to take it in her mouth. She wanted to enfulf the whole of it as she had done in the apple store. She wanted to feel the heat of his gush; trickling down her throat. But she resisted. Still it was not time.

Her own erotic centre wept profusely, becoming more sensitised as it flowed. Now she turned her back on him, just as she had when he had watched her from his window the last time.

Slowly she slipped her lacy triangle down her legs, driving the black elastic with her finger tips.

It dropped. She bent to pick it up, splaying her legs. It was just as she had done before. But this time it seemed a hundred times more exciting to be displaying the slick, most intimate leaves to the man sitting only an arm's length from reaching out and drawing a forefinger between them.

As she spread her legs wider, the stockings tight around her, the inside of her thighs trembled, the hollows of her loins taut from her erotic stance. She recalled that time when she had wanted to feel his shaft within her, and how frustrated she had been that he had been those feet away across the courtyard.

But this time he was not apart. This time he stood behind her, his phallus greater, seemingly longer and more fierce than ever she had seen it. This time she knew he would sink it into her waiting purse. In seconds she would sense its heat and feel its strength.

As Floy shed her G-string, Ramon nearly came. He restrained himself. Now she was presenting herself to him, her legs stretched widely as she bent to the floor. Contrasted with the blackness of her stockings her flesh

seemed white, the texture downy soft against the sheen
of black silk.

He shuddered at the intensity of feeling which the
sight of the two plump lips with their trim beard of
black hair created in his erection. His solar plexus
fluttered as if it held a thousand butterflies in full flight.

And on the inside of one thigh was a sticking plaster,
a small curl of black hair peeping out.

He sank to his knees behind her, putting his mouth's
lips to the soft sweet lips she was presenting to him.
Then he sucked. His tongue reached for contact with
her fleshy nub, swollen as if reaching out itself to be
savoured. She moaned. For some minutes he stayed
there, eating at the warm, erotic tissue; rasping at her
with his tongue. She shuddered with every move, the
lips opening and shutting with her spasms.

Now Ramon raised himself. He steadied her with his
hands around her buttocks. Shifting them to the top of
her thighs his thumbs prised the lips apart glistening
with his saliva and the seeping juice of her excitement.
Reaching his fingers deeply in, he wet them and ran
them down his shaft. Then he drove into her, as far as
it would go.

Floy felt the hot and rigid ram deep inside herself.
Bracing her hands against a chairback, she widened her
stance still tauter and thrust backwards onto the hardness, wanting every inch of its length.

He did not fuck. He did not pull out and plunge back
in again. He just stayed there, his fingers caressing at
her buttocks, his thumbs digging hard beside her secret
hole. It was as if he just wanted to experience her, to
give her that satisfaction of fulfilling her fantasy.

Floy could not stand it. It was not enough for her. He
had cheated her twice before. She needed to feel him
working himself inside her. She needed to feel it tense
and gush.

Her pelvis began to move, squeezing and sucking on
him as she rocked to and fro.

Ramon took her around the shoulders and pulled her upright, her back to his chest. He slipped his arms under hers and cupped her breasts. His ram was tight in her, the hairy base hard up against her rosebud. It felt delicious just to have him there; to know that he was captured. But he might still escape. She would not let him this time. This time he would be hers.

'Fuck me, Ram. Fuck me.'

Gasped out in hoarse whispers, they were the first words spoken since he had removed the necklace. She put her head against his face.

He whispered in her ear.

'Alright. I'll fuck you. But, although this is beautiful, I'm not going to fuck you like a ram tups a ewe. We can experiment another time.'

He plucked at her nipples sensuously.

Gently, he withdrew from her. Then he turned her and lifted her under the legs and around her back. Kissing her on the forehead, he carried her to her bed and laid her down.

She looked up as he towered above her, the purple head of his penis glistening in the dim light with her juices. Then, slowly, he lowered his mouth to hers, he lowered his body on to her, and he slid deeply into her again. Resting on his elbows, he studied her eyes.

'Have you forgiven me for abducting you?'

She kissed him tenderly in answer, her muscles squeezing at his intrusion for emphasis.

'Of course I've forgiven you, beautiful Ram. I found it impossible to stay away from you. I found that I needed you too much. Please forgive me for my prank.' She kissed his nose. 'I shut you out today just to make you want me more. But I had every intention of making you make love to me tonight, although I want to be an untamed animal with you sometimes.'

'I love you, Flo Pennington, and I want you to stay. Now that you've come back to me I couldn't bear to lose you. You could live here and write. We could do all those things you want to do, both in bed and out. And you would be free to create your fantasies and make your millions and educate your starving children.'

Floy looked up at the man who had his cockstem deep within her. 'I love you, Ram. I think you're the most caring, tender, randy and good looking male any female could ever have the fortune to mate with. But I love you for yourself, not just for your manimal.' She smiled that smile which lit her eyes with mischief. 'But I can't play any longer. Fuck me now; hard and long.'

Floy locked her mouth onto his. She began to gyrate her hips and bear her clitoris down on the root of his erection.

As Ramon's hands slid under her buttocks he lifted her. She drew back her legs tightly to widen his access, so that he could drive down into her without any restriction. She was giving herself to him just as she had offered herself before that dreadful morning after their shower.

As she felt the pressure of his finger on her small secret hole, a shudder of pleasure ran through her. Gently at first, he began to work his shaft and his finger in and out. She strained open, wider still, pulling back her legs to touch knees on breasts.

Now he increased his pace, driving deeper and harder with every stroke. She writhed to keep him captive while working to increase the contact of her ravenous lips on his groin. Her finger nails clawed at the small of his back as she pulled him to come down into her harder.

Ramon speeded his thrust.

Floy scored him deeply with her nails.

He drove into her again and then again.

Now she reached up and sank her teeth into his shoulder.

He let out a cry and thrust, deep and hard and long.

'Fuck me, Ram. Fuck me! Please!'

She was imploring.

It spurred him.

Out of control now, Ramon thrust, taking his shaft right out of her before he drove it in again, up to the hilt, his pubis grinding down on her, ramming so hard that she let out a grunt of air with each forceful intrusion.

Floy shuddered as each stroke became wilder and more aggressive, the fucking sound from their joining increasing too.

He panted.

She cried as energy pumped into her. His finger drove deep into her tight hole, shooting exquisite pleasure through her.

'Harder, Ram! Fuck me harder. Please don't stop. I couldn't bear it if you stopped again! Please!'

She was sobbing, the air panting from her lungs, expelled with the violence of each stroke.

Now, at every thrust, Ramon grunted 'Fuck', thrashing madly into her, pulling her tight to himself.

The tension built in Floy as energy accumulated at her coital focus. She strained to meet him on every stroke, trying to burst that dam which held the tension in.

Ramon cried out, 'Fuck . . . fuck . . . fuck . . .'

Floy gasped 'yes,' to every one.

Her stomach heaved, rising and falling as her hips rose to meet his charge and fell as he ebbed away from her.

The pace became frantic, he like a piston, unstoppable now in its power.

She bucked and writhed and ground herself upon him, her breasts heaving up and down with every arch of her torso.

'Fuck . . . fuck . . . fuck . . .'

'Yes . . . yes . . . yes!'

Finally the dam burst under the pressure of the motion and the words.

Together they arrived at a climactic explosion of fluids and flesh and flailing limbs and gasping breath.

The pump of his ejaculation and its heat inside her

made Floy writhe ecstatically. Rockets of sensation exploded through her body.

Together their stomachs went into spasm, each contraction causing one small fuck, until she subsided into a state of floating bliss.

He collapsed onto her, heaving; pumping still, moving his pelvis in little spasms.

Their mouths locked together. Now she worked his lips with small sucking movements, imitating with her tongue what he was doing with his repleted ram.

Floy sighed deeply and relaxed, relishing the ticking in her depths.

It was done. She had been loved and had been fucked and had loved and fucked in return.

Ramon was still inside Floy a half hour later. His erection did not die and he would not relinquish her until it did. They lay quietly. Her arms around his neck, his weight on his elbows, he studied her face, kissing her every few seconds. He was content. Mastering Flo Pennington was of little consequence now. She had given herself freely to him and he to her.

He pecked her on the nose.

'You didn't answer my proposal.'

She squeezed his hardness with her sex-lips, pleased that she was becoming expert with their use.

'I thought my body gave you its answer. How could I live without being fucked like that every day, several times a day?' She laughed lightly.

'Then it's yes? You'll live here with me?'

She kissed him tenderly.

'Of course it's yes. But I warn you, I'm a bitch to live with when I'm working on a book. And I shall need a lot more practical experience to get the sex scenes right.'

He laughed boyishly.

'Good. But the last book was very successful. I had a hard-on through most of it. And I felt so much a part of it. I recognised your description of my prick.' He grinned.

She laughed with him.

'Conceited pig!' She clenched her muscles around him again. 'But I'm glad you liked it, Ram. It couldn't have been written without you.' She squeezed again. 'Or without the help of your tongue and this wonderful animal.'

Ramon bit her neck and growled. Then he began to thrust again.

BLACK
lace

Already published

NO LADY
Saskia Hope

30 year-old Kate dumps her boyfriend, walks out of her job
and sets off in search of sexual adventure. Set against the
rugged terrain of the Pyrenees, the love-making is as rough as
the landscape. Only a sense of danger can satisfy her longing
for erotic encounters beyond the boundaries of ordinary
experience.

ISBN 0 352 32857 6

WEB OF DESIRE
Sophie Danson

High-flying executive Marcie is gradually drawn away from
the normality of her married life. Strange messages begin to
appear on her computer, summoning her to sinister and
fetishistic sexual liaisons with strangers whose identity
remains secret. She's given glimpses of the world of The
Omega Network, where her every desire is known and
fulfilled.

ISBN 0 352 32856 8

BLUE HOTEL
Cherri Pickford

Hotelier Ramon can't understand why best-selling author Floy Pennington has come to stay at his quiet hotel in the rural idyll of the English countryside. Her exhibitionist tendencies are driving him crazy, as are her increasingly wanton encounters with the hotel's other guests.

ISBN 0 352 32858 4

CASSANDRA'S CONFLICT
Fredrica Alleyn

Behind the respectable facade of a house in present-day Hampstead lies a world of decadent indulgence and darkly bizarre eroticism. The sternly attractive Baron and his beautiful but cruel wife are playing games with the young Cassandra, employed as a nanny in their sumptuous household. Games where only the Baron knows the rules, and where there can only be one winner.

ISBN 0 352 32859 2

Forthcoming publications

THE CAPTIVE FLESH
Cleo Cordell

Marietta and Claudine, French aristocrats saved from pirates, learn their invitation to stay at the opulent Algerian mansion of their rescuer, Kasim, requires something in return; their complete surrender to the ecstasy of pleasure in pain. Kasim's decadent orgies also require the services of the handsome blonde slave, Gabriel – perfect in his male beauty. Together in their slavery, they savour delights at the depths of shame.

ISBN 0 352 32872 X

PLEASURE HUNT
Sophie Danson

Sexual adventurer Olympia Deschamps is determined to become a member of the Legion D' Amour – the most exclusive society of French libertines who pride themselves on their capacity for limitless erotic pleasure. Set in Paris – Europe's most romantic city – Olympia's sense of unbridled hedonism finds release in an extraordinary variety of libidinous challenges.

ISBN 0 352 32880 0

OUTLANDIA
Georgia Angelis

At first, Iona Stanley longs for her temperate home of nineteenth century England. Shipwrecked on the remote South Sea island of Wahwu, she finds the exotic customs of the inhabitants alarmingly licentious. But her natural sensuality blossoms as she is crowned living goddess of the island. Her days are spent luxuriating in the tropical splendour, being worshipped by a host of virile young men. Suddenly, things don't seem so bad after all.

ISBN 0 352 32883 5

BLACK ORCHID
Roxanne Carr

The Black Orchid is a women's health club which provides a specialised service for its high-powered clients; women who don't have the time to spend building complex relationships, but who enjoy the pleasures of the flesh. One woman, having savoured the erotic delights on offer at this spa of sensuality, embarks on a quest for the ultimate voyage of self-discovery through her sexuality. A quest which will test the unique talents of the exquisitely proportioned male staff.

ISBN 0 352 32888 6

BLACK
lace

WE NEED YOUR HELP . . .
to plan the future of women's erotic fiction –

– and no stamp required!

Yours are the only opinions that matter.
Black Lace is a new and exciting venture: the first series
of books devoted to erotic fiction by women for women.
  We're going to do our best to provide the brightest,
best-written, bonk-filled books you can buy. And we'd
like your help in these early stages. Tell us what you
want to read.

THE BLACK LACE QUESTIONNAIRE

SECTION ONE: ABOUT YOU

1.1 Sex (*we presume you are female, but so as not to discriminate*)
     are you?
         Male   ☐   Female   ☐

1.2 Age
         under 21   ☐   21–30   ☐
         31–40   ☐   41–50   ☐
         51–60   ☐   over 60   ☐

1.3 At what age did you leave full-time education?
         still in education   ☐   16 or younger   ☐
         17–19   ☐   20 or older   ☐

1.4 Occupation _____

1.5　Annual household income
　　　under £10,000　　　☐　　£10–£20,000　　　☐
　　　£20–£30,000　　　☐　　£30–£40,000　　　☐
　　　over £40,000　　　☐

1.6　We are perfectly happy for you to remain anonymous;
　　　but if you would like us to send you a free booklist of
　　　Nexus books for men and Black Lace books for Women,
　　　please insert your name and address

　　　_____

　　　_____

　　　_____

　　　_____

SECTION TWO: ABOUT BUYING BLACK LACE BOOKS

2.1　How did you acquire this copy of *The Blue Hotel*
　　　I bought it myself　　☐　　My partner bought it　☐
　　　I borrowed/found it　☐

2.2　How did you find out about Black Lace books?
　　　I saw them in a shop　　　　　　　　　　　　　☐
　　　I saw them advertised in a magazine　　　　　　☐
　　　I saw the London Underground posters　　　　　☐
　　　I read about them in _____
　　　Other _____

2.3　Please tick the following statements you agree with:
　　　I would be less embarrassed about buying Black
　　　Lace books if the cover pictures were less explicit　☐
　　　I think that in general the pictures on Black
　　　Lace books are about right　　　　　　　　　　☐
　　　I think Black Lace cover pictures should be as
　　　explicit as possible　　　　　　　　　　　　　☐

2.4　Would you read a Black Lace book in a public place – on
　　　a train for instance?
　　　Yes　　　　　　　　　☐　　No　　　　　　　☐

SECTION THREE: ABOUT THIS BLACK LACE BOOK

3.1 Do you think the sex content in this book is:
   Too much ☐   About right ☐
   Not enough ☐

3.2 Do you think the writing style in this book is:
   Too unreal/escapist ☐   About right ☐
   Too down to earth ☐

3.3 Do you think the story in this book is:
   Too complicated ☐   About right ☐
   Too boring/simple ☐

3.4 Do you think the cover of this book is:
   Too explicit ☐   About right ☐
   Not explicit enough ☐

Here's a space for any other comments:

SECTION FOUR: ABOUT OTHER BLACK LACE BOOKS

4.1 How many Black Lace books have you read? ☐

4.2 If more than one, which one did you prefer?

4.3 Why?

SECTION FIVE: ABOUT YOUR IDEAL EROTIC NOVEL

We want to publish the books you want to read – so this is
your chance to tell us exactly what your ideal erotic novel
would be like.

5.1 Using a scale of 1 to 5 (1 = no interest at all, 5 = your
ideal), please rate the following possible settings for an
erotic novel:

Medieval/barbarian/sword 'n' sorcery □
Renaissance/Elizabethan/Restoration □
Victorian/Edwardian □
1920s & 1930s – the Jazz Age □
Present day □
Future/Science Fiction □

5.2 Using the same scale of 1 to 5, please rate the following
themes you may find in an erotic novel:

Submissive male/dominant female □
Submissive female/dominant male □
Lesbianism □
Bondage/fetishism □
Romantic love □
Experimental sex e.g. anal/watersports/sex toys □
Gay male sex □
Group sex □

Using the same scale of 1 to 5, please rate the following
styles in which an erotic novel could be written:

Realistic, down to earth, set in real life □
Escapist fantasy, but just about believable □
Completely unreal, impressionistic, dreamlike □

5.3 Would you prefer your ideal erotic novel to be written
from the viewpoint of the main male characters or the
main female characters?

Male □ Female □
Both □

5.4 What would your ideal Black Lace heroine be like? Tick
     as many as you like:

     Dominant   ☐   Glamorous   ☐
     Extroverted   ☐   Contemporary   ☐
     Independent   ☐   Bisexual   ☐
     Adventurous   ☐   Naive   ☐
     Intellectual   ☐   Introverted   ☐
     Professional   ☐   Kinky   ☐
     Submissive   ☐   Anything else?   ☐
     Ordinary   ☐   _____

5.5 What would your ideal male lead character be like?
     Again, tick as many as you like:

     Rugged   ☐
     Athletic   ☐   Caring   ☐
     Sophisticated   ☐   Cruel   ☐
     Retiring   ☐   Debonair   ☐
     Outdoor-type   ☐   Naive   ☐
     Executive-type   ☐   Intellectual   ☐
     Ordinary   ☐   Professional   ☐
     Kinky   ☐   Romantic   ☐
     Hunky   ☐
     Sexually dominant   ☐   Anything else?   ☐
     Sexually submissive ☐   _____

5.6 Is there one particular setting or subject matter that your
     ideal erotic novel would contain?

_____

SECTION SIX: LAST WORDS

6.1 What do you like best about Black Lace books?

_____

6.2 What do you most dislike about Black Lace books?

_____

6.3 In what way, if any, would you like to change Black
     Lace covers?

_____

6.4 Here's a space for any other comments!

_____

_____

_____

_____

_____

Thank you for completing this questionnaire. Now tear it out of the book – carefully! – put it in an envelope and send it to:

Black Lace
FREEPOST
London
W10 5BR

No stamp is required!